DREAMSTONE MOON

PAUL LEONARD

BBC BOOKS

Published by BBC Books
an imprint of BBC Worldwide Publishing
BBC Worldwide Ltd, Woodlands, 80 Wood Lane
London W12 0TT

First published 1998
Copyright © Paul Leonard 1998
The moral right of the author has been asserted

Original series broadcast on the BBC
Format © BBC 1963
Doctor Who and TARDIS are trademarks of the BBC

ISBN 0 563 40585 6
Imaging by Black Sheep, copyright © BBC 1998
Printed and bound in Great Britain by Mackays of Chatham
Cover printed by Belmont Press Ltd, Northampton

ACKNOWLEDGEMENTS

First and foremost I would like to thank my friends: Barb Drummond, for reading through the book and making many valuable suggestions; the BFW crowd – Mark Leyland, Chris Lake, Nick Walters and Simon Lake – for their consistent help and support during what has been a difficult time for my writing – in particular Nick, for doing far more than his fair share of our joint writing project and thus leaving me free to concentrate on worrying myself to death over this one.

Thanks also to my mother for telephone support and occasional free meals, and Nadia Lamarra for talking about other things (most of the time). Then there's (inevitably) Jim Mortimore – thanks for the pep-talks, Jim. Also many thanks to Kate Orman, Jon Blum and Lawrence Miles for writing good books to aim at, and Andrew Vogel (DW page at http://www.erols.com/vogell/), Dominique Boies (DW page at http://www.geocities.com/~boies00), Paul Beardsley, Jeremy Bement and others for email support! Jeremy's book of author interviews, *The Collective Consciousness*, is now available, contact him at: who1@darkmatter.planitia.net.

Lastly I must thank Steve Cole and Lesley Levene at the BBC for their patience and understanding, as well as their many helpful suggestions concerning the plot, the text and continuity matters. Not to mention the free lunches...

For John Bunting
(I know you prefer Stetsons to spacesuits,
but never mind... maybe next time!)

PROLOGUE

Hello
My name is Anton La Serre
This thing isn't working

Look there are supposed to be full stops where are the full stops what do you mean I

. .

So how do I?

Oh. I see.

Where did you get this thing anyway?

Where?

Where's that?

Look are you serious? You expect me to pay real money for this antique? I've got an Olivetti typewriter at home. Genuine 1960s portable. Real polymer plastic. Swiss–French keyboard. Wouldn't like to swap it for that would you?

No! I was joking! Look. I don't want it to take dictation. I want it to read my mind. Can't you understand English?

Oh. I see. Sorry. I didn't know you were using a translator. But I'm still not buying it.

I'm not surprised there's no call for them. I suppose there's no call for bells either?

Hang on. How do you

Yes. BELs. Not bells. BELs. Bio-electric connections. Dream machines. Nobody wants them any more. Nobody wants me any more. Boo-hoo. I'm very sad. Hey. How do you get this thing to do commas?

Three thousand is a bit steep. Will you take a part exchange? I can give you a Carnival 380.

OK. Two thousand and the Carnival. It's a deal. But show me how to do the commas. Oh. I see. Right.

Come on, then, Dictacom 400. We're going home.

Ali! I picked up this weird machine this morning, records what you say and spits it out as words.

Yeah. It's doing it now. Writing words in the air as I speak. Some sort of laser effect. Hollows, did they call them? Must be about a century old.

What does it look like? You mean the casing? Well, it's sort of greenish – you know, old organoplastic colour. Looks like it's been in the wars.

You reckon? Yeah, there's all kinds of ex-military trash around on Earth I suppose. Wonder how it got here? Look, I need a favour. I still haven't got that fund transfer from Ybrik from the Artificial Fish series, and I could do with –

OK. Yeah. I suppose I'll just have to give Ybrik a call. You don't know where he is?

OK.

Once upon a time, there was a dreamer called Anton. He liked his dreams. He liked them a lot. He liked them so much that he thought other people might like them too. He recorded them on computers and played them back into other people's heads.

And the other people liked his dreams and paid him lots of money. Well, OK, a bit of money. Well, in fact his girlfriend loaned him most of it, but then such is the life of an artist.

Then along came the big greedy dreamstone dragon, and ate up all the dreams. That is, he ate up all the market for dreams, because Dreamstone Dreams are Better Dreams.

Big, glittery, dreamstones. God how I hate them. But I suppose I'm going to have to learn to use them or I'll never pay Jono back that loan.

Dialogue setting, there's got to be a dialogue setting

'Yup, this is it,' said Anton.
  'Look, stop messing with that machine,' said Jono. 'We have to talk about this in a serious way. I can't continue funding you when you're not making anything.'

'I'm not asking you to fund me, just tide me over until the Artificial Fish series pays –'

'Anton, it isn't going to pay anything. Nobody wants BELs any more. All that hardware in your head. You can put a dreamstone on your pillow. And dreamstone dreams are –'

'"– better dreams". Yeah. I know. Hey! Look! It picked up the quotes!'

'*Stop* messing with that *machine*!'

'Sorry,' said Anton. 'Look. I'll get a dreamstone. I'll try it once. It won't work – I know it won't work. But I'll try it. OK?'

'OK,' said Jono. 'But not tonight. We do other things tonight.'

Anton laughed. 'OK. Not tonight.'

[non-verbal sounds]

'Hmm. Hang on – off. Oh. Umm, that is

Well, looks like I've finally found a use for this thing.

OK, Dictacom 400. Your mission, should you choose to accept it, is to sit there all night waiting for me to wake up, and then write down my first impressions of making dreams with dreamstone. Just in case the dreamstone doesn't work properly, which I'm sure it won't anyway. Got that OK?

Right, I'm going to sleep now – no I'm not, where's the –

OK. I think this stuff's in the right place. You know, it's quite pretty. All sort of glittery and yellow, with little bits of blue in it. And it shines in the dark, and the glittery blue bits move. I suppose it is like a dragon – ah, well, idle speculation. But I can feel something. There is something there, in the stone. They say that.

More in the morning. G'night.

[non-verbal sounds]

No. No! Oh God no help please. I've –

[non-verbal sounds]

Please don't – Please! No. *No!*

I –

[non-verbal sounds]

[non-verbal sounds]

[file closed]

CHAPTER 1

By her sixth 'morning' on the Kusk ship, Sam could barely unglue herself from the floor. She gritted her teeth, concentrated on it. On each movement.

Roll on to your front. Push up with your arms. Get a grip with your feet. Now push – push –

She fell back again, gasping, felt the mozzarella-like floor reattach itself to her clothes and her skin. She closed her eyes, decided to give herself a count of ten before trying again.

I'm going to come to a sticky end.

At first that had seemed like a good joke. A cool line for a dangerous situation. She'd looked at the thick, fetid air of the Kusk ship, the moisture crawling down the walls, the welded-in, unmovable controls, the heavy gravity gluing her feet to the organic slime of the floor, and she'd giggled and thought: a sticky end. Yes. If she sat down she would certainly get a sticky end. What do you get if you cross a Kusk ship with a paintbrush? What do you get if you cross a Kusk ship with a pitcher plant?

But gradually the jokes had begun to wear thin, especially since there was no one to tell them to.

What had Anstaar been thinking of, leaving her alone on this thing? She'd said there was food and water, but all Sam had managed to find was egglike things that looked as if they belonged in a horror movie and smelled as if they belonged in a drain. When she'd finally got one open – by dropping it repeatedly, kicking it, punching it, screaming at it – it turned out to contain a mushy green substance with a passing resemblance to pea soup, most of which had soaked into the floor. She'd scooped some up into her hands and forced herself to eat a little. It had tasted like vomit, and she'd promptly been sick.

Eventually she'd got hungry enough to try again, and had managed to keep it down. But she wasn't thriving on the diet. There were no mirrors anywhere on the ship, but Sam could feel the bones pressing through the skin of her face. The skin of her hands was white, with lots of small red blotches. An allergy? An infection? To think that all she'd had to worry about once was her new fringe.

– perhaps if I comb it back the blotches will go away will stop crawling on my skin perhaps I should find the medical kit but I don't know down this corridor somewhere the Doctor will know the Doctor the Doctor –

Sam opened her eyes, looked at her blotchy hands, realised with a shock that a lot more than ten seconds had passed. Had she fallen asleep again?

She had no idea how long she'd been on the ship. She'd slept six times, so it was probably only a few days, but it felt like weeks. There was no sense of movement. When she'd tried to use the controls they'd clung to her, oozing against her skin, searching presumably for the familiar pheromonal connections present in the skins of their Kusk masters. Whatever it was they were finding in Sam's skin, they didn't like it.

She struggled to get up again, forcing her body away from the floor, then forcing herself to walk the short distance through the gloomy air to the room where the food eggs were kept. It was like climbing out of a swamp loaded with a fifty-kilo backpack.

There were only four of the food eggs left. Opening even one seemed like too much effort. It would be so much easier to lie down and –

– cold, cold, with scratches along his cheeks and he wasn't breathing wasn't breathing pinching his nose watching for his chest to rise blowing desperate blowing wake up lips pressed hard against his –

'Please,' she told the ship, tears running down her cheeks.

'Please, I'd just like to go home.'

But if there was any sentience on this ship it either didn't understand her, or wasn't working, or simply wasn't switched on.

This is *stupid*, thought Sam. I can't die like this, stuck in an alien spaceship, just because I don't understand the control system.

She looked at the eggs again, decided that opening one really would be a waste of effort. She wasn't hungry. She had some energy. She would have another go at the control room, right now. Before it was too late.

With an effort, she lifted her left foot off the sticky floor, and lurched out of the food room towards the room where she slept. She had no idea whether it was really a control room, but it contained something that she thought was a viewscreen. It looked like a jellyfish strung up on wires, with little bits of metal in it, but it glowed slightly and showed her a grid and an image of a starfield. For all she knew it might be the Kusk idea of interior decoration – but the stars did move, if slowly, and occasionally a bright star appeared, bright enough to make her believe that she wasn't drifting in interstellar space, doomed to die.

The bright star was there again now, drifting across the screen – presumably the ship was rotating. And there was another star –

Sam felt her heart jump. That hadn't been there before. She must be drifting towards something – a planet, a moon, a piece of space junk. She struggled with the floor, adrenalin giving her a renewed burst of energy. The second 'star' seemed to be moving relative to the first, and changing in brightness. So she couldn't be far away from it. If only she could get something to switch *on* – radar, scanners, even a telescopic sight – then she might be able to find out what it was.

The star emitted a little tail of light, and began moving very quickly.

A *spaceship*.

Sam had an absurd impulse to shout, wave, jump up and down. But the other ship was already gone from the viewscreen.

'I'm here!' bawled Sam. 'I'm alive!'

She knew that there was no way they could hear her, but there was always the chance that they might be telepathic. Vocalisation might help them pick up her thoughts.

Or, failing that, at least it made her feel better.

'Help me!' she yelled. 'I don't want to die!'

Silence. There wasn't even an echo from the metal walls.

Then a voice spoke.

'Athshsish doshdoshdosh gurghdosh dshdsh gosh!' it said urgently.

The TARDIS translation system must be too far away, thought Sam. I should've realised this was going to happen.

'Ath*shsish* doshdosh*dosh* gurghdosh *dshdsh* gosh!' repeated the voice, with a good deal more emphasis.

She found herself giggling.

I should've stopped to pick up a translator when I'd finished trying to revive the Doctor and crying and being concussed and hysterical –

Yeah, right. And a toothbrush and a change of knickers would have been useful too. Life doesn't work like that, Samantha Jones. Not any more. It probably never did.

Clunk.

Sam's heart jumped.

That had felt a lot like –

Clunk.

'*Athshsish doshdoshdosh gurghdosh dshdsh gosh! Gurghgurgh pishtosh!*'

'Let me guess,' said Sam. 'Someone's going to board the –'

BANG!

Air began whistling past Sam's ears. A high-pitched whine, like a swarm of angry wasps, almost deafened her. A Kusk alarm system? A weapons system?

Sam became aware that the air was getting rather thin.

Very thin.

Her ears popped.

'Hey!' she yelled. 'I'm alive! I need air! I haven't got a spacesuit!'

She gasped, could barely suck in enough air to refill her lungs. Her ears popped again.

'Help!' she bawled. She could hardly hear the alarm now. The air was getting too thin to carry the sound.

There was a flash of light, and a hole appeared in one of the dark walls.

Sam could see stars through it.

– which means there's no air *and I'm not going to live much longer –*

Her ears were hurting, and something was bubbling in her throat. Mucus? Blood? She tried to jump towards the hole, towards the outside where there was at least a chance that someone might see her and pick her up before she died of oxygen starvation, but she was too weak to break away from the floor. Or it had hardened in the vacuum. Or something. Anyway she *couldn't move* and this *wasn't fair* and she should *never have left the Doctor –*

Something cold tingled on her face and hands, something cold and wet and she could *breathe,* she was sucking in vast gulps of air and they were hurting her throat and her lungs and she was coughing something up, yellowish gobbets floating in the air –

– mucus, great, at least I haven't burst a blood vessel –

And the cold wet thing was there again, another breath, and Sam could see the airline now, running back towards a big cylindrical object standing on heavy-duty legs. Some kind of robot?

No. It had an eye. A single big eye and rubbery skin and a big, beaklike mouth. And the 'airline' wasn't an airline at all: it was one of several long, rubbery tentacles.

The rest of the tentacles were wrapping themselves around Sam's body.

11

I don't believe this. I thought I was being rescued and now I'm going to be eaten alive.

'No!' she yelped, struggling frantically. 'Put me down!'

But the tentacles were pulling her towards the mouth, which opened wide to reveal several rings of long, sharp teeth. A blast of air that smelled like a particularly bad case of illegal pollution blew across her face, making her eyes water.

The mouth got closer. And closer. Sam felt the tentacles squeezing her tight against the hard beak, felt the slimy touch of alien flesh on her arms and face. She struggled, but could barely move against the powerful grip. And her lungs were bursting.

The cold, wet touch on her face again. A hiss of air. She gulped at it, felt a lurching motion, was almost blinded by light.

Sunlight? Lights from the other ship?

Before her eyes could adjust enough to see anything useful it was dark again. She tried to turn her head, but the tentacle wrapped around it wouldn't let her move.

She took another gasp of air, then made a determined, sudden movement. She managed to turn her face a little, saw a brilliant line of light.

Metal, she realised. Metal reflecting sunlight.

She saw what might have been a human figure in a spacesuit, drifting through jiggling afterimages of the light.

Then the world went dark again.

She tried to take another breath, felt the air sucked from her lungs. The red mist was back, and there was a ringing in her ears.

No. I'm going to get out of this. I've got to signal to that man in the suit. I've got to –

The tentacles holding on to her abruptly let go. Sam felt her body being pushed towards a cave of metal – no, a metal room, illuminated by bright lights – in fact –

An airlock. I'm OK, I'm alive, I've got a chance here.

She drifted for a moment, weightless, her ears still buzzing, as the airlock swallowed her up. A man in a spacesuit was straight ahead, paying out a line for her to – no, he was moving out of her way, attached to a line. He drifted within a couple of metres, but Sam couldn't reach him. The suit was gold, bright gold like some kid's toy, and the letters DMMC – O'RYAN were written in red across the chest.

An arm gestured towards the wall ahead of her: Sam looked, saw a series of plastic rings attached to the metal, getting closer. Getting closer fast.

I've got to grab the rings. Only one chance at this, or I'll bounce off and he might never catch me again. Especially if he's got the alien to deal with.

Her hands touched the cold, hard plastic and she grabbed with all her strength. The red mist was back, and she could feel sharp pains in her throat.

Decompression.

She felt the jolt as her arms straightened, but she couldn't see the rings any more. Her ears were roaring, and pain was shooting along her legs and her arms. She concentrated on solid plastic rings in her hands.

Hold on to them, just hold on as hard as you can.

But something was dragging at her body, dragging her away from the wall, and she had to let go. Then she was drifting, spinning, and the lights were everywhere, and she was breathing, *breathing again,* great gulps of cold, rich air, sweet as nectar, and coughing and choking and her throat hurt and her chest hurt and her legs hurt and her arms hurt and –

Something had grabbed her. The man in the spacesuit. He was holding on to her, holding her arms, holding her steady though the room was still whirling around them. She could see his face through the visor, shadowy, bearded, the eyes wide with amazement.

Sam became aware of a roaring sound, slowly receding to a hiss.

An electronic voice was talking, a jumble of syllables that could be any language. There was a jolt as she hit the wall, and another stab of pain. She saw the man let go of one of her arms to grab one of the plastic rings.

There was a moment's silence, then the man had sprung his helmet and was lifting it off. His face was beaded with sweat. His mouth was moving, but she could hear only a blurred mumbling noise.

He leaned forward, shouted in her ear.

'I said, are you all right?'

Sam tried to speak, coughed, choked, saw disconcertingly red gobbets floating in the air.

The man was shouting again. 'Where's Theo? We need him here right now!'

With difficulty, Sam managed to control her breathing. 'I'm OK,' she spluttered. She could scarcely hear her own voice.

Then she almost screamed in agony at a stabbing pain from her chest. She screwed up her eyes tight, waited for the pain to go away.

Thankfully, it did.

She opened her eyes again, saw the tentacles, cylindrical body and three stubby legs of the alien, floating behind the man in the spacesuit. She tried to pull back, tried to shout a warning, but could only manage to point with her free hand.

The man turned, and nodded at the creature. 'You still breathing?' he asked it.

A huge but otherwise disturbingly human eye opened in the slimy carapace, then closed again. Gouts of air were moving in and out of the alien's body, with a sound like the wind blowing through the branches of a large tree.

'Bit of...' (gasp) '...sunburn...' (gasp). 'Otherwise OK.'

It was then that Sam realised. Realised even before the man turned back to her. The alien hadn't been attacking her. It had been –

'Her name's Aloisse,' said the man. He was still shouting, and Sam was still having some trouble hearing him, but it was no worse than the average nightclub. 'Kind of a swamp-living alien. A pain in the butt, a stowaway, and a career troublemaker across half of human space. But, she's braver than I am, and she just saved your life. I'd never have got suited up in time to get over there.'

Sam looked towards the alien, took a deep breath, made quite sure she wasn't going to cough up any more blood, and then said solemnly, 'Thank you.'

'Are you really a stowaway?'

Sam and Aloisse were in what passed for a medical bay on the ship that had rescued her. It was a small plastic box of a room, with two beds in it, and a clutter of equipment on shelves, tucked into corners, or hanging from the ceiling. It was barely large enough for two humans, let alone Sam and the treelike bulk of Aloisse. Sam was lying on one of the beds with a piece of tubing attached to her arm, trailing up to a black Medical Support Unit fixed above her head. Aloisse was crammed into the space between the beds. Most of her cylindrical body was covered in a thick, grey shell that had the texture of a barnacle that has seen a long time at sea, complete with little pieces of green weed that Sam assumed were decorative. The tentacles sprang from the top end of the shell, about ten of them, weaving in the air like snakes. Both the beaklike mouth and the huge eye were in the midst of the nest of tentacles; each was tethered by a sinewy rope to the shell, but moved about on its own millipedal mass of tiny legs. Sam wondered if they had once been separate, symbiotic animals.

Large parts of the reddish skin around the base of the alien's tentacles were covered with a whitish cream, which bubbled and gave off a disgusting smell.

'Depends what you mean by stowing away,' Aloisse told her. Her native voice – a deep, wooden rumble, like logs falling down a distant slope – was audible behind the clipped, sanitised voice of the human translator strapped around her body just below the mouth. 'I'm not supposed to be on this ship, if that's what you mean. But I didn't hide or anything – I mean, that would hardly have been possible, would it? So I just told the boarding computer I was a mine inspector.'

Sam giggled. 'And it believed you?'

'Oh, computers will believe anything. Especially mining-company computers. They're specially built to be stupid.' Aloisse curled a tentacle in the air in front of her huge eye. 'Unfortunately, the crew were a bit more sceptical. But we were in interstellar space by then, and though they threatened to throw me from the nearest airlock, I don't think their hearts were really in it.'

'So you *did* hide?' said Sam.

'Well, I hung around in the cargo bay for a while. Inspected a few crates, just to keep the computer happy. Nothing very interesting in any of them, I'm afraid. How's your perforated lung?'

'Not as perforated as they thought it was.' Sam had spent a very uncomfortable half-hour with a tube down her throat, having the damaged part of her lung coated with some kind of intelligent membrane. It was doing the job – she wasn't coughing, or bleeding. But it hurt every time she breathed, and there was a dull pins-and-needles feeling in both her legs. 'The doctor told me I'm not seriously damaged. He said I'd be back to normal in a couple of days.'

'Oh, him! He'd say that to a miner who'd lost all four limbs and was suffering from plutonium poisoning. And probably has done, several times.'

Alarmed, Sam started to sit up. 'You mean I might be –'

Aloisse issued a deep bubbling sound which Sam guessed might be laughter. 'Don't worry, I think he meant it in your case. He's paid to deceive working miners, not stray teenagers rescued from decaying spaceships. What *were* you doing on that old wreck, anyway? If it's any of my business, that is.'

'There was an accident. I got stranded.'

'Ah, aren't we all.' Aloisse curled a tentacle in front of her eye again. 'These sucker-rims are hopelessly split – it's all that struggling around in a vacuum. I really need to visit a good tentaclist. You don't happen to know of one in this part of human space?'

Sam had to smile. 'No.'

'Oh, well, I don't suppose there are any males of my species for light years anyway. Hope not, in a way.'

Sam decided not to follow up this line of conversation. 'Did you say this was a mining company ship?' she asked. 'Where's it going?'

Aloisse's eye closed. 'Didn't anyone tell you?'

'Nope. They were too busy sticking things down my throat.'

'More likely they thought it might be a company secret and didn't want to risk disciplinary action.' Aloisse made a trumpeting sound that Sam imagined might stand for a contemptuous snort.

'So where are we going?'

Aloisse turned slightly, and pointed a tentacle at the complex, glittering display of the medical unit above Sam's bed. Next to the tip of the tentacle Sam saw the words DREAMSTONE MOON MINING COMPANY MEDICAL SYSTEM in silver on the black casing.

'So?' asked Sam. 'Where are we going?'

'Where do you think? The moon of Mu Camelopides VI. Otherwise known as the Dreamstone Moon.' Aloisse paused, as if for dramatic effect, but Sam was baffled.

'What's special about it?'

The floor started to shake, and Sam felt the first stirrings of alarm. Had the Kusk followed her? Was the ship being attacked? Then she realised that the vibration was coming from Aloisse.

'Ha! Ha!' said the translator suddenly.

Ah. So *this* was laughter.

'Lots of things are special about Dreamstone Moon,' said Aloisse at last. 'A wrecked ecosystem, exploitation of the miners, accidents, fatalities, lies, lies, lies –' She scratched at her damaged skin with a tentacle, then shuddered and flicked the tentacle away.

Sam wondered how much the 'bit of sunburn' was really hurting her. She was about to ask, but Aloisse spoke again.

'Come on, you *must* have heard of dreamstone. Where have you been for the last five years?'

Sam shook her head. 'You don't want to know. The list of places I've been in the last five *months* would take about half an hour to get through.' She hesitated, then added, 'And quite a lot of them had wrecked ecosystems, accidents, deaths and lies. You ever seen a Dalek war zone?'

Aloisse seemed to think about this for a moment. Then she said, 'You know, you're one of those people who gets more interesting every time you open your mouth. Not many people you can say that about, anywhere in–' She broke off suddenly and swivelled her body at the waist. The abrupt movement caused her tentacles to flail out: one caught Sam on the arm.

'Ow! Look what you're –'

Then Sam saw the open door, the figure standing there, watching them.

'Trying to corrupt her already?'

Aloisse's response was a hiss. 'No, Daniel. Just telling her the truth.'

'Well, whatever. But if you're fit you should get out of the medical bay. Remember you're supposed to be under arrest, now.' The man squeezed past the alien's body and looked down at Sam on the bed.

Sam realised that he was the crewman who'd helped to rescue her. Out of the spacesuit, he looked quite old, his face baggy and tired and his beard flecked with grey.

'We're landing in half an hour,' he told her. 'I came to see if you were fit to walk off the ship or whether we needed a stretcher party.'

Sam glanced at the tube attached to her arm, then cautiously swung her legs out of the bed and sat up.

A mild stab of pain. Pins and needles. Otherwise OK. She looked at Daniel and nodded.

Aloisse had shuffled over to the doorway of the room. 'You can hear the company propaganda now, Sam. Make your mind up and let me know at the port.'

Sam looked from Daniel to Aloisse and back again. 'Let you know about what?'

But Aloisse was already gone. Sam could hear her tripedal elephant's tread receding down the passageway. It sounded rather like a fair-sized dent being beaten out of a car.

She stood up, taking care not to dislodge the tube attached to her arm. But it seemed to follow her easily enough, curling like an earthworm to avoid tangling itself.

'What was she talking about?' Sam asked Daniel.

The miner shrugged. 'Aloisse thinks she's fighting a war. She wants to know if you're going to cross the lines and join her lot.'

Sam nodded. It sounded as if it was a familiar enough situation: a company out for what it could get, trying to keep labour costs to a minimum, and with no interest in the local ecology. Aloisse sounded as if she was brave, principled and honest. But – fighting a war?

Sam wasn't sure whether she needed to get involved in that.

She realised that Daniel was watching her face. Quite suddenly he reached across and clapped her on the shoulder. 'I shouldn't let it trouble you, kid. It's not your affair. I'll make sure they find some room for you on the next freighter out, whatever. Then you can go home, get yourself sorted out.'

Go home.

Oh.

– this is the twenty-third century and I can't go home, I haven't got a time machine and I can't ever go home –

'What's the matter? Not feeling well again? Sit down for a while. It's half an hour –'

'It's not that,' said Sam helplessly. 'It's just – home. I –' She swallowed, fighting an unequal battle to keep down tears.

'You have got somewhere to go?' Daniel's face was close to hers.

Sam hesitated, then said in a small voice. 'No. Not any more.'

CHAPTER 2

'Look, I almost died this morning. There has to be something you can do.'

The dreamstone salesman frowned. At least, Anton La Serre thought it was a frown. The insectoid face creaked and tightened, and the stubby antennae drooped. Behind the alien, dreamstones glittered against a backcloth of dark velvet, each with its subtle holo'd price tag glimmering in the shadows below it. The dreamstone that Anton had tried to use lay on the polished wood of the counter, its crystals dull and dead.

'If you had a negative reaction, sir, naturally we'll exchange the stone, or, if you insist, we can refund your purchase price in full. But I can assure you –'

'I'm not interested in the money!' snapped Anton. 'I could have had a heart attack! I really thought something was trying to kill me!'

The alien's antennae drooped still further, perhaps indicating its disbelief. When it spoke again the translated voice seemed to have gained a weary air. 'Such reactions are extremely rare, sir. And there's no evidence that they're any more dangerous than – well, than an ordinary bad dream. Obviously I'm extremely sorry that this has happened, but there's really nothing else I can do right now. Do you want a refund or an exchange?'

Anton took a deep breath, tried to think of another line of approach, one that might at least get the attention of someone in the company above the level of this front-desk person. He looked at the display of stones behind the alien. Most were small, no bigger than a human hand, and fairly irregular in shape, like the one that Anton had bought; but there were larger ones, and exotic shapes – crosses, dumbbells, cones, pyramids. The centrepiece of the display was a head-sized, hollow bubble of grey stone, shaped like a crested helmet, which oozed clumps of dreamstones.

Anton wondered if the lucky purchaser would be stupid enough to try to wear it.

The salesman's compound eyes were still watching him patiently. At least, Anton thought they were watching him. Without pupils, it was hard to tell.

'It's not just a matter of discomfort,' he said. 'I'm a working artist. These things –' he prodded the dead dreamstone between them – 'are supposed to take imprints of your dreams, not give you nightmares and then turn into dead lumps of rock. It's quite likely you've seriously disrupted my capacity to dream – it could be weeks before I can do useful work again.'

This wasn't quite true: one nightmare, however disturbing, was unlikely to affect his dreams for more than a couple of nights, and anyway Anton's skill lay in shaping them while he was awake.

'I'm extremely sorry if there has been any inconvenience. But as I've said –'

'If I lose any sales as a result, I'll sue the company.'

The salesman's short, leathery wings twitched. It swivelled its head with a creaking sound, as if looking for moral support. But the showroom was empty. Finally it said, 'Of course you must take whatever action you feel is appropriate, sir. But I can assure you that our company's policy is in full compliance with all the relevant human laws.'

There was a very slight emphasis on the word 'human': the Zmm-Zmm were the natives of Occam's World, and humans were, technically speaking, their guests and subject to their law. And for all he knew, by Zmm-Zmm law Anton might already have committed a cardinal insult on the salesman and be liable to forfeit a pint of his blood every week to feed the salesman's grubs. He'd heard of such things happening, since the Dalek war and the subsequent weakening of Earth's control in this sector. The Zmm-

Zmm *looked* respectable enough, with its clean, human-style wasp-striped suit – but you never knew.

Anton closed his eyes, wishing he'd brought Jono with him. His girlfriend wasn't afraid of anyone, or of any obscure native laws. She would have sorted the Zmm-Zmm out. But Anton was still feeling physically weak from the effects of the nightmare. He wanted nothing more than to sit down. Or, better still, go home, have a hot bath, a long nap, and then perhaps try to do some work.

Except that there was no point in doing any work. Nobody was buying his work. Everybody was buying dreamstones.

He opened his eyes again. The salesman was typing something into a desk terminal, using the handlike extensions on the end of its mandibles. It looked bizarre, as if the insectoid were trying to eat the desk.

'It's OK,' said Anton wearily. 'I know it's not your fault. I'll take a refund.'

The antennae twitched, but the Zmm-Zmm carried on typing for a full ten seconds before it spoke. 'Very well, sir.' It picked up the dead stone from the desk between them, then stretched its neck towards him and muttered, 'If you – umm – take another stone instead, I keep my commission.'

Ah, thought Anton. Obviously this thing thinks it knows a sucker when it sees one. Well I'm not going to be *that* stupid.

He opened his mouth to say no.

Then he had an idea.

If I can prove that these things are giving people nightmares, then no one will want them. Which will mean –

Which would mean he could make dreams the old way again, with BELs. Thoughts of sales, shows, commissions and universal adulation danced through his brain. All he had to do was try to use a dreamstone again, but this time hook up a BEL circuit instead of relying on that ancient Dictacom, so that he had proof of what the stone had done. It might not work – but it was worth a try.

He leaned forward and spoke to the salesman in a low voice. 'OK, I'll take another one.' He added, as casually as he could, 'I don't suppose you have any way of making it more likely that it'll have the same... effect as this one?'

The chitinous face creaked again. 'The *same* effect? But you said – you were complaining about –'

'I know,' said Anton briskly. 'I changed my mind.' He reached into his pocket, brought out his cash chip, and waved it authoritatively in the air between them, as if he really had a lot of money. He hoped the alien would be sufficiently impressed not to think about Anton's possible motives for his sudden change of heart – at least, not until he was out of the showroom.

'Well, if that's what you want, I'll see what I can do.' The Zmm-Zmm scuttled away, its wings twitching behind its back.

While he was waiting, Anton took his computer out of his pocket. 'Search: general,' he muttered quickly. 'References: dreamstone, bad dreams, insanity, artists.' He slipped the device back into his pocket as the salesman clattered back.

'This one has the same source label, sir. I can't guarantee that it will – that is, as I said, such occurrences are extremely rare, but –'

'That's all right,' said Anton quickly. He gave the alien his cash chip, wrote a twenty per cent gratuity on to the slate. 'But don't forget to refund the price of the original,' he cautioned.

The Zmm-Zmm nodded, then processed the transaction before carefully wrapping and packing the new dreamstone. As it handed the package to Anton it muttered, 'If there are any other services you want, I have connections with some of the Downtown hives –'

Anton felt the blood rushing to his face.

Now the bloody thing thinks I'm a pervert.

'No – that's OK, I –'

He turned away, still blushing, and hurried out of the showroom into the street. The daylight was dull, the sky leaden with a permanent winter haar. Occam's World had two suns, but both of them were currently about as far away as they could get. It was the best part of a year, by Earth reckoning, until spring. Anton stared at the grey fur-suited figures walking up and down the road, their pale, dull, inward-looking faces.

I'm tired of my world, he thought. I'm tired of people who only want cheap, tacky, rose-coloured dreams. I wish I'd been born on Earth, before the Daleks wrecked it – or even Earth now. Or anywhere else but here.

Anton had thought this sort of thing before now – frequently – but he'd never been so certain about it. So certain that something in his life needed to *change*. He started down the street, the new dreamstone heavy under his arm.

Now that he'd acquired the stone, he wasn't sure he could face going through with using it. OK, the nightmare might not happen again – but if it did –

He was going to have to live through it. Record it on the BEL.

He shuddered. It hadn't just been a bad dream. It had been a child's nightmare, a fever dream, a deep, primal, horror. *And something had been killing him –*

He became aware that his computer was ringing. He answered it, leaned against the marbled pillar of a clothing downloader's as he stared at the search results on the small virtual screen floating in the air above the machine. Over four hundred references, divided into categories:

Dreamstones – bad dreams 128

Dreamstones – nightmares 96

Dreamstones – terror 78

Dreamstones – horror 45

He frowned. Officially, bad dreamstones were extremely rare: but obviously the reality was different.

He thought again about what had happened in the showroom.

As soon as he'd told the Zmm-Zmm that he was interested in getting another nightmare stone, rather than just making a complaint, it had known what to do. And it had known where to make connections for 'other services'.

Maybe it hadn't been talking about sex. After all, that wasn't what he'd asked for. Maybe somebody was making an industry out of bad stones. Which meant –

Anton wasn't sure what it meant. He put the computer close to his lips and muttered, 'Refine search. Include: illegal trade, Downtown, sexual perversion.'

The list of references reduced to five. The first three were police public-access files. He read them, but they mainly talked about how to complain in the event of receiving a bad dreamstone. Anton noticed there was no mention of compensation.

The fourth file was a private address.

A Downtown address.

He touched a privacy code into the machine, then murmured, 'Arrange transport. Criterion: fastest route.'

One of the suns had set, and the leaden sky had turned the colour of smoke. It was darker in Downtown, because less of the sky was visible. Downtown wasn't just a name: the place was literally at a lower level than the human city, a jumble of native hives and semi-derelict human buildings spilling into a deep canyon that ran to the cold sea. From above, in the helicab, it had seemed almost picturesque: soft, friendly looking bioluminescent lights spotted around grey, ill-defined buildings. Close to, in the open air, it was shadowy, freezing cold, and full of strange whispers.

The building that Anton wanted was in the shape of a native hive, but made out of pieces of organoplastic and other leftover human materials. It was sprayed with faintly luminescent bactopigmentation, most of it blood-coloured.

He'd dismissed the helicab, not wanting to pay the waiting fee, but now rather wished he hadn't. Things moved in the shadows, scuttling, clicking, creaking. They might be harmless: beggars, children, native prostitutes – or just ordinary, poor, cold, humans or Zmm-Zmm going about their daily business. On the other hand –

– *click-click-click chatterchatterchatter ssss* –

– they might not be harmless.

Anton advanced towards the building, looking for an entrance, wondering why he hadn't just done his research in the library. Or called the police. Or told Jono where he was. Or anything.

A mechanical click. A whining sound, a motor running.

Anton looked around him, then saw the wire cage descending the walls of the building.

Of course. A *hive*. The entrance would be about a third of the way up. He watched the cage get closer, the creaking and banging sounds becoming louder until it landed with a sound like a scrapped heli being dropped in the dump.

There was a Zmm-Zmm inside. Huge, bloated, sick-looking. One eye was bubbled with white pustules, and probably blind.

'Is who you?' it asked, the rusty voice of its translator barely audible above the clicks of its native speech. 'Is want personal services? Is have appointment?'

Anton swallowed. The tension in his throat was enough to make the action hurt.

'I want bad dreamstones,' he said.

'Are bad? We have bad. Is choice bad lots. Is me up come see?'

Anton wondered how many languages the Zmm-Zmm's translator was going through before it got to English.

'Is me up come see?' repeated the alien, tapping the cage floor with ancient, chipped claws. 'Is good bad here, is promise.'

Anton swallowed again, wondered if he should at least call Jono and tell her where he was. There were spots of rust on the metal bars of the cage.

On the other hand, if it was *this* seedy, it was hardly a big-time operation. And making a call now would be the easiest possible way to annoy the old Zmm-Zmm, and perhaps scare it off a deal.

Anton got into the cage, tried not to feel sick as the contraption jolted its way up the blood-coloured walls of the hive. He quickly discovered that the best thing to do was just close his eyes.

He felt a spindly, chitinous arm descend around his shoulders. 'Is good bad,' clicked the alien voice. 'Is enjoy dream you lots.'

Anton ducked out of the embrace, leaned against the cold bars of the cage.

It jolted to a stop at last, against a stone platform decorated with Zmm-Zmm doing odd things that Anton supposed were intended to be erotic. The Zmm-Zmm opened the door, managing another attempt to feel Anton's shoulders in the process, then led the way through a narrow archway to the interior.

The first thing Anton heard was a scream.

A woman, screaming, begging for her life.

He felt his body begin to shake. He turned to the alien. 'Actually, I'll be honest with you –'

Another scream. Anton's eyes were beginning to adjust to the darkness now, and he could see lines of alcoves, the places that would be family cells in a real hive, could see the shadowy forms inside, twisting and turning, the dull blue glitter of the stones.

He turned back to the alien.

'I want to buy some of your stones.' *This is madness.* 'I want to buy all of them. I'll pay whatever you think is fair.' *I haven't got any money.* 'I'll phone my girlfriend –' *It doesn't need to know that.*

'Is buy stones all? Is nonsense! We have sell one. We have sell two. Is good bad, we sell. Is not sell all. Is business.'

A scream, horrifyingly near. It was impossible to tell whether this one was male or female. A series of gasps followed, then an ominous silence.

Anton wanted to scream too: *stop this, can't you see it's evil?* But he knew there was no point. The people here had come of their own accord, knowing what was going to happen. There probably wasn't much point in telling the police, either. They had to know about the operation: it was probably policy to leave small-timers like this alone, so long as not too many people died.

Feeling sick, he said to the alien, 'OK, I'll buy five stones. Five of the best, and all mined from the same place, right?'

'Is same place why?'

'Never mind why,' snapped Anton, disconcertingly aware that he wasn't sure of the answer to that question himself. 'Just get me the stones.' He handed the creature his cash chip, praying that there was enough left on it for whatever fee the alien saw fit to charge him.

The creature took the chip, verified it in a creaky digital reader built into its left mandible. Evidently the results were satisfactory, because it muttered, 'Is stones I get now,' then turned and shuffled away into an alcove. More screams echoed through the hive. These were definitely female. Anton thought of Jono. He had to suppress an urge to rush to the woman's rescue.

Eventually the Zmm-Zmm emerged from the alcove carrying a large cloth bag. 'Is five stones. Is label machine all same place.'

Anton lifted the bag. It was heavy, but didn't seem quite heavy enough. But when he peered inside, he counted five fist-sized crystals.

'Is alcove which you like?'

Anton lifted the bag. 'No, thanks, I'll take them home.'

'Is not home stones taken! Is not allowed!' squawked the Zmm-Zmm.

'I don't care what's allowed,' snapped Anton. 'I'm taking them.' He turned and walked to the door.

As he reached the outside platform, something barged into him from behind, and an ice-cold line formed across his throat.

It took him a second to realise that the something was the alien, and that the ice-cold line was a very long, very elaborately wrought knife.

'Is not good break house rules,' rattled the alien. He could feel the sharp punch of its mandibles against his back as it spoke. 'Is bad results.'

Anton could feel his body shaking, but he was quite unable to move, to struggle, even to talk.

'Is return stones or die.'

Anton moved. He swung the heavy bag of stones towards the place behind him where the alien's head must be, swung it *fast* –

– *this is insane, what am I* –

– there was a dull splintering sound. The knife at his throat was gone, clattering on the spit-and-ceramic platform. Fluid was splashing the back of his neck and his arms.

He turned, saw the Zmm-Zmm slumped against the doorway, amber fluid leaking from its broken carapace. It was making a terrifying hissing sound, like a balloon deflating. Its antennae twitched feebly, then suddenly stiffened. The hissing stopped.

Anton waited, half expecting more Zmm-Zmm to spring from the interior of the hive and fry him with blasters. But nothing happened, except faint clicks and pops as the flesh stiffened under the fallen alien's chitinous exoskeleton, and a single, raucous, human scream from inside the building.

Eventually Anton realised that there wasn't going to be any immediate retribution. That quite possibly the ramshackle old alien had been running the operation on its own, and that there wasn't going to be any retribution at all.

He knew then that he was going to live the rest of his life with the knowledge that he had killed someone.

CHAPTER 3

Matthew O'Connell always held on to the wheel of the excavator, even though it steered itself. It made him feel better to know that he had at least nominal control over the machine. Ahead, dust and fragments of rock danced between the cutting blades: sharp greys and black shadows, shifting constantly in the forward lights. Glints that might be crystals. In the old days, he would have stopped, checked the slurry around the treads, looked for dreamstone. Looked for gold. Looked for iridium...

He blinked. 'God, I almost fell asleep at the wheel there.'

No reply. They'd stopped double-shifting miners after the first year, and the computers weren't set up to talk back. O'Connell didn't mind the solitude, but it was difficult to stay awake sometimes.

He stared ahead into the whirling dust, realised that the number of glints had increased. It looked as if he might have hit a vein of dreamstone. He glanced at the readouts on the panel, feeling a faint undercurrent of excitement. It was habit: a leftover from the days when it made any difference what you found. Now, you got paid the same, whatever. A testament to your irrelevance. But it was still nice to find something.

The panel showed a crystal: high refractive index, some internal luminescence. 'Dreamstone, Quality 3 [40%] or 4 [60%]' according to the computer. O'Connell took a look at the magnified samples and took a personal bet on the 40% option. Not that the computer's quality rating really mattered – there was no way of it telling the 'quality' of a stone in any sense except appearance, and in practice the artists who bought the stuff were more usually interested in obscure arty qualities like emotional resonance and something they called 'colour', but which had nothing to do with anything visible to the eye. Stones were batched by area, samples tested, and the rest of the batch priced accordingly. Until the tests happened, there was no way of telling the final asking price. The stuff O'Connell was looking at might be practically worthless, or priceless beyond dreams.

He became aware that something had changed ahead. The light was brightening, as if he'd cut through into an artificially illuminated area. He checked the instrument panel, but it showed only rock ahead. The cutters went on cutting.

But the light was still brightening.

Well, this is what I'm here for, thought O'Connell. He put the brake on, damped the cutters, watched the whirling blades slow.

Then he saw what was beyond them.

For a moment – just for a moment – he tried to be rational. These things couldn't possibly be down here. There was no air. No means of sustenance.

But then they started to advance, shadows becoming real, eyes staring, long tentacles and chitinous limbs waving.

The monsters were here.

O'Connell screamed.

The gravity on Dreamstone Moon was low. Lower even than the centrifugally generated false gravity of the medical bay area on the *Dreamstone Miner*. Sam guessed it was about ten per cent of Earth's: a small moon, then.

From space it had looked tiny: a jagged lump of rock, bubbled with craters that seemed too large for it. The base, a ring of domes and radar towers, had looked temporary, small, an encampment.

Inside, it was huge. The landing bay alone was the size of a small town, and the gentle slope of the girder-strung roof above her told her just how big the dome was. And this was just one of the domes. How many had there been? Ten? Twelve? Looking up dizzied her: she stumbled, started to fall. She scrabbled for a rail, didn't find one. She put her hands out, found herself shooting away from the floor, sailing over the heads of Daniel and the other miners. She yelped, even though she knew she could hardly hurt herself in this gravity.

'It's easier to hop,' said Daniel, grabbing her arm. Sam felt herself being dragged back to the ground. 'Legs back – that's it – *jump*! And again! Pretend you're skipping!'

Within a couple of minutes, Sam had got into the rhythm of it. By then, they'd crossed the cavernous space of the landing bay, and were fast approaching a strip-lit door labelled PERSONNEL AIRLOCK FOUR.

Through the airlock was a long, noisy room full of people and spacesuits: people getting into spacesuits, people getting out of spacesuits, people leaning against spacesuits with cards or holoflicks in their hands. There was a clattering of metal, a creaking of plastic, a hissing of air supplies. Everywhere there was the ubiquitous, unimaginative, red-on-gold DMMC logo. Sam noticed a shadowy man dressed in black, hovering in midair, suspended by a harness of thin silver cables, muttering into a small silver box.

'Shift controller,' muttered Daniel. He raised his voice. 'Hiya, Kran, you old spider! How's the web?'

The 'man' looked down, and Sam saw that 'he' wasn't human at all. Daniel hadn't called him a spider for nothing. He had an extra pair of arms – or, rather, three sets of undifferentiated limbs, all double-jointed and sheathed in a shiny black skin. The rearmost pair were folded up behind his back. As she watched, he shimmied down to them, paying out the gossamer cable behind him. His head swivelled, revealing a total of perhaps half a dozen catlike eyes and a continuous, fine-mesh surface which might be something to do with breathing, but, on the other hand, might not.

He emitted a curious bubbling noise, and after a moment a

translator squawked, 'Hiya yourself, Daniel. Who's the girlfriend, now?'

'Picked her up on a dead ship out by the slip point. Look, can you give me twenty minutes? I have to take her up to Tiydon's office.'

The alien waved a free arm. 'Sure. Take your time. Number Four's all blocked up again anyway.'

'*Again?*'

The alien's head extended abruptly, revealing a jointed neck inlaid with runelike symbols in green and gold. 'Some kind of infall, or so they said. Couple of guys trapped down there. Tekeneke – you know, the old Krakenite – and Matthew O'Connell.'

'They all right?'

'They should be. It was the beginning of their shift –'

'*Should* be?'

'They won't let us near the place. You know what it's like. Base Security only.'

Daniel shook his head, swore quietly. 'It's not good enough, Kran,' he said. 'You spoken to Tiydon?'

Kran ducked his head, a gesture that must have meant no, because Daniel said, 'OK, then, *I'll* speak to him.' He took Sam's arm. 'Come on, kid. I think we should get you off this place as fast as possible.'

He pulled her through the maze of suits and miners. Sam saw faces – mostly human, a few alien – then there was another airlock; a maze of crowded passageways; a lift which they shared with a creature that looked like Aloisse, but whom Daniel greeted as Igermonitos; and finally a path floored with a bright mosaic and flanked with real palm trees, a swimming pool off to one side and a miniature tropical forest growing on the other. At the end of the path was a pointed arch containing a big, polished, wooden door.

Inside the door was an office – not as big as Sam had expected it to be – full of glittering crystals and the smell of rock dust. Two round windows showed views of a long plain of bare rock, with a scattering of boulders casting long, dark, sharp shadows. Framed by the windows was a desk, carved from a single piece of rock, flat and polished as a tombstone. Various pieces of electronic equipment were scattered on it, together with a couple of piles of paper, each one weighted down by more of the ubiquitous yellow crystals.

Behind the desk was a man.

The man was dark-skinned, bald, with small brown eyes that fixed on Sam at once, with a sharp, judgmental gaze that she didn't like. He wore a business suit. At least, Sam assumed it was a business suit: the sea-blue material had the texture of woven grass, and the magenta-and-gold tie was more like a small rosette. But she put that down to changes in fashion. It had the perfect fit, the artificial smartness, of any business suit from any era she'd yet experienced.

'Good day,' said the man, with a false smile that went perfectly with the suit. 'I'm the Mine Overmanager, Aril Tiydon. So you're our young stowaway?'

'I'm *not* a –' began Sam indignantly, but Daniel was speaking over her.

'No, this is a kid we picked up on a wreck near the slip point. The stowaway's an alien, and she's still on board. Says she won't come off until she gets concessions.'

'What concessions?' snapped Tiydon.

'Oh, the usual thing. Close down the mine, pay millions of interbucks to start up a nature reserve.'

Tiydon laughed. 'Send us all home without a job, she means. What does she really want?'

The miner shrugged. 'I haven't a notion. You know these crazy aliens.'

Sam decided she'd had enough of letting Daniel do all the

talking. 'She's not crazy. She saved my life.'

Tiydon glanced at her. 'Did she?'

'Went into vacuum without a suit,' put in Daniel. 'Me, I didn't even believe the heat trace was real until she dragged the kid out alive and kicking.'

'And she's probably right about the mine and the local ecosystem,' hazarded Sam.

'Is she now?' Tiydon winked at Daniel. 'I think we'd better get you out on the first freighter home, young woman. Don't you think so?' Without letting her get the breath for a reply he turned back to Daniel. 'What d'you reckon? Sit it out? She can always stay on till the ship goes out again. That's one way of getting rid of her.'

'She'll find some way or other of causing trouble, whatever we do,' said Daniel.

It was at this point that Sam realised they were talking about Aloisse, not her. She just wasn't that important.

'Better lock her up, then. Who's captain on the *Miner* at the moment? Tina?'

Daniel nodded.

'D'you think she'd mind if we kept our alien friend in clinkers on the ship?'

Daniel shrugged. 'Probably not. But you'd better ask her about it yourself. You know how Tina is about official channels.'

Tiydon nodded. 'OK. When are you on shift?'

'Now,' said Daniel.

'Make it twenty-two hundred hours, and get this kid on a spaceship first,' said Tiydon, gesturing at Sam without looking at her.

'I'm not sure I want to go,' said Sam, her voice showing her annoyance. But they were treating her like an *object*, and she didn't have to like it.

Tiydon's sharp eyes fixed on her again. 'It isn't a matter of what you want. This entire base is a commercial premises, y'know.

We're not running an interplanetary hotel or a mission for runaway children.' He smiled, went on in a less severe tone. 'Don't worry, we won't charge by the light year for taking you home. Where is home, anyway? Ha'olam? Ryman's World?'

Sam choked off an impulse to tell this stuffed suit exactly what she thought of him. If she did that, she might well be handcuffed and dragged off to whatever transport they had in mind, kicking and screaming. She satisfied herself with looking sullen, like the runaway teenager Tiydon obviously thought she was. It wasn't too hard.

Daniel was already standing by the door. Suddenly he looked back and said, 'I heard about the cave-in on number four. What happened there?'

The miner's tone was casual enough, but Tiydon's expression changed. His face tightened, closed in. Sam was sure she saw a flicker of fear in his eyes.

He sighed and shook his head. 'I wish I knew, Daniel. But we're shutting it off for the time being. Until we find out.'

'Did you get everybody out of there?'

'There's one still missing – O'Connell. But Security are on to it.'

A pause. Sam could see the blush of anger on Daniel's face, but all he said was, 'Let me know if they need any help.'

'I'll do that, Daniel.' Tiydon sounded dismissive.

The miner nodded, frowned, and left. Sam followed.

'Why are you so chummy with him?' she said to Daniel once they were outside.

Daniel glanced at her. 'He's the boss. And he's not too bad, either. Goes down the bar with the lads, sometimes, which is more than you can say for most of the above-ground set.'

'But Aloisse is fighting for *your* rights. And you just sold her out.'

Daniel glanced at her. 'You're worried about Aloisse?' He clapped her on the back, laughed. 'I didn't sell her out, kid. I passed the buck. Didn't you hear me passing it, now? "Talk to Tina yourself," I said.' He glanced at Sam, saw that she was still angry, and quickly went on, 'I told you, I like Aloisse, but she's a darn nuisance. I want to keep my job, and my mates' jobs. These creepy-crawlies she goes on about, the ones that're supposed to breathe vacuum, I'm sure they're great and all that – but I've got human mouths to feed back home.'

Sam looked down at her trainers, still covered in sticky fragments from the Kusk ship, clumping along on the too-clean mosaic of this executive environment or whatever it was. She was both embarrassed and angry: embarrassed because she understood exactly why Daniel was doing what he was doing, angry because she still thought he was wrong.

'Well, *I* don't have anyone to feed back home,' she said at last. 'And I think Aloisse deserves some support. I think we should go back to the ship to talk to her.'

Daniel patted her shoulder in a fatherly way. 'Sorry, Sam, but you're going on the first freighter out of here, just like Ri Tiydon said.'

' "Just like Ri Tiydon said",' echoed Sam. She stopped walking, turned to face him, forcing him to stop too. 'Do you do everything he says? What about the cave-in? You told your friend you were going to speak to Tiydon about that – and did you? I mean, you just believed everything he said. Do you really think that these security people are going to be able to save your friends? Or don't you care any more?'

'Sam, you don't know anything about it,' he said, quietly, his blue eyes meeting hers. 'If there was anything I could do, if there was anything Tiydon could do –'

'He's the boss, isn't he?' But Sam's voice was uncertain: she could already see that it wasn't quite as straightforward as that.

Daniel just shrugged.

Sam looked away, saw two fishlike aliens dancing in the

swimming pool. Water splashed in slow, high, low-gravity arcs. 'I'm not leaving,' she said.

Daniel caught her arm gently, turned her to face him. 'Now, tell me I didn't hear that.' There was a weary expression on his face, and a kindness that almost made her give in.

Almost.

'OK, you didn't hear it,' she said. Then she snatched her arm free of his and set off at a steady lope down the corridor to the lift.

'Level zero,' she told the machine, hoping she could remember the rest of the way back to the landing bay.

'Hold it!' called Daniel. He was bounding towards the lift, great low-gee hops: in his tracksuit he looked slightly ridiculous doing that, like a giant rabbit. The doors shut just before he could reach them.

Sam felt the low gravity diminish to near-zero as the lift descended. She wondered if Daniel was going to call out security. Probably he would. She realised that she'd got herself into a more serious situation than she'd intended. 'Crossing the lines' and joining Aloisse's side didn't just mean making Aril Tiydon her enemy: it meant making Daniel her enemy. And all the other miners.

Was she so sure that Aloisse was right? The big alien had saved her life, but that didn't necessarily mean that her political views were correct. Perhaps the mining operation wasn't harming the ecosystem as much as Aloisse thought it was. What were dreamstones, anyway? The base was huge: somebody must be making a lot of money. But that didn't necessarily make it a good idea.

Sam realised that the lift had stopped. The doors opened on to a corridor full of people. She looked at them closely as she stepped out. It was hard to tell with the aliens, but most of the humans looked poor and tired: their clothes basic, their faces lined and pale.

She remembered what Daniel had said: 'I've got human mouths to feed back home.' The miners, she guessed, didn't have much choice. Other jobs might be even worse. Or there might not be any other jobs, if the economic situation was bad enough. Sam wished she'd paid more attention to the Doctor's historical ramblings on the early twenty-third century. All she could remember reading from this period was a whale song book.

The Doctor.

No time to think about him now, she decided.

She let herself be carried by the flow of the people in the corridor, found herself in a dining area. The smell of food made her realise how hungry she was. The last time she'd eaten properly had been – had been –

A very long time ago.

She'd joined the queue, looked over the shoulders of the others at the various hot ready meals on offer, tried to work out which if any of them was vegetarian, and decided to go for a salad and bread roll just in case, before she realised that she had no money and no means of getting any money. She had no way of getting anything to eat, anywhere to sleep, even a change of clothing.

It was either Daniel or Aloisse, she realised. The mine company or its opponents. She didn't have the option of staying nonpartisan here.

OK, she thought. Given no choice…

She turned away from the food dispensers, ignoring her rumbling stomach, and looked for signs to the landing bay.

At the entrance she ran into Daniel.

He smiled. 'Thought you might be here,' he said. 'Come on, kid, there's time for some dinner before we go.'

CHAPTER 4

The spaceship was empty. The Doctor was sure of that.

It was tumbling end over end, a silent, blotchy home-grown thing. There was a hole in its side, and the long ropes of cabling that had escaped had wrapped themselves around it. The entire structure was dusted with ice crystals.

The TARDIS console room hummed around him, full of power. Power that was doing him no good at the moment, because he couldn't find the only thing he wanted to find. The Doctor rested his hands on the console, silently interacting with the TARDIS systems to find out where he was.

'Mu Camelopides,' he muttered. 'That's interesting.'

There was something he knew about the Mu Camelopides system, but he'd mislaid it in the huge, ill-ordered warehouse that was his memory. He looked at the library, the vast shelving stretching towards the ceiling, the elaborately carved doors that led to the main reference room. But the 'M' section was half an hour's walk away. And it could take hours more to find the book he wanted, since the library had stopped being cooperative and moving them around for him. Then it might not have information about the right century. He looked at the cat he'd been given on Earth after his most recent battle against the Daleks. It was curled up asleep in a chair, and ignored him. He sighed.

'I should write things down more often. Remind myself.'

Well, no use worrying about that now. He'd made inquiries at every post office and missing-persons bureau he dared visit: human, Draconian, Tractite, Chelonian, Besiddian, Arachnon, Krakenite... the lot. He'd visited Threadworld, wrapped himself in the toffee-like Thread Helmets and traced sightings of humanoids anywhere in the Centrum.

Nothing. This wreck was all he had left. The only Kusk ship in the right time, in the right place. It had to be the one.

He looked at the dead, tumbling spaceship again. Could Sam still be alive, somewhere aboard? It seemed unlikely. More likely she'd been picked up. There was a warp-drive slip point nearby – the Doctor could almost feel the subtle, superficial twisting of space that the primitive human machines made for themselves.

But –

'Was Sam's ship going in, or going out?' he asked.

He looked at the cat again, but the cat was still asleep.

The food in the miners' canteen was like everything else at the DMMC base: basic but adequate. Most of it had turned out to be vegetarian: on Daniel's recommendation she'd had some Vithiliskan Savoury Fruit, which looked like basted tennis balls and tasted like chickpeas. For some reason they were served with a sweet mint sauce.

Sam ate two portions, watched over by an indulgent Daniel. During the second portion, she had time to speak. She told him quietly that she didn't really have anywhere to go, so there was no point in shipping her out on the next freighter.

'I…' she said. 'My family are –' *in a different century* – 'dead.' She gave him an edited version of the events on Hirath, told him that her companion had been left for dead, without saying who he was or why.

To her immense relief, Daniel didn't ask any questions, just nodded gently from time to time.

Afterwards, over dessert, she asked him about his family, and was told that he had a wife, Shelly, and two kids, Clarissa and Nadine, both much younger than Sam.

'Never make important decisions when you're tired or hungry,' he told her as she tucked into the pink flesh of a split Tiu-Tiu root, covered in something that ordinarily would have been too sugary for her taste. 'How d'you feel about going with Aloisse now?'

'Still the same,' said Sam. She looked up, meeting his eyes. 'Has she been locked up?'

Daniel did his patient shrug again. But then he said, 'I suppose I'd better be finding out for you, then.'

Sam grinned.

Captain Tina Ffrench of the *Dreamstone Miner* was indignant. She didn't put her end of the call on visual, and Sam guessed from the slightly confused sleepiness in her voice that they'd just woken her up.

'No, of *course* I haven't locked her up!' she protested, when she'd got the gist of what Daniel was telling her. 'Aril thinks he runs the Universe since he got that promotion. I just don't take any notice of him. For a start I haven't got a cabin big enough to lock her up in, and anyway she has actually locked herself *into* Hold B, which if I did it from the outside would be illegal. So all in all I'm probably stuck with her till the end of recorded history. I mean, if Aril would like to send about five security guards with a set of metal cutters in, he's more than welcome to try and haul her off –'

'He's got other things on his mind,' said Daniel. He told the captain about the accident in Shaft Four, keeping his voice low so that the other miners in the comms bay wouldn't hear. Sam guessed that the information wasn't officially released yet.

'Oh, hell,' said the captain. 'That's bad. OK, so what *are* we going to do with our tentacled friend?'

'Sam here says she's going to negotiate with her. If that's all right by you.' Daniel pushed Sam in front of the comms-booth camera.

There was a pause. Then: 'Jesus, she's a bit wet behind the ears for a negotiator, isn't she? And isn't she the kid we picked up –'

Daniel laughed. 'That's her. But she's smart for her age, she likes

Aloisse, and better still Aloisse likes her. And –' he did his shrug –
'she's all we've got.'

A momentary silence.

'I've travelled a lot,' supplied Sam. 'And I owe Aloisse a favour,
since she rescued me and saved my life. I think she's being stupid,
and I think I can get her to change her mind.'

Another pause, then a sigh.

'OK then, Sam. Do your stuff. If you can get her off my ship I'll
give you a campaign medal.'

'Aloisse?'

Silence.

'Aloisse, it's Sam.'

Silence.

'I came back to talk to you.'

Silence.

'Are you all right?'

'I'm fine, thank you very much. And you?' The familiar wooden
rumble of her voice was muffled by the insulated door of Hold B,
but audible enough. It reverberated in the metal walls of the
passageway for several seconds, an odd, almost mechanical noise.

One of the light fittings overhead started flickering. Sam had to
grin: Aloisse really was a bit of a disaster area on ships built to
human specifications.

'You're going to have to come out eventually,' she said.

Silence.

'I want to join your lot. But I can't do it unless you come out and
help me. I don't even know where they are.'

A very loud click, followed by several interesting thumps. The
overhead light died altogether. Fortunately, there was enough light
from others along the passageway to see fairly well.

Sam looked at Daniel, who raised his eyebrows. 'Looks
promising,' he muttered.

The door swung open, revealing Aloisse, her skin looking rather dusty, her huge eye open and already fixed on Sam. Warm, rather musty air blew gently past her from the dark space of the hold beyond the doorway.

Her big eye fixed on Sam.

'I was wondering when you'd make up your mind,' she said.

'You mean you locked yourself in the hold and everything just to make sure I'd take your side?'

'Oh no,' said Aloisse. 'Not just for that.'

Sam and the alien were making their way across a rough, grey plain. It was utterly dry, and airless: the shadows were as sharp as knives.

'I needed to make a point,' Aloisse said. 'The things that company gets up to are terrible, you know.'

'They let us out of the base.'

'Only because they knew I'd be less trouble off the base than on it. Oh, I know Daniel's nice enough, but – look!' She raised a tentacle – now encased in a long, ring-jointed spacesuit appendage – and pointed at a bizarre, treelike crystalline formation on the horizon, full of tall spikes. 'You don't often see them this near the equator.'

'What is it?'

'Exanaxi. If you wait you'll see it breathe.'

'It's *alive*?' She frowned. 'What does it breathe?'

'Air, of course,' said Aloisse. 'It makes it from the rock. At least, that's what the biologists think is happening. What no one understands is – ah! There!'

The outline of the Exanaxi blurred; Sam realised after a moment that this was because dust had risen up around it, obviously blown up by the release of the gas the – plant? animal? neither? both? – had exhaled.

Slowly, the blurring went away. Sam waited, expecting

something else to happen, but nothing did.

'That's it for another day,' said Aloisse after a while.

'How did you know it was going to breathe if it only does it once a day?'

'Crystals were up. See? It's not glittering so much now. They only glitter when they're getting ready to breathe. Or sometimes when they're fighting off predators.'

'What sort of predators?'

'Oh, zaxix, Higgs's cortenenda, that sort of thing.' Aloisse had started out across the plain once more. 'I told you, it's a complete ecosystem. And they –' she jerked a tentacle back towards the mining camp, still visible as a jumble of plastic blisters on the horizon behind them – 'are systematically destroying it.'

Sam tried to remember if the Doctor had ever mentioned a vacuum-living ecosystem. Certainly she hadn't run into one.

'Is it silicon based?' she asked Aloisse.

'No, carbon.' The alien seemed surprised at her suggestion. 'The outer coating's diamond, intercellular membranes are bucky tubes, mostly. Given a chance the company would probably be mining the wildlife directly. At least we've managed to stop that from happening. So far. Though you've got to look out for wildcatters. Do you like Cetacean?'

Aloisse's sudden changes of direction reminded Sam of the Doctor. It was oddly reassuring, but it also brought a lump to her throat.

'Umm – not sure. What is it – um, they?'

Aloisse laughed, raising a small dust storm of her own. 'You *are* a bit strange, aren't you? They're a musical band. A lot of young humans are into them. I'm *amazed* you haven't heard of them. You aren't a time traveller, are you?'

Sam froze. 'I – that is –' OK, heart in your mouth time. 'Yes. Or at least, I was living with one.'

Aloisse laughed again. 'Well, that excuse should cover pretty well everything.' A pause. 'Gallifreyan, I suppose?' Sam nodded. 'Yes, we've had dealings with them. Arrogant lot. Very strange political system. And *obsessed* with time travel.' The visor of her spacesuit moved to face Sam: she couldn't see the shadowy eye inside, but knew she was being looked at. 'I shouldn't go around telling everyone about it. Some people will kill for that kind of power.'

'I know. The Doctor says he's had a lot of trouble. People wanting to know too much, do too much.'

'Why did you leave him?'

Sam felt herself blushing. 'There was an accident. I –'

I should have gone back.

But she couldn't say it.

Aloisse must have sensed Sam's discomfort, because she quickly changed the subject, pointing out a line of silver posts a few hundred metres ahead. 'That's it. The edge of company property, in this direction at least. Beyond that Mu Cam VI-One is still free space. Theoretically.'

'And the protesters' camp?'

'Just at the bottom of that hill. Can't you see it?'

Sam realised that she could. It was the same bright dust colour as the plain, but the regular shape gave away its artificial origin: it was a half-doughnut, a broken torus with the ends covered in scalloped metal sheeting. Looking closely, Sam could see a few small windows, and the pie-dish shape of an antenna pointing at the stars.

'I think it used to be a bit of an old orbital station,' said Aloisse. 'But for us it's home. For the next few weeks at least. Months, maybe.'

Or maybe years, thought Sam. This is my life. Here. Now. This little piece of metal on a random moon in the middle of twenty-third-century nowhere.

Home.

Until further notice.
She started down the slope towards the camp.

CHAPTER 5

Jono had a place under the Pythagoras Dome, in the mild humidity of an eternal, artificial summer. Sun lights floated over the gardens of the low houses, their tethers glinting occasionally. Flowers grew under the pearly sky: big pink hydrangeas, blue and yellow trumpetflowers, even a native clzz-wzz tree covered in tiny, silver blossoms. The buildings in the dome were reconfigurable, made up from plug-in cubical units in various floral colours: Jono had her house stacked up at the moment, a mini-skyscraper with the porch and front door on top, accessible only by heli, or, if you were brave, a rope ladder hanging down into the upper branches of a small tree in the front garden. Anton directed the helicab to the roof, jumped down on to the fake wood of the porch. The security system inspected him, bleeped, let him in.

He found Jono in the climbing room, slouched on a dry branch of the indoor candabdab tree she used to keep her claws and muscles in trim. Her tail twitched when he came in, then after a moment her eyes opened and she yawned, revealing her five rows of serrated teeth and a long, pink tongue.

'Hello, human playmate,' she said sleepily, then swung off the branch and brachiated across the room to land at his feet and enclose him in a hot quasi-feline hug. She licked his face a couple of times, her fur prickling against his cheek, then met his eyes. 'What's up?'

Anton stepped back out of her embrace.

'Come on.' She winked. ' "I can tell by the smell." What's the problem? Ybrik bothering you again?'

Anton swallowed. Now he was here, he had no idea what to tell Jono. Perhaps he should just forget it, have a drink, spend the evening here.

No. She'd talked him into this dreamstone business. She ought to know what had happened as a result.

And he needed her help.

'I had a bad dream.'

'And you've come to tell me about it?' She stepped back, pulled a green robe from its hook near the door, slipped it on, then began combing her mane with her claws, dragging out fragments of leaf and tangles with a crackling sound.

Anton swallowed again. His mouth felt as if it was full of glue.

But it was no good. He had to tell her.

'I had a bad dream and then I killed someone and now I'm afraid to go home.'

She froze, for a full second, utterly motionless with her hands on the belt of the robe, which she'd been in the middle of tying. The pupils of her eyes narrowed to slits, then widened again.

Finally she finished tying her robe, then began combing her mane again.

'How can I help?' she asked.

Anton felt as if a huge weight had been lifted from his back. He knew it was an illusion: he had still killed the Zmm-Zmm, and he was still going to have to face the consequences of that. But at least Jono – practical, confident Jono – was going to stay on his side.

He thought of the questions she *hadn't* asked before deciding to side with him – who was it? why did you do it? did they deserve it? – and felt his eyes filling with tears.

Jono stepped forward, gently licked his cheek with the tip of her tongue.

'You need a drink,' she said.

The five nightmare stones seemed oddly at home in Jono's living room, amid the elaborately wrought hunting masks and wooden models of primitive Zmm-Zmm hives that filled most of the available space.

'Are you sure you want to do this?'

Jono was sprawled on a green baize couch underneath the window, idly lapping at her fourth or fifth bowl of crème de menthe. Her eyes glowed slightly in the light from the lamp on the low table; outside, it was dark.

'I have to,' said Anton. 'I killed a sentient being for these things. I want to know why I did it.'

Jono shook her head. 'Anton, I've *told* you. If I'd been there, and seen what that "sentient being" was doing to make money for himself, I wouldn't have waited for him to pull a knife. I would have *eaten* him. Slowly. Painfully. While still alive, as far as possible.' She opened her formidable jaws and idly plucked at one of her serrated teeth.

Anton smiled back. After she'd heard his story, Jono's support for him had gone from absolute and unconditional to absolute, unconditional and enthusiastic. She seemed to think he'd done the city a favour, that he'd advanced the entire cause of sentient civilisation. He was sure it was at least partly genuine, and not just the product of her love and loyalty: but at the same time, he wondered what she *would* have done if she'd been there.

Handled it better, probably.

Not got anyone killed, almost certainly.

'I wish you had been there,' he said. 'I should've asked you along.'

'Mmm.' Jono lapped at the crème de menthe. 'You always were impulsive.' Her pupils narrowed to slits, and her robe shifted around behind her, a sign that her tail was thrashing to and fro underneath it. 'What are your impulses telling you now?'

Anton looked at the tiny, detailed pattern of tiles on the floor. 'I think I should use these stones. Now. Tonight.'

'Are you going to be able to sleep?'

'I don't know – maybe –'

Jono gestured at his glass, which still contained a mouthful of the milky green fluid. 'More of that?'

Anton shook his head. 'I know it sounds strange –'

'But you'll need to concentrate. Yes.' She stretched her long-toed feet

51

against the thick green fabric, ran her tongue around her lips and her flat, dark, nose. 'Perhaps there is another way I can help you to sleep.'

Their eyes met, and Anton smiled. He got up from the chair and joined her on the couch.

His head was on fire, it was huge like a balloon and it was burning burning burning and the monsters were coming – huge, grey, steel-shiny monsters with red coal eyes – dreamstone eyes –

'They're going to kill me! They're really going to –'

The blow hit Anton in the face, hard.

He jolted upright, saw Jono staring at him, her lips drawn back to show her front teeth, her fingers still stretched out where she had slapped him. The stones were in a ring around him, and all of them were flaring with light, as if there were flames inside them.

– burning burning burning –

Anton shivered with remembered terror. He became aware that, far from burning, he was terribly, terribly cold. As if he was alone, losing heat, dying.

He felt vomit rising in his throat. He tried to stop, to move, but it was too late – he was sick over the side of the bed, the green-stained fluids spattering over Jono's plum-coloured bedroom carpet.

Jono sat on the bed, put an arm around him. 'How do you feel?' she said.

After a while, he nodded. 'I'm OK.'

'You go clean yourself up, I'll see to this mess.'

Anton tottered to the bathroom, his head still full of half-formed images that kept taking on semihuman shapes. Bizarre, crippled little hairy things ran down tunnels, screamed, died messily. Yet they were utterly terrifying, their faces, their blazing, greedy eyes.

Was that what he had dreamed, or was he thinking of it now, in response to his feverish condition? Anton's instinct – and his long practice with dreams – suggested the former. But what were these creatures? They were humanoid, but not human. Not even dream-human. He was sure of that.

When he returned to the bedroom, Jono was supervising a stain remover. The little machine hissed and frothed as it crawled, cockroach-like, across the carpet. Jono whistled at it occasionally, to encourage it to turn around, or to intensify its efforts.

'Did the dream tell you anything?' she said after a while.

'Monsters – pain – confusion. It was like a fever dream.' He sat down on the edge of the bed, trying to get his thoughts together. Only then did he notice that it was already starting to get light outside. It was the early, false, eternal-summer dawn of the Pythagoras dome, but it was still dawn. Someone would have found the body of the Zmm-Zmm by now. The police would be looking for the killer.

The killer. I killed someone.

Anton was amazed to discover that he didn't feel as bad about that as he had the previous night. The shock of the nightmare seemed to have dislocated his feelings. Or maybe he really didn't care. Maybe his conscience wasn't so disturbed; maybe its deep-down voice was telling him that it was only a Zmm-Zmm he had killed, after all. Not a real person.

Anton shivered. He hadn't thought he was like that.

Jono whistled the stain remover away and sat down beside him. 'What now?' she asked.

Anton looked at the dreamstones. They were dead now, all the light gone.

'I think I should take them back,' he said. 'Go to the Dreamstone Moon.' Before Jono could speak he clattered on: 'I know it sounds mad, but it felt as if those nightmares were structured. Not just random images. Somebody had already imprinted the stones. I need to find out who.'

Now he'd said it, he was absolutely sure about it. It made sense: it was the *only* rational explanation.

Wasn't it?

'I suppose it's possible,' Jono was saying. 'But I don't think the place has got any intelligent natives. I suppose the miners could be doing it. Or someone who works there. But why? And why would they produce such horrible dreams?'

Anton shook his head. 'I don't know, but I need to go there.'

Jono slipped an arm around his shoulders. 'And I suppose you want me to pay the fare?'

Anton felt his face redden. 'I'm sorry, I hadn't even thought about – I don't know what I spent on the stones –'

Jono laughed aloud. 'Anton, you never, ever know what you've spent on anything.' Then Anton felt the muscles in her arm bunch with tension. 'Do you want me to come with you?'

Anton looked at her profile, the flat nose, the heavy, catlike jaw, the wise eyes.

She would come, if he asked her.

But he couldn't do that to her. She had a life to lead, here. Her own life. This was his problem, and he wanted it to stay that way.

'No.'

She turned her face to his, settled her chin in his ready outstretched hand. The fur was rough, like stubble.

'I'll pay your fare,' she said. 'I'll even let you have my reserve cash chip. But please try not to spend it all. And go on the lunchtime shuttle.'

'Why?' said Anton, thinking of police, of bad dreamstone merchants, of getting off Occam's World as soon as possible.

Jono's eyes narrowed to slits, and her long whiskers twitched slightly.

'Because I don't feel I will ever see you again,' she said softly. 'And I want to say goodbye.'

CHAPTER 6

'It doesn't happen for years.'

'I mean, we have full, happy lives.'

'Full, happy and fulfilled lives.'

'Anyway, only one of us gets eaten.'

'The other one helps bring up the children.'

Sam looked from one of the knee-high, delicate-looking, only vaguely spider-like beings to the other. Two triplets of dark eyes on short, jointed stalks stared back at her. They were called Arachnons by the other protesters; their personal names were Kekkikk, and, well, Kekkikk again, only you held your eye stalks in a different position. Not having eye stalks Sam had resorted to calling them Kekkikk-1 and Kekkikk-2, but it wasn't much help, since they looked identical: the same leg markings, the same delicate shade of duck-egg blue on the abdomen, the same feathery amber gills protruding from their necks.

And, she suspected, the same warped sense of humour. She just didn't believe this. However much they *looked* like spiders, surely the females didn't *really* eat the males after they mated?

'You're having me on, aren't you?' she said finally.

The eye stalks twitched, which might have meant anything.

'No, we're not,' said Kekkikk-1, or, well, possibly Kekkikk-2.

'That's why we're so much like each other,' said the other one.

'You never know which one's going to make it, so our wife wouldn't want us to be too different.'

'Not that we've chosen a wife yet.'

'We won't do *that* for a while.'

'No way. Not till we've had that full, happy and interesting life.'

'Perhaps never.'

'With luck.'

Sam looked around the crude steel box littered with plasteel benches that served the Dreamstone protesters for a canteen and general meeting hall, hoping that someone would be watching and would give her some sort of clue about how she was supposed to react. But there weren't very many people about: a couple of feline Besiddians were sharing a drink and conversing in low voices; a human in his thirties had his feet up reading a folding computer; and a white, six-limbed Chorodoron was brachiating from the steel rails that ran across the length of the ceiling. But nobody was paying any attention to Sam and the Arachnons. Outside the windows it was dark, the two-day night of Dreamstone Moon.

Oh, well, if she was going to make a fool of herself anyway…

She turned back to the pair of Arachnons. 'I suppose all your literature must be about love and death,' she said, trying not to sound too sceptical, just in case.

'Most of it. But isn't most of yours?'

'*Romeo and Juliet.*'

'*Tender is the Night.*'

'*The Transmigration of Timothy Archer.*'

'*The Affirmation.*'

'We're reading Mortimore right now. All his characters die.'

'Horribly.'

'But then so do most people. Even humans.'

'So it doesn't make any difference, not really, does it?'

Sam didn't reply. She still had a sense that the Arachnons were just waiting for the punchline. She was immensely relieved when the heavy door at the end of the room clanged open, revealing the tentacled figure of Aloisse.

'Ah, there you are,' she said, fixing her eye on Sam. 'Have you read Junsequat yet?'

Sam struggled to think which of the many e-books she'd been given was Junsequat. She'd quickly found out that protest had become something of an exact science since the twentieth century: Sam had spent her four days in the base cramming on everything from general stuff like Interorganisational Relations Theory to the specifics of Protest Management. At first she'd thought she was going to be bored, but she'd quickly realised that the material Aloisse had selected wasn't at all dry and academic, despite the titles. A lot of it referred to real protest situations, some of them going back to her own time. After a couple of days' reading – or, more accurately, interactive viewing – Sam had realised that Aloisse wasn't blinding her with science: she was simply trying to equip her with the basic knowledge she needed in order to be able to participate without becoming a liability to the others.

'Junsequat was the paper on "The Statistical Maximisation of the News Items Promotion System through Interview Keyword Techniques",' Aloisse informed her.

Sam blushed. That was one where she *had* let the title put her off. 'Sorry,' she said. 'There was just so much stuff.'

'That's OK, but can you read it before tonight? Cirbnekk's organising a dig-in at one of their new sites.' Cirbnekk was another Krakenite (a human name for her species, she'd explained contemptuously; but her own version was unpronounceable, which didn't leave Sam with much choice). As far as anyone was, Cirbnekk seemed to be in charge around here. 'With any luck we can bring them to a halt, get arrested, get on into the top ten news items, at least locally. We might even make the hundred on Earth, I'm told everything else is really quiet. But it'll help if you look at Junsequat's Interview Keyword tables first, so you know what to say to the police and the lawyers. You're not worried about spending a few days in a cell?'

Sam felt her heart beating faster. This was what she was here for, not playing guessing games with aliens about their mating habits. 'I'm in,' she said.

'Me, too,' said the two Arachnons simultaneously.

Aloisse eyed them. 'Are you sure? It might get a bit rough.'

'We're OK with that.'

'Life is short.'

Sam just looked at them, then turned back to Aloisse.

'Can I have a word with you?' Sam asked. 'There was something I wanted to ask about the management of the anti-Weather Control demonstrations in the 2040s.'

Aloisse twitched her tentacles. 'Yes, but you'll have to walk with me to do it, I've got to be at the Media Relations Unit ten minutes ago.'

Sam grinned. She'd been rather hoping that Aloisse would say something like that.

As soon as the heavy door had shut behind them, she asked, 'The Arachnons don't really get eaten by their wives, do they?'

Aloisse's eye waved towards Sam. 'Yes. Terrible thing, but nothing you can do about it. Hormones, you know. Now what was it you wanted to know about the anti-Weather Control protests?'

But Sam had frozen in the middle of the corridor.

'What's up?'

'I didn't believe them,' she said. 'I thought they were joking. They must have thought I was –'

'Oh, don't worry, nobody ever does believe them, the first time. I suppose they get used to it.'

But the reassurance was too late. Sam was already dashing back down the corridor, rehearsing an apology.

The Doctor stepped out of the TARDIS doors and looked around.

Ah. A corridor.

Question was, where did it lead? This was the nearest habitable area to the Kusk ship: the time was only a few days later. If Sam was anywhere local, she should be here. And if she wasn't, well, perhaps at least he'd be able to find a record of the incident, or the shipping, or something.

For the time being, it was his only lead.

He started along the corridor, slowly. He found himself smelling the air from time to time, and frowning.

After a while, he stopped and looked around. Plain, standard-issue metal walls. Air-conditioned, much-recycled air, faint smell of tropical plants and a rather stronger smell of oil.

No. It wasn't the smell exactly, he thought. It wasn't even the air. It was more like – *the feel*.

Yes. The feel of the place was wrong.

But then it usually was.

He only hoped that Sam wasn't involved in anything dangerous.

But then, he knew she probably would be.

Digging holes in the ground wasn't quite as easy as Sam had expected. She'd thought there might be a spade involved, for instance. In fact, she was in charge of a bulldozer.

A bulldozer armed with high explosives.

'This still doesn't feel right,' she protested to Aloisse, who was, thankfully, the one who was actually driving the thing. 'I mean, we're supposed to be against damaging the environment.' She gestured helplessly at the big twin blades of the bulldozer's power drilling attachment, and the red explosives launchers fitted above them, barrels aimed at the holes they'd just drilled in the ground. Beyond, a steely plain shone in the noon sun, ending at a black, knife-sharp horizon.

'You heard the brief,' said Aloisse. 'This whole area is due to be nuked next week to make a rubble dump. The only way we're going to stop it is by standing in the way – and for that we need radiation-proof shelters. You have to be realistic about these things, Sam.'

She handed Sam a firing key.

Sam still hesitated. This felt more like making war than making a point.

'I know how you feel, Sam,' said Aloisse. 'I feel the same. But this is all we can do.'

'What about the Exanaxi and things?'

'There isn't anything living round here. The nearest Exanaxi is over six kilometres away at the moment. That's more than a safe distance. Believe me, I've studied the life here more than anyone else except Higgs. I know what I'm doing.'

Sam bit her lip. This was a bit like working with the Doctor. You never quite understood everything he was doing, either, but –

Yes. He would have found a different way. Something less violent, but just as effective. But, right now, Sam couldn't think what it would have been.

'OK,' she said at last. She inserted the key.

'On my mark – three – two – one –'

They turned their keys, and the dozer shook as the explosive-tipped rockets shot home into the churned rock.

The surface shuddered. Loose fragments clattered down on the hull, disconcertingly loud. As they settled, Sam could just see the flicker as another dozer fired its explosives a couple of kilometres away. That would be the two Kekkikks. Somewhere beyond the horizon – that was more than four kilometres away – a man called Jess and a Besiddian called Sono were doing the same job. The idea was to confuse the base authorities, and overstretch their resources – Aloisse didn't want all three units arrested: she wanted some of them back at the base preparing the next phase of the protest.

'Now we wait for all hell to break loose,' said Aloisse. She pulled at a lever with a spare tentacle, and the dozer rolled forward to the edge of the blast site. Sam watched as steel blades ploughed into the broken rock, then as the shovel turned on its arm and dumped the first load of fragments at a safe distance from the hole.

A buzzer sounded, and a red light lit up on the panel. Sam looked at the readout screens, saw the words PROXIMITY ALERT – EXPLOSIVES ARE NEGATIVELY INDICATED.

'It's only the company coming to arrest us,' said Aloïsse, pulling the blade down for the next load. 'The machine's just warning us not to blow them up.'

A cylindrical steel object rushed overhead, startlingly close, absolutely silent. Sam caught a glimpse of the DMMC company logo, a dazzling flicker of rocket exhausts, and it was gone.

'Doesn't look like they were after us,' she said, surprised at how disappointed she felt.

'They might be back. Or they might not be anything to do with it. It *was* a bit of a quick response, especially for this dozy lot.' Aloïsse twitched a tentacle in the direction of the Kekkikks' dozer. 'Looks like they missed them too.' A pause. 'Hmm, that's odd.'

Sam looked up sharply. Aloïsse's tone of voice hadn't changed – that was coming from the translator. But her eye was out on its stalk, peering through the curved screen of the dozer.

'He's suiting up. What's he doing in there?' She flicked a switch on the panel. 'Squid One to Spider Men, Squid One to Spider Men, what's happening?'

Silence. Sam could see it now: a tiny, silver shape glinting in the sun as it descended from the cab of the dozer.

A spacesuit. No. Two spacesuits.

Of course. They did everything together.

Sam blushed, remembering her earlier conversation with the Arachnons. They'd accepted her apology happily enough – as Aloïsse had said, they seemed to be resigned to being misunderstood – but even so, Sam wished she'd just taken the trouble to do a little research before deciding that they were out to make a fool of her.

Aloïsse was fiddling with a keypad on the control panel. 'You don't remember the code and frequency for the suits, do you? I can't get anything here –'

Sam looked at the panel, saw a paper label stuck to the side of one of the screen units, with the figures 100773,35.54 written on it.

'That it?' she asked.

Aloisse tapped the numbers into the keypad, and was rewarded with a hissing sound, through which faint clicks of Arachnon dialogue could be heard.

'Bloody interference,' snapped Aloisse. 'I'll bet that's the company jamming our –'

The hissing got louder, and broke into a series of clicking, gurgling noises.

Suddenly, a translation system cut in. The volume was far too loud: it hurt Sam's ears in the confined space.

'Help!' it roared. 'Help us!'

Sam looked, but she couldn't see the tiny suits any longer. There was no movement near the Kekkikks' vehicle.

Aloisse whipped a tentacle out to the keypad. 'Where are you?'

More clicks and gurgles, then something that sounded very like a scream.

'Under the Moon!' roared the translator. 'It's under the Moon!'

On the radio, there was the sound of something tearing, another scream, followed by a roar of static.

Then silence.

Daniel O'Ryan didn't very often get drunk, and he never got drunk alone.

At least, he hadn't before today.

Today he'd gone down to the Wildcatter, got himself a bottle of Jameson's, and drunk a quarter of it before he even got back to his room. He'd locked the door, sat down on the pale-blue, standard-issue chair by the pale-blue, standard-issue table, and started to drink the rest.

Matthew O'Connell was dead. Daniel could still see Tiydon's

face as he'd made the announcement over the base vid: *embarrassed* God help him, as if what the Dreamstone Moon Mining Company and its employees thought of him was more important than the fact that he was responsible for someone's death.

'After four days of making every effort we were just too late to save him.' Tiydon's words echoed in Daniel's brain. *Every effort?* Why hadn't they brought the miners in to help, then? Why let security handle a mine-safety problem? It almost made you believe what Sam and that tentacled git Aloisse had said: the company were wrong, they shouldn't be mining here, there was something going on that they wouldn't admit to.

There was a faint chime from the comm system. Daniel glanced up, decided to ignore it. He'd watched the faces of the other miners after the announcement, and had seen the anger there. Kran was talking about a strike. More probably, there would be a riot. No doubt this was someone who wanted him to join in, or one of Tiydon's people trying to get him to help them calm things down.

Daniel wanted none of it. None of that being caught in the middle. Not now. He was off duty, and his time was his own. He didn't have to talk to anyone unless he chose to.

He stared at the sea-green wall of his room, the antique copper plates, the holovid of his wife Shelly and their two daughters, which had long ago been frozen on one eternally smiling frame. The happiness in the children's faces, the green leaves and flowers behind Shelly's golden hair, mocked him with their safety, their freedom. It was for them that he was here. For them, he would stay here, until his pension was due, or until – until –

He didn't want to think about dying like his friend.

'Perhaps I should just go home,' he said aloud. 'Give up and go home.'

'I don't think so,' said a voice behind him.

Daniel was on his feet and facing the intruder before he'd finished speaking. He relaxed a little when he saw a friendly, relaxed face: a man perhaps a little younger than he was, wearing a strange costume, like something out of a previous century.

Daniel stared for a moment, confused: then the whiskey he'd drunk caught up with him and he swayed, almost fell. The man caught his arm, smiled. 'Sorry, but you weren't answering the door comm.'

'That's because I intended to get drunk,' said Daniel. 'In private.'

The man's eyes went to the bottle on the table – now almost half empty. 'Yes, yes, I see. Can I ask you a few questions first?'

'Questions? You're not with the press, are you?' Daniel stared at the man. He didn't look like a reporter. But then, he didn't look like anyone sensible at all. More like someone in search of a fancy-dress party.

'No, I'm looking for a friend.'

'So am I, but he's dead.'

There was a slight pause, and Daniel absorbed the look of sympathy on the other man's face.

'Mine isn't, I hope. She's called Sam. They told me that you've met her.'

'Um, I don't know.' Daniel struggled to remember. Sam. The teenage runaway. So this was her dad. Funny, he didn't look old enough. And why *was* he wearing those ridiculous clothes? 'She went off with Aloisse's lot. The protesters. Couldn't stop her. You know what kids are like.'

'And where can I find these protesters?'

Daniel shrugged. 'Another time, I'd take you to them. Just now, I don't want to be drunk in charge of a spacesuit.'

The other man's face fell. 'Oh, *please*. I've been looking for her everywhere.'

He sounded more like an abandoned child than anyone's father. If he was like this all the time, Daniel could begin to understand why the kid had left home. But on the other hand…

Daniel's two were a bit young to get up and go wandering round the galaxy, but he wondered how he'd feel if they did, when the time came. Not too good, he guessed.

'Look, I'll get you a map.' Daniel pulled his computer from his pocket and laid it out flat, forced his whiskey-fuzzed brain to concentrate. He called up the local map, scaled it to show the base and the surrounding terrain.

'The protesters' camp is there, just outside the perimeter. It's not marked on this, but it's by that little crater, at the bottom of the hill slope. You can see it easy enough when you get close enough.'

'You don't approve of these protesters, do you?'

The question made Daniel swing around again. 'You sure you're not from the press?'

'Why, have you got something to hide?' The man's voice was firm, almost cold, his gaze level. Not any longer the abandoned child – more an avenging angel.

Daniel looked away. 'I'm not sure. There have been some… incidents.'

'Like the one that killed your friend?'

Daniel nodded. 'It's just that they won't tell us anything about it. They would only let the security people down there – they wouldn't let the miners near the place.'

'Ah.' A pause. 'I think we're going to need to take a look at this, Daniel. Where was the accident?'

'Shaft Four, but we'll not get down there without –'

The man was already leaving.

Daniel hurried to catch up, surprised to find that he felt almost sober. 'We'll need permission from –'

'No we won't. I'm the Doctor.' The man was almost running towards the lift at the end of the corridor.

Daniel finally caught him up as the doors opened.

'What about your daughter?'

'Sam? She'll be safer where she is, I think.' He got into the lift, smiled at Daniel. 'Come on, we've got people to see, places to break into.'

Bewildered, but strangely hopeful, Daniel followed him.

Aloisse's voice was so loud that it was making something on the control panel rattle.

'I didn't pull you out of that ship to get yourself killed in a hole in the ground here! At least wait –' The translator went silent as Aloisse's suit unfolded itself around her.

Sam ignored the alien, because she'd noticed that Aloisse wasn't physically trying to stop her. She was just proving that she cared: she knew as well as Sam did that both of them were going to be needed outside if either of the Kekkikks was injured.

Which seemed likely.

Sam pushed the clips on her suit helmet home, checked the power, the water, the oxygen, the insulation.

All OK.

Sam hit the switch that opened the inner lock door. It slid back slowly, creaking and grinding.

'Should get those seals checked,' muttered Aloisse's voice, now coming through the suit radio.

In the airlock, Sam used the eyeblink pad on the suit, rather clumsily, to set the radio to the Arachnons' frequency and code.

A brief hiss of static, then nothing.

She closed the lock door: Aloisse hadn't finished suiting up, and anyway the tiny chamber was too small for both of them.

The lock cycled, the outer door opened. Feeling absurdly like Neil Armstrong – perhaps because the dozer with its polyhedral control module and rocket lift system looked a little bit like a lunar escape module – she clambered down the ladder on to the powdery surface.

Aloisse had raced the dozer across on its emergency rockets, and put them down only a few metres away from the Arachnons' machine; the blast hole was between the two, a star-shaped fracture in the rock. The side nearest the Arachnons' dozer had been excavated, leaving a steep slope covered in loose stones.

A thin, white arm waved from the top of the pit.

No. Not an arm. It was mist, thin streamers of vapour scattering into the vacuum.

There was air escaping. From one of the Kekkikks' suits? Sam moved cautiously around the pit until she could see down the slope.

A sharp hiss from her headphones. Sam jumped, but it was only Aloisse, who was now climbing out of the dozer, causing the whole vehicle to rock slowly on its four stubby legs. 'Don't go down there on your own!'

'I wasn't planning to,' said Sam, peering over the edge. At the bottom, she could see something gleaming.

A spacesuit arm – long, delicate, Arachnon-shaped. 'Kekkikk!' she called.

'The radios must be out,' observed Aloisse. She was standing by Sam's side. 'I'm going to see if I can reach –'

She stretched a tentacle into the pit. But Sam could see it was hopeless. Aloisse's heavy body was teetering on the edge of the slope. If she fell, even in this low gravity, she was as likely to kill the Arachnon – and possibly herself – as to be of any help.

'Lift me up,' said Sam. 'Lift me up and lower me in. Head down, then I'll be able to push some of the rubble out of the way and grab him.'

Sam half expected that Aloisse would argue – half hoped she would – but she simply said, 'Right-oh!' and grabbed hold of Sam with two or three tentacles and heaved her off the ground. For a moment all Sam could see was a confused swirling of the silver ground and knife-shadowed rocks. Then she was halfway down the pit, head downward.

'See anything?'

Awkwardly, Sam used the eyeblink pad to switch on the suit's lights.

Straightaway she saw the helmet of the Arachnon's suit, and the head inside it. The eye stalks were stiff, motionless, the eyes an amber pulp.

Life is short.

'He's dead,' said Sam. Her ears were buzzing, and she could hear a quiver of shock in her own voice. 'He's dead and I can't see the other one.'

'Are you sure? I thought he moved just a minute ago.'

Sam looked at the pulped eyes, the bubbling fluids inside the helmet. 'His suit's broken.' She could see the breach now, a raw ragged tear, fluid boiling away, droplets rising in the wind.

He'd died with air around him, but not enough air to save his life.

The world started to rotate again, as Aloisse hauled Sam up.

'No!' yelled Sam. 'The other one might be alive! I've got to –' But she was already landing on her feet in front of Aloisse.

'We've got to get some proper help,' said Aloisse firmly. 'Right now. I'll call the security chief at DMMC.'

But Sam pushed her way out of the alien's grip and began to pick her way down the slope. She had to be very careful where she put her feet. Some of the freshly cut rocks were probably sharp enough to damage her suit. Others might simply give way beneath her.

'Sam!'

'I'm nearly there,' said Sam, trying not to think about how afraid she ought to be. But if the other Kekkikk was still alive, she *wasn't* going to let him die. Not if he could be saved.

As she pushed her way past the gruesome contents of the broken suit, her own suit buzzed at her. She checked the panel, saw that it was a meteor-impact alert. She felt a moment's panic, then a gentle click on her faceplate made her realise the truth. The thin air escaping from the ground was just sufficient to carry small pieces of grit. Some of them were hitting her – hopefully, not hard enough to do any damage.

The rear of the Arachnon's suit was simply missing: by turning her suit's lights up to full power and peering forward, Sam saw the broken piece some distance away and a couple of metres below her, resting on a smooth, polished surface that looked a little like marble.

It was leaking pieces of frozen blood.

Not grit, then. Blood.

Sam realised that her legs were shaking. She made herself jump down to the polished stone. Her lights showed a long passageway, the walls glistening. She could feel the faint push of the escaping air against her back, though it was clear that it was at nothing like normal atmospheric pressure. When she thought to ask the suit, it informed her that the pressure was four millibars.

There was no sign of the other Kekkikk.

She turned, saw that the passageway behind her was different. The walls were covered in thick, dark, tangled roots. As her eyes adjusted, she could see that they were cracked open along their length, leaking whitish fluid which quickly boiled into vapour: Sam guessed that this was the source of the 'air'. Further down, the roots seemed to grow together, forming a solid mass that blocked the passage.

The ground trembled, and pebbles clattered down around her. Sam jumped, turned, saw Aloisse. Furious, she gestured at the broken roots.

'You knew what you were doing, did you? There was nothing alive for miles, was there?'

'Steady on, Sam, we don't know –' She broke off and at the same moment Sam saw a new movement ahead of them.

The roots were moving.

The roots were moving *fast*.

One slammed into Sam's body, and she realised too late that they weren't roots, they were *tentacles*, and the thing they were connected to was moving, moving towards them, and *it had an eye in it –*

Her suit buzzed, red lights lit up all over the panel. Her ears popped.

SUIT INTEGRITY BREACHED! INSTITUTE EMERGENCY PROCEDURE ONE!

'I don't know what it is!' bawled Sam. Something was squeezing her legs, another something had hold of one of her arms. She couldn't see: the visor was blocked. She heard the sound of cracking plastic. She tried to breathe but there was *no air* and *what am I going to do now –*

'Aloisse!' she yelled. 'Help!'

There was no response, but the shout drained the last of the air from Sam's lungs. She felt a tearing pain in her chest.

No I am not *going to die –*

She made an effort to break away, but her arms and legs seemed to have turned into warm cotton wool. They wouldn't move. She had a brief, whirling, red-misted impression of stars and rocks and the dead eyes of the Arachnon in his suit.

Then she was on the marble floor, staring at Aloisse, motionless in the grasp of a dozen or more of the tentacles.

She tried to call the alien's name, couldn't. Orange blood spattered her visor. Aloisse? One of the Kekkikks?

She knew she had to move, or she was going to die. But she couldn't. Her body wouldn't obey her.

A warm mist descended over her vision.

– no I am not *going to –*

CHAPTER 7

'So that's the extraction shop,' said the guide, a tiny, metal-winged Esqueekeemmian. 'As you see, we have some very skilled robots in here.'

A pause. A few dutiful giggles.

Anton guessed that he was supposed to giggle, too, but he didn't find it funny. The guided tour had so far been exactly what he'd expected: a waste of time. Everything he'd seen so far could have been VR'd from Occam's World. But he hadn't been able to think of any other way to start his exploration of Dreamstone Moon, and everyone else on the Dreamship *Excalibur* was booked in for the tour.

He looked at the crowd. Mostly humans, with a scattering of dreamstone-sensitive aliens, Besiddians like Jono, a slimy-skinned Borlog, a couple of Geomydes. All of them were staring through the row of vacuum windows at the metal hammers of the machinery that pulverised the dreamstone ore. Anton pressed forward, saw a dusty conveyor belt rocketing along, covered in head-sized fragments of rock and a lot of pebbles and dust. The conveyors vanished into a series of square mouths from which a pale violet light flickered.

'At the end you see the Dream Machine,' said the Esqueekeemmian, with a fluting giggle. 'At least that's what we call it. The fragments are checked for density, and X-rayed. If a dreamstone shows up, they're shunted onward for speed erosion in the Melter. And that's where we're going next!' The guide pressed a key on his belt and the conveyor carrying the party moved on, slightly more slowly than the one carrying the rocks, past the Dream Machine. After a few minutes, the view changed. Rock was melting, falling away in slices around lumpen yellow crystals.

'Microbots do the work here. You can't see them, but they eat you all the same!' ·

Anton was getting a little bit tired of the Esqueekeemmian's 'jokes'. He looked at the raw crystals, saw men working at the end of the chamber with cutters and water jets. Finished crystals were piled up in bins. As Anton watched, a loader robot rolled in and wheeled one of the bins away.

'Takes away a bit of the romance, yes?' said a voice somewhere below Anton's shoulder.

He looked down, saw a short, stout but apparently human woman, wearing a blue overall covered in pockets.

'I don't feel very romantic about them,' said Anton. 'The only one I ever tried to use gave me a nightmare.'

The woman raised an eyebrow. 'No surprise. So are you one of these dream artists, then?'

'No,' said Anton quickly. He'd quickly realised on the trip out that he was going to have to be careful what he said to the other tourists. Most of them were dreamies – dreamstone users who were incapable of creating their own dreams. They regarded anyone who could as a sort of minor god. The woman would be asking for his brainwave print next.

'So why were you using a dreamstone, then? Unhappy marriage? Tired of your job? Masochistic tendencies?'

Anton looked down at the woman, feeling himself blush. Did *everyone* here know about the nightmare stones?

The woman was watching him with small brown eyes – so small, and so far apart, that Anton suddenly realised she wasn't human. A Vorsedd, perhaps? But didn't they have horns? Perhaps she was half human. Her cheeks were red, flushed deep with blood. If she was Vorsedd or human, she was either permanently embarrassed, or an alcoholic. Her hair was short and – ah. Not hair. Spines. Definitely Vorsedd, then. Must've had her horns clipped. Or perhaps the women didn't have them.

He realised she was still waiting for a reply.

'I – er – just thought I'd give it a try. Since I was coming here.'

'Uh-huh.'

Anton became aware that the tour appeared to be over. The rest of the crowd were shuffling into the lift. He started to follow them, and the woman started to follow him.

'Are you sure you're not an artist?' she was asking him. 'You look like that man – the one who did those lonely-boring-little-planet BELs, a couple of years ago. La Sade, wasn't he?'

Oh, hell.

'No. I've heard people say I look like him.'

'La Serre,' said the woman suddenly. 'Anton La Serre. That was it.'

'Not me, I'm afraid. Sorry!'

They were pushing their way into the lift now. Everyone could hear their conversation. Anton became aware that he was sweating.

Don't tell anyone who you really are.

Those had been Jono's last words to him at the spaceport. His brisk, practical girlfriend had provided him with an untraceable cash chip, and a link to her mother's firm of lawyers in case of arrest. Then she had kissed him goodbye, with no more said about its being the last time.

But he had felt her sadness, even so.

The Vorsedd woman was still talking. 'I'm sure you're not an ordinary dreamie. I've met too many of *them*.'

Go away. But Anton couldn't quite bring himself to say it.

The lift doors opened, and the crowd spilled out. The Esqueekeemmian guide was chittering about the gift shop. Anton hurried out, then stopped dead as he realised something.

The way the woman had talked about dreamies meant she almost certainly wasn't one. He looked back, saw that she was still in the lift. For the first time he registered her blue overall, her large, calloused hands.

She wasn't on holiday.

'You work here, don't you?'

Tiny brown eyes twinkled at his. 'And you're Anton La Serre.'

He walked back into the lift. The woman was standing in the door, blocking it so that it wouldn't close. The last of the tourists, the Besiddian couple, squeezed past her, hand in hand.

'What were you doing on the tour?' asked Anton.

A grin. 'Following you.'

Anton swallowed. Was she a fan of his art? Did she just fancy him? Or did she have some more complicated, and possibly dangerous, motive? Anton never had been too good at handling people, and right now trying to work out this strange woman's intentions was the last thing he needed.

'I – umm –' he said eventually.

She leaned over, touched his arm. 'Why don't we discuss this over a drop of whisky?'

Her eyes were still fixed on his. It sounded like a good idea. Or a very bad one.

'Think about it. I'll be in the Wildcatter, Level Four-down. It's the only place round here where they serve the kind of drink I like.' She leaned back into the lift. 'Name's Innell, by the way, since I already know yours.'

The door closed in front of Anton's face.

Daniel wondered if he was mad, or drunk, or just dreaming. No way was this going to work. The guard was a male Besiddian, about two and a half metres high. He was staring in an unblinking feline manner at the man who called himself the Doctor. The Doctor had a hand extended towards the guard, and had a quite ridiculous smile on his face.

'Jelly baby, officer?'

Amazingly, a huge front paw lifted up slowly, and a big, purring grin appeared on the Besiddian's face.

'Thank you! Like human sweets! You party?'

'Yes, we're from the party,' said Daniel quickly. He was unable to prevent himself from adding bitterly, 'O'Connell's wake.'

The huge alien didn't seem to notice. 'Another sweet? Yellow one?'

The Doctor extended his hand again, at the same time winked over his shoulder at Daniel. 'Sexual dimorphism. Besiddian males are twice as heavy as the females, and half as intelligent. The corresponding ratio for humans is one point two. Keep him talking.'

Yes, thought Daniel, maybe. He knew male Besiddians weren't all that bright. But what about the surveillance cameras? And the lock on the pithead access door behind the guard? Anyway, the guard might be a bit dim, but he was hardly going to let them past just because –

The Doctor had vanished.

The guard seemed unperturbed, and after a moment Daniel realised that this was because he had the bag of sweets cradled in his huge hand and was licking them up, several at a time, with a large pink tongue.

'Boring down here,' he observed, looking at Daniel and talking through a mouthful of jelly babies. 'Better to fight and party.'

Wouldn't we all, son? thought Daniel. From the glossy look of the alien's silver coat and the rippling look of his muscles, he guessed that the Besiddian was less than ten years old.

'I fight good. Have lots of wives.'

Keep him talking. Ah.

'Oh, that's great for you,' said Daniel. 'What are their names?'

The Besiddian swallowed a mouthful of sweets. 'Gono, Noji, Kifo, Bello and –' a blink – 'next week, Katyo.'

Daniel could see the Doctor again now. He was squeezed into the recessed frame of the lift door, doing something to the electronics of the control panel.

'Next week, eh?' Daniel said to the Besiddian. 'You got to knock someone down to get her, then?'

'Becarridicosdix,' said the big alien instantly. 'Kill him good.'

'Oh, yes, that's the – er – big one with the green stripes, isn't it?'

'Blue stripes,' corrected the alien. 'And I'm bigger.'

'Door's open!' called the Doctor.

The guard turned. 'Hey! You're not supposed to go in there!'

'That's all right, we're aliens too, or at least I am.'

Daniel dodged past, was surprised when the guard didn't stop him. He glanced back, saw that the alien was holding a gun – one-handed, with the bag of sweets still in the other.

'You have to stop or I shoot you!' he said, totally without conviction.

'No, I don't think that's right,' said the Doctor. 'Check in the manual.'

Then he shut the door behind them. Daniel punched the descent button, felt the light gravity vanish as the lift free-fell down the shaft.

The Doctor rubbed his hands together and smiled.

'He'll call for help,' said Daniel, as the lift jolted to a stop.

'But he'll probably check in the manual first. By which time we'll be somewhere else –' the Doctor was already out of the door – 'or at least we'll have found something out – oh.'

Two women were standing in front of them. Both of them were in the gold-and-grey uniform of Earth Special Reserve Forces. Both of them had guns.

And both of them were pointing the guns at the Doctor.

'I think you'd better come along with us,' said one. She wasn't young: a fringe of iron-grey hair was just visible around the edges of her grey helmet. Daniel noticed the gold starburst insignia of a Captain on her shoulder. 'And I suggest you forget the bag of sweets this time. I *do* know what's in the manual.'

'Ah,' said the Doctor. 'Time for Plan B.'

Daniel glanced at the Doctor. How could he be taking this so lightly? What in God's name were the Specials doing here?

The Doctor grinned. 'Cooperate with the local authorities.' He extended a hand to the officer, who ignored it. 'Hello, I'm the Doctor, and I used to be a Special Scientific Adviser to UNIT, when there was one. I wonder if I can be of any assistance in the present situation.'

The Wildcatter was easy enough to find. It was the noisiest place on the base: you could hear it as soon as you stepped out of the lift on Level Four-down. In fact, you could hear it *before* you stepped out of the lift, or even before the lift arrived. Anton had a strong feeling that it was noisier than anywhere he'd ever been, at least recently. He supposed that the extraction shop might have been worse, if he'd been standing by one of the machines, but it would have been a close-run thing.

First, there was the music, which sounded like a piledriver. Then there was the crowd noise. Two male Besiddians were fighting, throwing each other against the walls of a metal pit, while around the edges, holding on to a perilously thin rope, a mixture of other species jumped up and down and waved cash chips in the air. Anton saw the faint stroboscopic flicker of data moving around, and guessed that bets were being placed.

He saw Innell leaning against the bar. She was wearing a white leather vest studded with gold sequins, and her blue overall trousers. She'd put a halo on, abstract silver galaxies growing quickly and dying. The spines growing out of her scalp glinted with the fibres of the holonet supporting the projection.

'Like it?' She gestured at the halo. 'I got it in the tourist gift shop. Just wanted you to know I was on the side of the angels.'

Anton had to laugh.

Innell switched the halo off. 'What're you having?'

Anton peered across the bar at the dark potions on offer.

'Q'q'fot wine,' he eventually concluded.

Innell keyed instructions into her computer. Then Anton noticed the drink in her hand. It had the nauseous caramel colour of faked whisky, and there was far too much of it.

'Perhaps on second thoughts I'd rather –' he began.

Too late. The datalight on the bar flickered, and machinery came to life. A glass appeared, and a dark red fluid issued into it. It looked about as much like wine as Innell's drink looked like whisky.

'Now then,' Innell bawled in his ear as she handed him the drink. 'I know that you dream for a living. Don't you want to know what I do here? Or would you rather guess?'

Anton grinned. Now that he'd given up trying to hide his identity, he knew that he rather liked this person. 'I think you're a cocktail waitress,' he offered.

She laughed. 'What, with muscles like these?' She flexed her arm, and Anton saw a substantial biceps and a triceps and various lesser muscles moving. 'I suppose you could get them carrying drinks, if the drinks were heavy enough. But rocks are a lot heavier.'

It was then, rather belatedly, that the penny dropped.

'You're a *miner*? But –'

'Hush! Don't tell everybody about it! I'm not supposed to be here!'

Anton frowned, then blushed. 'Er – that's my line, isn't it?'

'Well, you were making it rather obvious.' She took a sip of her whisky, and winced. 'Actually, I'm not an official miner. I'm what the company likes to term a "wildcatter". That is, I live here, I dig holes in the ground, and I pay the company fifty per cent of what I get – which isn't much – for the privilege of drinking in their overpriced bars.'

Anton felt a rush of excitement. This was too good to be true! 'You're just the sort of person I need to talk to!' he said.

'Uh-huh,' said the woman noncommittally.

At that point, the background noise took a turn for the worse, becoming a sort of unearthly screaming. The floor shook so violently that Anton spilled part of his drink.

Innell mouthed something that Anton knew he had no chance of understanding, but rather hoped meant, 'Let's get out of here.'

His computer flickered: he looked at the screen, saw that she'd sent him a message.

'Yajiculuivsiwen won again. 10-1 on, not worth placing a bet. Never mind. Are you looking for more nightmares or more dreams?'

Anton stared at her. 'Both,' he shouted.

She frowned, gestured at his computer: obligingly he typed in the message, but showed her the screen instead of sending it. He didn't want any risk of a record being made of the conversation.

'You want to see a vein of dreamstone,' she sent, her gloved hand wriggling as she typed. 'Pure, raw, stuff, still in the ground. Then you'll find out what it's all about. *And* why I don't work for the company, by the way.'

'When can we go?' asked Anton, almost spilling the rest of his drink in his eagerness to get the words typed.

Innell looked up at him with raised eyebrows. 'Hold on!' she bawled aloud (the background noise had reduced a bit). 'I didn't say I'd take you!'

Anton's disappointment must have been written on his face, because Innell just grinned and grabbed his arm. 'I didn't say I wouldn't, either. But how up are you on heavy-duty spacesuit-control procedures?'

'You're a very lucky human, you know that?'

'Mmm.'

'This is the second time I've pulled you out of a dangerous situation that you shouldn't have been in to start with. What's the matter with you? Are you normally like this, or just temporarily suicidal?'

'Wha– Mmm?' Sam opened her eyes, blinked fiercely. The alien was leaning over her, the tentacles reaching for her, the *tentacles* –

No. It was only Aloisse.

'Waa!' She struggled to sit up, but couldn't move. Something was holding her down. Straps. 'Lmm – o!' It hurt to talk, a tight band of itchy pain across the whole of her chest.

'You can't move until the lung patch is healed,' said Aloisse. 'At the moment a machine's doing most of your blood oxygenation, and it needs you to stay horizontal. But you'll be OK in a day or so.'

'K'k'sss?'

Aloisse moved out of her field of vision. Sam got a blurry view of a metal ceiling, old and pitted, and realised that she was in the protesters' base.

She tried to ask the question again. 'Waa – oo –' *What happened to*?

'We never found the other Kekkikk. He's dead, I suppose.'

A short silence. Sam found herself blinking back tears.

Life is short.

'Base security came out and sealed off the whole area.' A pause. 'I don't think they'll be rubble-dumping there now.'

Sam wondered for a moment whether exposing the underground creatures had been a deliberate part of the protest. If Aloisse had lied to her. But it didn't make sense. Why should the alien lie? And why should she risk her life and Sam's? Not to mention getting the two Arachnons killed.

No. It was nonsense.

But Sam had the distinct sense that *something* was wrong.

She flexed a hand, wriggled the fingers.

'Eeb! *Eebrd!*'

'I think you need to have a rest.'

'*K – ee – brd!*' snapped Sam. Every syllable hurt.

'Oh. Umm – there might be one –' A tentacle reached across Sam's field of vision. Plastic moved under her left hand, then under her right. Sam felt the curved shapes, suddenly very glad that she'd taught herself to use the post-2020 bowlboards that had replaced the twentieth-century QWERTY layout. The curvature itself told you where the letters were, and the layout was infinitely more logical.

'What was the thing that attacked us?' she typed quickly, wondering whether Aloisse had the boards connected or whether she could key-read. Key-reading was next on Sam's list of useful skills to acquire. Though, knowing her luck, as soon as she'd done it, the Doctor would stop travelling in the centuries where –

Oh.

No Doctor. Just the centuries.

Just *this* century.

She realised that she'd missed Aloisse's reply, and asked the alien to repeat it.

'I've no idea. Those tunnels shouldn't be there. The company might be something to do with them. We don't know.'

'Did that thing look like a company official to you?'

'Of course not. But it didn't look much like anything from the local ecosystem either. They might be trying to introduce a predator species to wipe it out, "by accident", so that there won't be any restrictions on exploitation. Disgusting trick, but common enough. I don't know how they'd do it in this system – it's too strange to be very susceptible to external predators. But it might not stop them from trying.'

'Yes. Maybe. But it must have been brought from somewhere where there are similar species. Somewhere like –'

Sam stopped typing, as she realised what she was saying.

Tentacles. One eye.

It had been a lot bigger than Aloisse, but –

Sam struggled to put the facts together in her head. The protest seemed to be run almost entirely by Aloisse and the other Krakenite, Cirbnekk. What if they weren't protesting at all, but *protecting* their own?

Did their species have its own plans for the Moon?

Whatever it was, she couldn't talk to Aloisse about it. Not without doing some thinking first.

'I'm tired,' she typed.

The keyboards were removed from under her hands. Tentacles moved across her field of vision. One gently touched her forehead, and a huge eye appeared above hers.

'Actually, I'm glad you went in there,' said Aloisse. 'You're very brave. I'm only sorry we didn't save them.'

Sam felt the warmth in the rumbling behind the translated voice, saw it in the big eye. Surely Aloisse couldn't be lying to her.

But then the eye was gone, and Aloisse's steps were clumping away across the floor, and Sam wasn't sure any more.

CHAPTER 8

'Sorry, Daniel. I realise that meeting the Specials like this must have been a bit of a shock for you. But you shouldn't have been down there.'

Aril Tiydon looked different, thought Daniel. Something had shaken him. Outwardly he was still the casual boss, the smart suit with a smile behind a big desk. Everything was neat as usual, the heavy dreamstone pinning down a pile of hardcopy, the computer folded in front of his folded hands.

But his eyes were frightened. His gaze wasn't settling on anything. Particularly, it wasn't settling on the heavy, uniformed figure of Captain Isobella Cleomides.

She just stood there, her eyes unmoving, staring into the middle of the wall as if no one else were in the room.

Daniel noticed the movements of the Doctor's eyes, making the same observations. He was counting something off on his fingers as he did so.

Finally the Doctor asked, '*What* is it you're hiding down there?' He spoke quietly, but with emphasis.

Cleomides answered before Tiydon had a chance. 'We can't tell you that.' Her voice was clipped, almost artificial. Like a robot. Like a –

Don't even think it.

'Why not?' the Doctor was asking. 'I'm here to help.'

Tiydon spoke: 'With all due respect, Doctor – um –'

The Doctor turned on him. 'Let me guess: you don't know who I am, I shouldn't have been there and now you don't know what to do with me. Am I right?'

Daniel found himself smiling, and saw a faint answering echo of that smile in Tiydon's face, quickly suppressed.

'Well, what you could do is *tell me what's happening*. Then I might be able to help you.'

'It's classified,' snapped Cleomides, still without moving her eyes.

It was Tiydon who turned to face her. 'Since when?'

'It's a military decision.'

'I see.' Tiydon's gaze swung around the office, settled on Daniel. 'What do you know about the Doctor?'

'He's that stowaway's father.'

Tiydon nodded, though he was clearly puzzled. 'Have you told him where she is?'

Daniel nodded.

'I'm not her father, just a friend,' said the Doctor unexpectedly. 'And it doesn't matter where she is now. As long as she's on this moon I suspect she's in some considerable danger – and so are the rest of you.'

Tiydon's gaze fixed on the Doctor. 'What do you mean?' he asked quietly.

'I'm not sure yet. And if I'm going to find out I'll need proper facilities.'

'My advice is that he should be removed from the base at once, under armed guard,' said Cleomides. 'He's not human. We did a retinal scan – it suggests he might be of Partriscisnad origin.'

'That's a new one,' muttered the Doctor. He turned to Cleomides. 'Look, perhaps if we could just talk about this –'

'I don't talk to aliens!' barked Cleomides.

A pause. At last Tiydon said, 'Well, I do. I have to, round here. And I'm making this decision, OK?'

'The military position is –'

'The military aren't running this base!' snapped Tiydon. 'These are still commercial premises and I make the final decisions!'

Cleomides didn't reply, just swung on her heel and walked out of the office. Her gold-and-black uniform brushed against Daniel's arm as she passed.

When she'd gone, Daniel asked, 'What's going on, Aril?'

Tiydon shrugged. 'Head office asked them in after the business in Shaft Four.'

'What business?' asked the Doctor sharply. 'Do you know what really happened down there? It wasn't a normal accident, was it?'

Tiydon glanced at Daniel, and sighed. 'If I knew, I wouldn't be able to tell you, for security reasons. But I don't know, so I can tell you that I don't know, and you have to believe me.' A smile, directed at Daniel. 'That Irish enough for you?'

Daniel laughed, but he didn't really think it was funny. He noticed that the Doctor didn't think so either. He decided that Tiydon was, in fact, lying, which meant that things were worse than he'd thought.

'Have you got a lab?' the Doctor was asking. 'I'll need some of this dreamstone, a scanning EM at a magnification of about ten to the sixth, and some kind of AI, preferably the sort that doesn't talk back.'

Tiydon looked at Daniel again, and Daniel realised that he was being asked for advice.

'Trust the Doctor,' Daniel said instantly. 'I certainly don't trust Cleomides.'

Tiydon nodded slowly. 'I'm not sure I do. But she's here at Earth's request – I can't guarantee to keep her off your back for long.'

The Doctor rubbed his hands together. 'Oh, I'm not worried about her,' he said. 'There are too many real problems.'

'Clamp – manual oxygen – *then* breathe. It could save your life, OK?'

Anton nodded, then remembered that this was little use inside a suit helmet. 'OK.'

Innell had used most of the buggy trip to the wildcatters' huts to talk about safety procedures. Only about half of it was going in, but since Innell must have said everything about three times by now, Anton reckoned he'd taken in enough to be safe.

As safe as you could ever be, with raw, radiation-streaked vacuum less than thirty centimetres from your face.

He'd used suits before, but the ones that Innell's lot used seemed to be unusually crude. There was a retinal pad control, but it was strapped on by a piece of cabling, a late addition. There were palm switches, and chin contacts as well.

All three worked. 'Better safe than sorry,' as Innell had said, perhaps five or six times.

Ahead, the ground was dropping away from the hilly territory where the DMMC base was located to a broad plain. Once flat, it was now covered with excavations: this was the main area where the company mined. Anton was impressed with the scale of it. From the hills, they could see a twenty- or thirty-kilometre horizon, and all of that territory was covered in heaps of rubble. The horizon shimmered with dust. Anton noticed Mu Camelopides VI, Dreamstone Moon's mother planet, close to the horizon, a big, featureless brownish-grey disc.

'This is the *real* extraction shop,' said his new guide. 'And this isn't half of it. They've got sites like this covering half the plains.'

'I've seen the pictures,' said Anton. 'But it wasn't quite – I mean –' He couldn't complete the sentence. The scale of the destruction was making him feel queasy. 'Where's your place?'

'Wouldn't you like to know?'

Anton grinned. The way that Innell had looked at him when they'd suited up had made it quite clear that she wasn't after him because she was a fan of his dreamscapes. And he was sure it was fairly uncomplicated lust: not the sort of thing that Jono would object to. Meaningless jealousy wasn't one of her faults. But he wasn't sure he wanted to get involved with anyone, even at that level. It seemed untrue to his mission, somehow, though he wasn't sure how that could be, or why he felt that way, or even why he thought it was a mission at all.

'I meant the place where you found the pure dreamstone,' he said.

'Oh, that!' A pause. 'About another five minutes. Fifth slagheap to the left of the road.'

Anton looked, saw the road running across the plain, counted the slagheaps. The fifth one was distinctly smaller, not a neat cone like the others but a scattering of loose rock. Small, glinting figures moved around – Anton was too far away to tell whether they were people or machines.

'Wildcatter territory,' said Innell, answering the question he hadn't asked. 'Now – time to make sure you've been listening properly. What do you do in the event of an air-supply failure?'

They'd made the protesters' meeting hall into an improvised Arachnon chapel by draping the windows in blue plastic and setting up a spotlight in the middle of the room. Sam wished she'd been able to help, but, although they'd let her sit upright, talking still hurt her and walking around was difficult – she got out of breath quickly, and painfully, despite the oxygen pack on her back. But she'd been determined to come to the service.

To her surprise, two media reporters were there, one a black-faced, vaguely reptilian person – Sam didn't recognise the species – one a woman in dark blue; both of them had the long snouts of autocams strapped to their foreheads. They were obviously there with Aloisse's permission, and they were discreet, keeping to the back, filming quietly, but Sam felt irritated by them nonetheless.

The bodies of the two Kekkikks hadn't been recovered – the company had one, the other had never been found – so they were represented by two finely carved and painted bone statuettes called klikklekks, which Aloisse had translated as 'soul totems'. There was one on each side of the altar, connected by a metal track. Bizarrely, they looked a little bit like model steam engines.

When everyone was settled in and quiet, Aloisse went to the improvised rostrum in front of the light-altar, somehow managing to make her clumsy tripedal walk quiet and solemn. She spread eight of her tentacles in a radial pattern, the shape of the Arachnon Great Web, and slowly moved her body from side to side so that it faced everyone in the room in turn.

'Two brave young people died yesterday,' she said. 'They died doing what they had volunteered to do, against the wishes of their families, possibly against those of most of their people. I know that according to the Arachnon belief system, those who die an avoidable death when they're young, before they're married, are sinners – unless they are defending the honour of the Web. Well, I say that Kekkikk and Kekkikk –' she used two spare tentacles to make the eye-stalk distinction – 'were doing just that, out here, five hundred light years from home. They were defending the honour of their people, by proving that Arachnons can care about others, and defending the honour of their religion, by proving that it makes them big enough to feel that way. And I'm sorry, truly sorry, that following their belief and their honour in this way cost them their lives.'

She stepped down from the rostrum, said quietly, 'Does anyone else wish to speak before the last cocooning?'

Sam hesitated. She hadn't known the two Kekkikks at all. But if nobody else was going to step forward, she felt that she should try to say something, even so. She was about to stand up when Kyono, a tall Besiddian, walked to the rostrum. She, too, talked about the Kekkikks' bravery and commitment to the cause, '…and if anyone doubts that this protest is worth the sacrifices we have made, they only need to look at how these two young people died, in the jaws of a creature planted there by the Dreamstone Moon Mining Company!'

The reporters were still filming. Aloisse was standing next to them.

Sam felt a jolt of shock and anger as she realised what was happening. The memorial service was being turned into a propaganda exercise. Another speaker, a man called Jess, got up and began speaking; now that she knew what was happening, Sam could run the speech against a checklist of Junsequat's Interview Keywords. There was a tick in almost every box.

She looked accusingly at Aloisse, but Aloisse had moved to the back and was talking to the reptilian reporter.

When the man got down, Sam stepped forward. The light-altar was almost uncomfortably bright, and she could feel its heat when she stood close to it. Close up, the klikklekks didn't look so much like steam engines: the carved and polished curves of bone had a way of trapping details within details, as if it had been assembled atom by atom, painted molecule by molecule. They seemed almost alive. Sam wondered how old they were. And how they had got here – did the Arachnons carry them around everywhere they went, just in case they died?

She looked up at the audience, took a breath. 'I barely knew the Kekkikks personally,' she said. 'But I was near them when they died.' She paused to get another breath, wincing at the pain in her lungs. 'They were lively, and funny, and they faced death with – with a sense of humour, and I'm sorry they died. That's all.'

She walked to the back where Aloisse was standing, feeling weak and dizzy. She half expected the big alien to tell her off for not being publicity-conscious enough, but she only said, 'Well done. That was just right.'

Cirbnekk was speaking now. The other Krakenite was bigger than Aloisse, and the skin around her body was loose, its surface subtly creased, like elephant hide. Again, Sam was reminded of the creature that had attacked them in the tunnel. It *could* be a coincidence, but…

When Cirbnekk had finished, the 'soul totems' were solemnly cocooned by the two Krakenites. Somehow they managed to make their movements *look* spider-like, as their translators pronounced the clattering words of the Arachnon language. Sam didn't understand a word of it, but she bowed her head respectfully nonetheless, hoping she wasn't also supposed to contort her limbs into a strange position.

When the cocoons had been taken away and the congregation had started to disperse, Sam caught hold of Aloisse, nodded at the reporters. 'Did they have to be here?'

The big eye regarded her. For the first time, Sam noticed that there were two pupils set in the deep-blue iris, separated by about ten centimetres, and joined by a threadlike structure that might be a nerve.

'The Kekkikks would have wanted it, Sam.'

'You're sure?'

'It'll help us. It's not much, for two people's lives, but it's better than nothing at all.'

'I don't think it's –' Sam paused for breath – 'respectful. They're *dead.*'

A hesitation. 'I'm trying to get their deaths investigated, and the publicity will help! Look, I have a lot of things to do.' She started to clump away towards the door.

'Things that you can't tell me about!' snapped Sam. Then she blushed deeply as she realised what she'd said. 'Sorry.'

Sam saw the reporters hovering, the woman in blue muttering into a notepad. She lowered her voice. 'Look. I need to know. If your people are involved in some way.'

'What are you talking about?'

'The thing that killed the Kekkikks. The thing that attacked us. It looked like you. Bigger, but physiologically similar.'

There, she'd said it.

'Oh, for heaven's sake! Sam! Half the living things in the galaxy are "physiologically similar" to each other! My body type – which your people call Krakenoid – is one of the commonest biological forms there is on low-gravity planets. And how many humanoid species are there? It must be thousands! I know that humans are instinctively afraid of things with tentacles, but I thought you knew better!'

Sam felt the blush return to her cheeks, but this time she was genuinely embarrassed. What if she was wrong?

Aloisse had turned to the reporters. 'This is off the record!' she snapped. 'Right off! Is that clear?' She whirled back to Sam. 'Sam, there *is* definitely something going on here that shouldn't be. But I'm not in charge of it, right? Maybe the DMMC isn't either. I don't know. I simply *don't know*.'

'Then how did you get me out of the tunnel?'

Aloisse slipped a tentacle lightly around Sam's arm. 'I pulled,' she said. 'Very hard.'

Sam thought about the rickety slope, the sharp rocks, her damaged spacesuit.

'I don't believe you.'

Aloisse let go. 'Well, that's your privilege.' She started to walk away again.

'I just want the truth!' Sam shouted after her. Then a wave of pain and dizziness hit her. For a moment she thought she was going to faint.

A hand touched her arm. Sam turned, found herself facing the woman in blue, the reporter. Her skin was dark, her eyes a startling green.

'Are you OK?'

She had an American accent, an East Coast twang.

'I'm fine.'

'You seemed pretty angry there. What exactly do you suspect –'

Sam shook her head. 'Can't tell you.'

The woman grabbed Sam's arm a little harder, leaned forward. 'We can do a deal.' Sam raised her eyebrows, waited. 'If you can give me the story on what happened to you out there and why you think the Krakenites are involved, I can tell you something I think you'll find useful,' she said.

'What?'

The woman smiled, showing even, slightly pointed teeth. 'Well, I can't tell you that without giving you the information, can I?'

Sam looked down at her shoes, the same battered trainers with dried, hardened bits of the Kusk ship still adhering to them. Aloisse had saved her life. And now she was thinking of trading her suspicions with this reporter for... what? And why? Because she needed to know the truth?

No. She remembered Daniel, with his family to feed back home. If the mining operation was in danger because of Aloisse's activities - if *miners* were in danger - then someone needed to know about it. But...

She looked at the reporter's face. The woman didn't seem unfriendly. Didn't seem polished, hard, cynical.

'Come on, kid, I haven't got all day,' she said.

Sam swallowed. What would the Doctor have done?

Thought of another way.

Well, sorry, Doctor, I can't think of another way. And Aloisse was right about one thing: if it helps the cause, then the personal considerations don't matter.

'OK,' she said, staring the woman coolly in the face. 'But your information had better be good.'

'Here it is. Look right ahead.'

Innell and Anton had switched off their suit lights. They were only a few metres underground, but the blackness was absolute.

'I can't see -' began Anton. Then his vision started to adjust, and he could make out the glowing nodules of dreamstone in the bare rock.

He stared at them. 'It's this easy to find?'

'Uh-huh. Why do you think the Dreamy Muddleheaded Muckraking Company is so rich? Most dreamstone mining's just automatic processing. You saw it on the guided tour. Microbot trawls, autodozers, processing plants. Their miners are structural engineers, really. They keep a few shafts open under the base for show, but wildcatters are the only *real* miners.'

A flicker of light dazzled Anton for a moment, and he saw that Innell was holding a laser cutting tool.

'No!' he snapped, putting a hand on the machine.

The light went out instantly. 'Careful with that,' said Innell. 'You could get us both killed. That beam doesn't just cut through rocks, you know.'

'Then don't –' He waved at the dimly glowing crystals. Dazzling afterimages of laser fire danced in front of them, making him feel sick. 'It's the flickering,' he said. 'Makes me feel a bit ill.'

'My God, you're not epileptic, are you? You should have –'

'No! I'm not sure what it is. Perhaps it's just –' He waved at the stones.

'OK,' said Innell. 'You're OK. Breathe evenly.' He could just see her face inside the visor, soft colours shining on her skin. He realised she was probably looking at his medical diagnostics. 'If you want to leave, just say so.'

'I'm OK now.'

He looked back at the stones, and saw that Innell was right. The stones were very different *in situ*. The glow wasn't constant: sparks of light moved across each stone, and sometimes between them, leaving brief trails in the crystal, like miniature meteors. The trails made patterns, and the patterns changed. Squares – hexagons – cubes. In some ways it was like watching the lights of a city from above.

On impulse he leaned forward, touched his suit helmet to the softly glowing stones.

'Careful,' said Innell. 'Some of those things have sharp edges.'

But dreams were chattering at the edge of Anton's mind.

Starkly familiar dreams.

– *Mummy Mummy Mummy help me Mummy Mummy the monsters are here Mummy Mummy pleeease don't let them kill me Mummy help me help me help me* –

He pushed himself away from the stone. He could feel his body shaking, sweat prickling in his armpits. His suit's blowers cut in, a low mechanical drone.

'You OK? Your pulse rate's up again.'

'Fine. It's just –' He turned to look at her. 'Do you ever feel anything strange when you go near the stones?'

'Strange?' She paused. 'Sometimes. Your imagination gets a bit carried away down here. And the stones are – what is it? Pseudosomnopsychic? That's how you people can use them, isn't it?'

Anton shook his head. 'I read up on that on the ship. It's just scientific language for "we don't know how they do it". But you can *feel* –'

He lowered his head to the stone once more.

– *hurts it hurts it hurts it hurts it hurts* –

And Anton could feel the pain, a deep throbbing in his temple. A bad dream? Who had made this storehouse of dreams and nightmares? Did he have nightmares because every stone he touched happened to be a bad one, or because he *made* the stones bad in some way? He realised he was no nearer an answer here in the mine, with living dreamstone right in front of him, than he had been in Jono's house on Occam's World.

Suddenly, light flickered in Anton's face. He jumped back, to see Innell at work with the cutter.

'If I can cut the rock here, we should be able to get the whole cluster out intact,' she said. 'Did you know that the Dreamy Muddleheaded et cetera actually waste ninety-five per cent of the dreamstones they bring up? Just break 'em to pieces in the production process. I always get them out –' She reached in with a gauntleted hand, yanked at the rock – 'intact.' Her hand came back, with a fist-sized, multifaceted bubble of dreamstone in it. 'Is this the one that you thought was talking to you?'

Anton stared at the broken stones with an inexplicable feeling of horror.

'You shouldn't –'

He felt his stomach heave, and stopped talking, swallowing hard – but it was too late. An alarm went off in his suit as vomit spattered out of his mouth and over the various chin controls.

'What the –' began Innell. 'Oh, Jesus, you picked a good time to get spacesick!'

Anton tried to speak, to explain that he wasn't spacesick, that it was something to do with the dreamstones. But he couldn't move his jaw. A tiny suction hose was wandering around the lower part of his face like a snake as he was sick again, his stomach cramping and –

– *the monsters are killing me* –

He heard Innell catch her breath. 'Come on, that was a quake! We've got to – *What the hell?*'

Anton felt the ground shiver. Condensation was blurring his visor: he could barely see Innell. The suction hose was still hissing around his chin. It tickled.

'Anton – *get out of here! Right now!*'

He saw a searchlight behind him, realised it was Innell's suit. But there was something strange about it. He turned, saw that it was half obscured by ropes of pale flesh –

– *the monsters are killing me* –

Had it been a warning? What had he done?

'Innell!'

'*Get out! Get help!*' She was being dragged backward. Anton saw the laser cutter on the ground, picked it up, waved it helplessly at the retreating suit. If he could cut her free –

Except that he had no idea how to work the thing, no idea how to stop it from cutting through Innell's suit, or even his own. And she was gone before he could even begin to look at the controls.

Shakily, he took a step forward, saw a large, ragged hole in the ground. A hole that he was quite sure hadn't been there a moment ago.

One of the tentacles whipped across his face.

He jumped back, saw several others trailing on the ground around him. But they were pulling back through the hole, making no attempt to attack him.

Innell's voice rattled in his earphones. 'Get *out*, Anton!'

'What's happening?'

'I don't know, it's pitch-black and –'

A snapping sound and a cry of pain.

Anton rushed back up the tunnel, suddenly conscious of the stench of the vomit sloshing around in the neck seals of his suit. There were splashes of it on the visor.

'Emergency channel!' he yelled into the radio. 'I'm at forty-two-slash-sixteen and –'

But then his entire body jolted and the tunnel did cartwheels around him.

– Mummy Mummy the monsters are going to kill me Mummy help please –

Another jolt. This time he felt the impact of his head on the back of the helmet, the pain shooting through his neck. The suit bumped across the stone floor for several seconds, then slid to a halt.

A couple of red lights showed on the panel. Anton had no idea what they meant. There was a cold, wet feeling on the back of his head. Blood? Vomit? Water?

'Innell?' he called.

No response, not even static.

He sat up. He was shaking, and his head throbbed with pain. An alarm began beeping in the suit. But there didn't seem to be anything in the tunnel with him. He thought about what had happened, realised that he hadn't been attacked: he'd just jumped too high and hit his head on the ceiling.

Oh, God, he was so *stupid*. No wonder Innell had kept on at him about safety procedures.

He tried to remember what she had told him about suit diagnostics. Chin tab one – he found it, was rewarded with a master diagnostic. It was clear from the diagram that the radio was out, and the secondary air supply had a leak – which was OK, because the primary was still working and he had three hours' air. And the distress beacon, independent of the radio, was signalling, set off automatically by the damage. But he had no idea whether the signal would reach the surface from here – quite probably not. He needed to walk out of the tunnel.

He tried to stand up. The pain in his head immediately got worse, and he almost sat down again.

He made himself take a step along the passage, then another, then another. 'Keep it slow,' he muttered to himself. 'Don't hurt yourself again. You have to get out of this. You have to get help to Innell. You have to get back to Jono.'

She said she would never see me again.

Something was blocking the corridor ahead. Pale rock – no –
Pale flesh.

A wall of pale flesh, creased like elephant hide, surrounded by trailing tentacles. A huge, single eye opened, and examined him patiently.

'Oh no,' moaned Anton, as the tentacles reached out towards him. 'Oh no oh no oh no oh no.'

She said she would never see me again –

CHAPTER 9

Daniel watched as the Doctor examined the dreamstone samples recovered from the cave-in site at Shaft Four. There was a gas spectrometer, with its input connected to a beaker full of crushed dreamstone heated over an electric coil, and another sliver of dreamstone under a microscope, which was displaying its output on a computer screen. Daniel noticed flickering lines of input moving between the spectrometer and the computer, and between both of them and a mysterious silvery egg-shaped piece of apparatus that the Doctor had produced from his pocket.

The computer screen showed patterns, crystalline but constantly changing, like an image Daniel had once seen of salt precipitating out of a solution. The Doctor stood in front of it, his hands in the pockets of his archaic jacket.

'Have you got a neutrino scanner?' he said suddenly.

Daniel looked around the clutter of the lab. It wasn't really a properly equipped facility at all: more a glorified storeroom where some of the bits of apparatus just happened to be plugged in. Most of the 'lab work' at the mine was automatic – the scientific staff were on-site people and spent their time underground with the miners. Daniel had still been surprised, however, to find the lab area deserted, all the scientists apparently seconded by Cleomides's military friends.

'I wish I knew what was happening to this place,' he said to the Doctor, as he rummaged in a head-high plasteel locker labelled FLUID REVERSING PRISMS, NEUTRINO SCANNERS ETC. 'It's like the military are taking it over.'

'Yes, very probably,' said the Doctor abstractedly. 'But I don't think that's the major problem.'

Daniel swallowed. He didn't like the sound of this at all. He found the scanner, a grey plastic tube about ten centimetres long, and took it across to where the Doctor stood.

The screen had changed, he noticed. Now it looked more like a city, long streets with pulses of traffic moving down them, splitting up at junctions.

The Doctor took the scanner from him without a word, and applied it to the sliver of dreamstone under the microscope, holding it awkwardly so that he could watch the picture and the scanner reading at the same time.

He counted on the fingers of his other hand. One-two-three-four-five. One-two-three-four-five. One-two-three –

Suddenly he said, 'Did you know that in the twentieth century they had to go about a mile underground to detect neutrinos?'

'Really?' said Daniel.

The Doctor glanced up. 'Yes. They got some very interesting results, too. Most of them wrong, but –'

The detector beeped. The Doctor looked at the reading, looked at the screen, then turned back to Daniel. His expression was serious.

'Daniel, I need to speak to Tiydon again. All the mining has to stop. Now.'

Daniel stared at him. What was the man talking about? 'I don't think he'll let you do that, Doctor. I know there are problems, but –'

The Doctor turned to face him, grabbed his shoulders. Daniel felt the shock of his stare, the force of his personality almost physically pushing him back.

'You *have* to stop. Don't you realise what these dreamstones of yours might be?'

Daniel shook his head. 'Whatever they are, Doctor, we have to keep mining them. Otherwise I'm home with no job, and four thousand other people with me.'

The Doctor slapped his forehead. 'Humans! Always worried about where your next meal is coming from, aren't you? Can't you ever manage to remember that you're out of the jungle?' He broke off, frowned, looked at the floor.

Daniel felt it then. A slight, but definite quivering under his feet. The sort of quivering that preceded a cave-in or –

'A quake!'

'Quite possibly.' The Doctor was looking at the screen again. 'Don't worry, this one's survivable, I should think.'

The whole room was shaking now. A plastic box full of data crystals slid off the edge of a table and clattered to the floor. The picture on the computer screen juddered out of focus. Outside, an alarm began to blare.

Daniel was already moving towards the door, following the tiny red arrows on the wall that had automatically illuminated to indicate the way to the nearest safety shelter, when the shaking stopped, quite suddenly.

'That's interesting,' said the Doctor. He was looking at the neutrino detector.

Daniel grabbed his arm. 'Come on! I've got to get you to a shelter now! This might not be the end of it!'

The Doctor looked up at him. 'No,' he said solemnly. 'It most certainly isn't the end of it.'

'Warning,' said the soft voice in Anton's ears. 'Suit rebreather functions compromised. You have six minutes' air supply remaining.'

It didn't taste like six minutes' worth to Anton. It tasted as if the air was already exhausted. His pulse pounded in his ears, and his lungs strained. He knew that he was probably panicking, that he could survive twenty minutes or more on the air in the suit after the supply failed if he would just *calm down*, but his body refused to obey that instruction. His legs and arms were shaking. He wanted to *get out, get out of this horrible place* – but there was nowhere to go. Just fifty metres of stone-walled passageway.

The way up was blocked by the tentacled creature. The way down was blocked by a solid wall of dreamstone. He had walked up and down perhaps a dozen times, examining the walls for cracks, listening to the dreamstones for clues, *anything* that would show him a way out.

Nothing. Just the slowly decreasing numbers on his air-supply reading. The hole in the floor, where Innell had been dragged down, had disappeared.

He looked up at the creature again. It looked back at him, the same unblinking stare. The tentacles twitched. There were mouths all around the eye, four or five of them: every so often, one would open, to reveal several rows of crystalline teeth.

The crystal looked remarkably like dreamstone.

Anton giggled helplessly. As a child, he'd wanted to be a scientist – but he'd never been able to master any mathematics beyond the level of simple algebra. He just didn't seem to be able to concentrate on it. Well, now he had his chance to make public the scientific discovery of the century: 'The Crystalline Relationship Between Dreamstones and the Big Murderous Tentacled Things that Live on Dreamstone Moon'. That sounded like a good title for a scientific paper. Perhaps he would write it in the –

'Warning: suit rebreather functions compromised. You have five minutes' air supply remaining.'

Anton giggled again. He could knock up a scientific paper in five minutes, sure. It wouldn't matter if he made a mess of it, because he wouldn't be around to hear the reviews. He would be *dead* because he couldn't get out of this bloody tunnel he was *dead dead dead* and the suit alarms were going off and he *was going to die* and he was punching the wall of wrinkled skin and the mouths were opening, all of them, and the teeth were glittering and the condensation from the thing's breath was running down the outside of his visor.

Anton stopped, breathing hard.

'Warning: suit rebreather functions compromised. You have two minutes' air supply remaining.'

Breath. The thing was *breathing*. Of course it was. *There was air outside the suit!*

Anton giggled wildly at the thought that he might easily have suffocated himself with air all around him. He stepped back from the creature, treading on several of the tentacles as he went. The animal didn't respond; the huge eye didn't even blink.

It occurred to him that it might be very weak, or dying. Perhaps the air wasn't breathable after all.

'Suit?' he asked, then remembered it wasn't set up for voice commands. Desperately he tried to remember what Innell had told him about external diagnostics. Chin tab two? He tried it, was rewarded with a diagram of the suit's electrical circuits.

Chin tab three produced a series of readings: 380 mb, 17% O_2, 44% CO_2. A flag advised him that it was dangerous to breathe.

'Warning: suit rebreather functions compromised. You have one minute's air supply remaining.'

Well, it can't be any more dangerous than what I'm breathing now, thought Anton. He began to loosen the helmet seals. A red light lit up on the panel, and the voice warned him again that the external air wasn't safe to breathe. He ignored it.

The seals broke. Anton's ears popped. For a moment he thought that the suit was right, and the air was unbreathable: then he managed to draw the thin, ragged stuff into his lungs. It smelled clean and stony after the stale-vomit stink inside the helmet.

He thought about stripping the rest of the suit off, then decided against it. It was hard work just to breathe the air: his lungs were heaving as if he'd been for a marathon run. He looked at the tentacled creature. What was it? It looked like a Krakenite – there were a few working in the mines – but surely it was far too big for that. And it showed no sign of intelligence.

Anton closed his eyes for a moment. It was hard to think in this air. He needed to rest, wait for rescue. For something.

He staggered down the tunnel towards the dreamstones. His legs felt heavy and weak at the same time. Twice he almost fell.

Finally he reached the stones, saw their welcoming glow in front of him. He slumped down, his body shaking with the effort of staying awake. His head flopped back against the glowing crystals.

Immediately, he fell asleep, and began to dream.

'So?' said the reporter, when Sam had finished her story.

Sam frowned at her. She'd thought she'd told the story pretty well, considering that she had to pause for breath after every fifth word or so. But the woman – she'd said her name was Madge – seemed unimpressed.

They'd gone to a tiny room, a former airlock that now faced inward and was being used as a storage cupboard. It was windowless, and lit by a single striplight that was too bright. They were sitting on two plasteel crates, Madge with a plastic voicepad open on her knees, a red recording light flashing in the top corner. Upside-down words were laid out on the screen, neatly justified, like the pages of an open book. Sam's words. Just seeing them printed like that made them seem like the truth, but Sam wasn't sure any more.

'Well,' she said. 'The thing that attacked us looked like a Krakenite, and I just don't know how Aloisse got me out of that hole.'

But Madge shook her head slowly. 'Kid, that doesn't make any sense at all. Your friend's right – there are species all over the galaxy that look like her, or enough like her to confuse people like us. And she could easily have pulled you out. They're enormously strong. Remember the gravity's only ten per cent Earth normal round here.'

Sam blushed, looked down at her shoes again.

'Aloisse and I have worked together for years, Sam. She's a bit strange, even for a Krakenite, but I trust her. If her people are up to anything – and frankly I don't think they are – I'm sure she doesn't know about it.'

Sam bit her lip. 'Sorry.'

'I think it's Aloisse you should apologise to, not me.'

Sam stood up, nodded, opened the door. Then she thought of something. 'Why were you so keen to hear my story, if you didn't believe –'

'I didn't want the competition to get it. And *he* might have published.'

Sam was halfway out of the door when Madge caught her arm. 'Hey! Don't you want that information I promised you?'

Sam hesitated. So far all she'd done with any information she'd come across was make mistakes and make a fool of herself. It had seemed so easy when she was with the Doctor: now, on her own, it seemed nearly impossible to make sense of things. It must be some magic of the Doctor's, she decided. It must extend to cover me, somehow, when I'm with him, and now –

And now it's gone.

'I don't really deserve it,' she said eventually.

Madge stood up, faced her through the narrow doorway. 'Look, kid, some of what you said about the Kekkikks was real exciting, a good story. It'll be a great help. And Aloisse'll forgive you what you said – she knows it's easy to jump to the wrong conclusions. I do it all the time. The trick is to know when to run the story. And when *not* to run it, OK?' Her eyes met Sam's.

Sam nodded. 'OK.'

'So you want the information?'

Sam nodded again.

Madge pulled her back into the storeroom and shut the door, then spoke quickly and quietly.

'Earth Fleet are on manoeuvres in the area. Five hundred ships.'

Sam frowned. 'Meaning…?'

Madge shrugged. 'I don't know for sure. But I have a little friend in the fleet, and he tells me that they're practising land-and-destroy routines, over and over. On airless little chunks of rock just like this one.'

'So we could be in the middle of a war?'

'I don't know.' She leaned closer. 'But I can tell you, I'm getting out tomorrow. I'm not paid to be a war correspondent – the guy in black can take care of that if he wants.'

'You think I should get out too?'

'Up to you. Come along with me if you like. I can get you to Ha'olam or Occam's World.'

Sam hesitated.

Then the room started to shake.

Sam half fell, saw Madge's voicepad cartwheeling towards a wall. She grabbed it, then saw that the wall was buckling.

The room was crumpling, like a cardboard box someone had stood on.

Madge was scrabbling at the door. It opened – no, buckled – outward, the shock jerking the woman on to her knees. Sam flung the voicepad aside, pulled Madge up.

She was shaking, breathing far too hard.

'I've left it too late – we're all dead. I *knew* I shouldn't have come to this thing –'

'OK,' said Sam, holding on to Madge's arms, hard. 'Don't panic.' She was panicking herself, her heart hammering double time, but she wasn't going to show it in front of Madge or they could both end up dead.

A distant crash and a scream. Air was blowing past in the passageway outside, carrying rock dust and fragments of paper. An alarm began to shrill.

But the floor wasn't shaking any more.

'Right,' said Sam, letting Madge go. 'We move. Suiting-up room.

Now.'

Madge looked at her, nodded.

Sam moved out into the corridor, slipping the oxygen mask over her face and taking a deep breath. She paused to check the supply, saw there was about five minutes' worth of oxygenated air in a backup tank. Good. That would keep her and Madge going for a few minutes if they had to cross vacuum to get to the spacesuits.

She peered into the corridor, assessing the damage. As she did so, the ground quivered under her feet and Madge gave a little gasp of fright. 'They're bombing us!'

'I'm not sure.' Sam had felt a few bombs land near her and this hadn't felt like that. The corridor was buckled, the metal walls warped. In one place the metal had broken, and Sam could see cracked rock. The ceiling met the floor some way short of the doors to the common room. In the other direction, the way to the suiting-up room and the airlocks, it seemed to be clear.

Sam took another breath of oxygen, then shut off the supply. They might both need it later.

'All clear,' she said to Madge, and started down the corridor.

The floor began to shake again. Then all the lights went out, and Madge screamed.

Sam reached back, grabbed her hand. 'It's not far,' she said, trying to sound brave and competent, and, to her amazement, succeeding quite well.

Gradually they made their way down the corridor. Sam kept a hand on the wall, took one step at a time. She didn't remember seeing any large pieces of fallen debris, but she couldn't be sure. The dust swirled around her face, forcing her to use the oxygen mask again. Behind her, she could hear Madge coughing. The air was becoming painfully thin, and was starting to get cold.

Then, ahead, she saw a light.

It was an emergency light above the door of the suiting-up

room, the intercultural symbol for a spacesuit flickering in outline red.

Madge didn't need encouraging any more, was staggering ahead of the wheezing Sam.

They arrived to find three people there before them: the man, Jess, who'd read at the ceremony, and Kyono and Sono, the Besiddians. Sono was hurt, blood leaking from a twisted arm. Jess and Kyono were helping her into a spacesuit. The red emergency lighting made the plastic parts of the suit seem curiously formless, almost like a fluid.

There was no sign of Aloisse or Cirbnekk, or anyone else.

Jess glanced up at Madge and Sam. 'OK? Not hurt?'

Sam shook her head. She found a human spacesuit about the right size on the racks and put it on. She checked the air supply before deciding that she could risk fully oxygenated air for a few minutes.

Her lungs started to feel better as soon as the warm, rich air came through the plastic mouthpiece. The pain in her chest receded to a dull ache.

'If we circle round the outside,' she said, half to herself, 'we should be able to help the others. Dig them out or something.' She began looking round the room. There had to be emergency tools in here somewhere – she was sure that she'd seen them.

'Not much chance of digging anyone out,' said Jess quietly.

Sam stared at him.

He met her eyes. 'Whole far end's squashed flat. I saw it happen from my window. The hill just fell on it. I think we're the only ones. I was surprised to see you.'

'You mean – Aloisse –'

He shrugged.

Sam felt her throat tighten.

So much for my new friends. Does everyone around me die like this?

She was suddenly glad that she had her spacesuit on, the dark visor over her face. She didn't want the others to see her crying.

CHAPTER 10

The damage was worse than Daniel had expected. In the lab area, it had seemed no more than a shaker: worrying, but, as the Doctor had said, survivable.

By the time they got to Level Three-down, however, it was clear that things were worse than that. The plaza area, around the canteen, was solid with people, humans, aliens, some half suited up. There was pushing and shoving, an anxious babble of voices, distant screams of pain. The main lights were out over half the area. Nobody seemed to be making any effort to evacuate, despite the obvious damage.

Daniel shoved his way through the crush, assisted by the Doctor, who seemed to be able to make even the most solidly jammed people move aside with a polite 'Excuse me'. When they reached the area where the lights were out, the Doctor produced a pen-sized flashlight from his pocket. It was surprisingly powerful, almost too powerful: Daniel was dazzled for a moment by its glare.

Then, ahead, he could see uniforms. Black-and-gold Space Marine Specials uniforms. The shouts had become more clearly defined: 'Let us in there!' 'We can help, damn you!' 'We'll dig them out with our hands!'

Daniel and the Doctor looked at each other. Daniel elbowed his way further into the crowd. 'What's going on?' he shouted.

'Canteen roof fell in, mate,' said a voice Daniel half recognised. 'There are people in there injured. They'll be done for if we don't get some props under it, but the bloody troopers won't let us through.'

As if to back up the man's statement, there was another scream, a woman's voice, much closer now. Daniel still couldn't see anything except a wall of backs in overalls and, bizarrely, a group in brightly coloured fancy dress, all plumes and golden glitter.

The Doctor was ahead of him. 'Excuse me, I'm the Doctor. If you could let me through – thank you –'

And suddenly they were at the front, facing the line of marines. Daniel recognised the blonde sergeant who'd been with Cleomides when she'd arrested them earlier. She glanced at him, then stared at the Doctor coldly.

Behind her, the canteen was wrecked. The far wall appeared to have given way completely on both levels, and the upper balcony section had collapsed on top of the lower section.

Under one of the half-collapsed tables, less than ten metres behind the line of soldiers, was a familiar spidery shape.

'Kran!' shouted Daniel.

One of Kran's eye stalks turned, and his gaze met Daniel's. 'Thought I'd come and have a bite. Got bitten instead.'

'Are you OK?'

'I could do with this table off my abdomen, but I'm not hurt, no. At least, not badly. There are some people further in – I'm not sure about them. What's happening? Where are the paramedics?'

Daniel looked around, saw the Doctor haranguing the sergeant, obviously trying to get past the line. But she was just shaking her head.

'Let me guess,' said the Doctor. 'There's something big and alien crawling about behind the wreckage and you don't know what it is, so you're not letting anyone in unless they turn out to be either friends with it, in which case you might be letting the enemy win, or eaten by it, in which case you've not done your duty to protect Earth citizens. So while you dither about the best course of action, people are dying unnecessarily. Is that right?'

The woman stared at him. 'I have my orders,' she said. But Daniel could hear the doubt in her voice.

'Look, I'm not friends with it,' said the Doctor. 'But I know what it is, I know it won't eat me, and I'm sure that in the unlikely event it's still there at all I can get it to leave you alone while you get your people out. Now are you going to let me do that?'

The sergeant touched her lapel, muttered into a throat mike.

The Doctor looked over his shoulder at Daniel, rolling his eyes.

'Cleomides says you can go through,' she said at last. 'But if there's any trouble, we're authorised to use deadly force. Clear?'

'Well, just don't use it without checking what you're firing at first,' snapped the Doctor. 'Come on, Daniel.'

Inside, it quickly became clear that more people were trapped in the wreckage than Daniel had imagined.

It was also clear that some of them were dead.

Dusty faces, still, stiff. Arms, pools of blood.

Daniel turned back to the troops. 'Where the hell's the medical team?' he roared.

'Dealing with another situation, I should think,' said the Doctor quietly. 'Give me a hand here.'

There was a woman half buried in rubble, her lower body crushed. Daniel guessed that she was the one who'd been screaming. Now she was quiet, but still conscious: her eyes opened when Daniel took her wrist, looking for a pulse.

'Krakenites,' she whispered.

'What?'

'Never did trust 'em.' Her eyes closed.

The Doctor was holding her other arm, injecting something from a silver hypo.

'Smart procoagulant,' he said, answering the question Daniel hadn't asked. 'She's got internal injuries. It should keep her going long enough for the team to get here. Come on.'

Behind them, Daniel noticed that a few other miners were through the line. To his surprise, he saw Tiydon there, shouting into a radio. Three or four people were helping to shift the rock pinning Kran's table down. The marines watched the scene suspiciously.

'Come on!' shouted Daniel. 'There's people dying back here!'

The Doctor was already several steps further forward, almost up against the crumbled rear wall of the canteen. Broken rock hung perilously over his head: in a higher gravity it would have fallen, and even here it was dangerous. But the Doctor seemed unconcerned. He was scrabbling something out of a knee-high pile of dust at the base of the wall. Something white and tube-shaped. At first Daniel thought it was a severed human limb, and recoiled, but then he saw the suckers.

A tentacle.

And the injured woman had talked about Krakenites.

At last, Daniel began to see what the Doctor was getting at with his talk of aliens. And why the Specials were here.

And why Tiydon was afraid.

Daniel walked up to the Doctor, who was examining the tentacle with a magnifying glass. 'It wasn't a quake at all, was it?' he said, keeping his voice low. 'We're being attacked.'

'Not exactly,' said the Doctor. 'Have a look.'

Daniel looked through the magnifying glass at the severed tentacle. It had been sheared through, as if cut by a knife. He could see droplets of blood glittering –

No. Wait a minute.

Glowing. Glowing with the same yellow and glittering blue as dreamstones.

That was because, Daniel slowly realised, they *were* dreamstones.

He looked up at the Doctor, incredulous. 'Krakenites *eat* the things?' It seemed impossible, but he couldn't think of any other explanation for what he was looking at.

The Doctor shook his head. 'This isn't part of any Krakenite. The structure is wrong. And the dreamstones weren't ingested, they're a natural part of the biology. If you look closely, you can see the neural connections.'

The Doctor poked around in the broken flesh for a moment, apparently looking for something. Suddenly he looked up at Daniel. 'Wait a minute! Did you say Sam had joined a protest? Where? What were they protesting about? I need to ask them some questions.'

Daniel frowned. He'd forgotten about the teenager. 'Over by Tepee's Crater.' He shook his head. 'Their place was pretty flimsy. I hope she's all right.'

The Doctor looked at him sharply. 'Then we've got another reason to go and visit them. Come on.'

'I don't think so,' said a voice behind them.

Daniel turned, and saw Isobella Cleomides.

The grey-haired captain was carrying a standard-issue light anti-Dalek gun, and it was pointed straight at the Doctor.

'Entity known as "the Doctor",' she said. 'You are under arrest on suspicion of sabotage against the property of Earth nationals, cooperation with alien or aliens unknown, and being a party to an act of terrorist murder. You are not obliged to say anything –'

'Never mind all that,' snapped the Doctor. 'If you're going to insist on arresting me I'm certainly going to say something. I just hope you'll listen this time.'

'I told you,' said Cleomides. 'I don't talk to aliens. And I don't listen to them, either.'

Her finger tightened on the trigger.

The airlock doors wouldn't open.

As far as Sam could see, there was nothing wrong with them: the walls were straight, although tilted a little. The metal didn't appear to be buckled in any way.

But the doors wouldn't budge. They couldn't get out of the suiting-up room.

Sam had turned the air supply in her suit down to normal. There was two hours' air, but even if they could get out she had no idea how long it would take them to find a place of safety. If Madge was right and they were under attack, the DMMC base might have been nuked. Or it might be occupied by alien forces. Anything was possible.

There was still no sign of Aloisse, or Cirbnekk, or any of the other protesters, and there were no voices on the suit radios other than their own.

The man, Jess, came over and looked at the airlock panel, then touched the wrist panel of his suit to it.

He scowled. 'Outer door thinks it's got a leak.'

'Has it?'

'Only one way to find out, that's jemmy the inner door.'

Sam glanced at him. He was blond, with hair in a short ponytail, and could have been any age from mid-thirties to mid-fifties. She wondered whether his competence was real or just bravado.

'If we jemmy the inner door,' she said, 'and the outer door integrity's breached, anyone else left in the base is going to die.'

'*If* there's anyone alive,' snapped Jess. Then, more quietly, 'Kid, they're trapped and going to die anyway. This stuff won't be breathable for much longer.' He waved a hand through the thinning air.

Sam imagined herself trapped in the room where she and Madge had been talking. It could easily have happened, if the room had been a few metres nearer the common room. She imagined air thinning around them. Then suddenly rushing out. Because Jess had jemmied the airlock. Because nobody had bothered to go back and check.

But going back was risky. There could be another attack – or quake, or whatever had happened. What if they all died just because she'd insisted on going back to rescue people who were probably dead already?

Sam realised that there was no simple right answer. This was another one of those decisions that Sam would rather have left to the Doctor. Or Aloisse. Or anyone.

But now she had to make it herself.

Jess was wandering around the locker room: with a shock, Sam realised he was looking for something to jemmy the door with. As she watched, he picked up a power cutter lying by the arm of one of the suits, and tested it. She could hear the roar of the blades even through the thin air and the suit's insulation. So the decision wasn't going to be hers after all.

She thought about Aloisse, trapped without air, helpless, dying. *She saved my life. Twice.*

'Wait,' she said.

Jess looked at her.

Sam set off back into the base. 'If I'm not back in five minutes, jemmy the door.'

'Sam! Wait!'

Madge's voice. Sam heard the fear in it, and felt a momentary doubt.

Footsteps, heavy, booted, slow in the low gravity. Then Madge was by her side, helmet on, the power cutter in her hand.

'It's gonna need at least two of us to get anyone out,' she said. 'We might have to carry them.'

Sam looked at the woman's face, shadowy through the visor, more relieved than she would have thought possible.

'Thanks,' she said, struggling with tears again.

There was no possibility of getting through the collapsed main corridor to the common room area. As Jess had said, it seemed to be squashed flat. All they could do was try the rooms on each side. Most of them were sleeping quarters, and empty. Then there was a small lab facility. Machines were tipped on their sides, and a pool of purplish fluid bubbled silently.

The next door wouldn't open.

Sam hammered on it. 'Anyone in there? Anyone need help?'

Madge touched the power cutter. The blades whirred.

A scraping sound from the door. Then an electronic voice spoke, the words hard to distinguish through metallic resonances. 'This is Aloisse. There's no air in here. Don't open the door.'

The message was repeated. Then silence.

'Are you suited up?' asked Sam, then realised that the alien might not be able to hear her.

'She isn't,' said Madge. 'Both the Krakenite suits were in the locker room.'

They looked at each other.

Sam heard Madge call the others on the radio, telling them to seal their suits. The blades of the cutter whirled again, touched the door in a flurry of sparks.

'We'll never get through it if it's a pressure door,' said Sam. But, even as she spoke, she was looking at the door. It wasn't a pressure door – there was only plastic sealing round the edges. There was no way that it would hold tight against a vacuum.

Which meant that –

'Careful!' bawled Sam. 'Aloisse is sealing the door with her tentacles!'

'She would.' Madge put her helmet against the door. 'Aloisse! If you can hear me, back off! We're cutting through!'

Sam felt a tugging sensation at her feet, saw rock dust moving.

'I think she's –'

The door exploded inward. Sam saw Madge falling, startled, saw the cutter, blades whirling, smashing into the door frame.

Saw a blade shatter Madge's visor. Heard Madge scream.

Aloisse was there then, wrenching the remains of the door off its hinges, wrapping Madge's head in something blue and rubbery, almost pushing Sam back down the corridor. Air was rushing past them, making progress difficult. Sam had a glimpse of Aloisse's eye, bloodshot, the heavy beak that covered her mouth leaking more blood, but she stumped on, carrying Madge. Sam thought about trying to help, decided it wasn't worth asking. Anyway,

Aloisse wouldn't be able to hear her. Even in these few seconds, the remaining air was all but gone.

They reached the locker room. Jess was already at work on the airlock door with another cutter. One of the Besiddians grabbed Aloisse. Jess put the cutter down and helped Sam with Madge. With a shock, Sam realised that the woman was unconscious.

Then she saw the expression on Jess's face, and felt her guts lurch.

'Her suit says she's not breathing,' he said.

They pulled back the blue plastic that Aloisse had wrapped around the visor.

The helmet was dark, Madge's face invisible. After a moment Sam realised that this was because the visor was covered in blood.

It started to bubble out into the near-vacuum of the locker room.

'She's dead, Sam,' said Jess after a while. He went back to the door.

A buzzing began in Sam's head, and a little, whispery, hysterical voice: *You could have just told her to go back, handled it on your own...*

Aloisse had finished suiting up. Even through the thin air remaining in the room, Sam could hear the roar of air coming from the suit's tanks as the big alien refilled her lungs.

Sam fiddled with her radio. 'Aloisse, I –' she began.

'She needn't have come back for me,' said Aloisse. 'I can stand vacuum for half an hour. I was just waiting for the pressure to equalise, so that I wouldn't endanger anyone else by opening the door. Then I'd've walked through.'

'Oh,' said Sam.

There didn't seem to be anything else to say.

Pain, there was only pain, pain and more pain and the monsters were here, here inside his head, treading on his

thoughts, uprooting his mind, and it was burning, it was
burning, burning, burning –

Anton screamed, as the huge dark hand closed around his throat. He tried to struggle, but he couldn't move his body. He felt sweat prickling, heard a voice.

'OK, OK, give him a jab or he's going to burn up.'

A face appeared in front of his. It seemed huge, like a thundercloud, the features vaporous and strange. The eyes stared, like lakes pooled with clouds. The cheeks seemed to tremble, beading sweat like small suns.

'No –' moaned Anton.

A cold touch on his neck. A banging of plastic, like thunder. Anton shivered.

'Come on, mate, we'll get you out of here.'

The plastic cover was zipped up over his head, then inflated like a cocoon. Anton heard a hiss of air, and suddenly he could breathe properly again. At the same time the fever diminished.

His head started to clear.

He remembered what he had to do.

He tried to sit up, to unzip the plastic bubble, but the zip was on the outside and anyway, he couldn't reach it: he was strapped to the trolley protected by the bubble.

'It spoke to me!' he yelled to his unknown rescuers. 'The dreamstone spoke to me! It told me –'

He trailed off, frowning.

'It told me to kill you all,' he whispered, at the same time realising how ridiculous that was. He didn't want to kill anyone.

Then he remembered the old Zmm-Zmm, dying on the crumbling balcony.

'It can control people!' he shouted. 'It can control me! It made me come here! It killed Innell! It made me kill someone!'

A hissing sound in his ear. Static. A radio.

'OK, mate, OK. Just take it easy now. You haven't killed anyone.

No one's dead. There wasn't anyone down there with you. There's been a quake, that's all. We'll get you back to the company base, get you patched up.'

'You don't understand,' whispered Anton.

At the same time, he was thinking about what they'd said.

The base.

Yes. The base was the biggest threat of all to the dreamstones. If he could destroy that –

'I'm dangerous,' he said aloud. 'I called the monsters. They killed Innell. Please listen.'

But there was no reply.

CHAPTER 11

In contrast to Tiydon's office, Isobella Cleomides occupied a tiny, neat room, with a tiny, neat desk. It reminded Daniel of his own quarters, except that the holovid on the wall was moving, and showed a husband and three sons instead of a wife and two daughters. The smiles were the same, though. The smiles of home, of safety. The boys were throwing a blue-and-white beachball from one to the other, endlessly, a seamless loop of childish happiness.

Cleomides saw Daniel looking, met his eye coolly. 'I'm hoping to get back to them alive,' she said. 'And you're not helping me.' She touched a key on the computer in front of her. 'Now, tell me. This Doctor – if he was the UNIT Scientific Adviser working with Brigadier Lethbridge-Stewart, from my information he'd be about two hundred and fifty years old.'

Daniel shrugged. 'Well, he's lying, then. But he seemed OK to me.'

'Obviously he did.' Cleomides drummed her fingers on the desk, just once, a funeral roll. 'Why *did* you trust him? Why did you go along with him to Shaft Four, even though it was a restricted area?'

'He seemed to know what he was doing.'

'So when someone seems to know what they're doing, you defy company regulations and military law and follow them about like an idiot. He could have done *anything* – and you would have been his accomplice!'

Daniel felt himself getting angry. 'My friend had died. The company wasn't doing anything about it. I thought I'd take a look, and the Doctor offered to help. I'm sorry if that was against military law, but I thought I was working for a private company.'

'You're still working for Earth!' snapped Cleomides. She hesitated. 'You were looking at the holovid. My husband is very much older than me, you know. I know he doesn't look it, but he takes antiagathics and –' she smiled – 'he dyes his hair.' A pause. 'He was married before. He had a whole life before he met me, but he lost it. His first wife was a Dalek Killer, you see. It was the only way out, in those times. And so he lost her, and then he lost their child, to one of the plagues. I bore his children, you see them there. Three fine sons. Then the time came to build the space force, they were asking for volunteers who had fought in the resistance. People they could trust. And my husband wanted to go! At sixty-nine! To defend his children, he said. To make sure it never happened again. The only way to make him stay was to say that I would go instead, even though I was only a child in the war. I would defend them. Now I'm here on this rock, defending my people and people like *you* are consorting with *aliens*! Do you know what they have done to us? Have you seen what they have done? Or was your country spared, perhaps? Was your country not turned into a wasteland?'

Daniel had met people like Cleomides before. Too many of them. Using the experience of suffering as a justification for inflicting more of it on others had always seemed a weak argument to him.

But he knew it wasn't logic that counted in things like this. So he met Cleomides's gaze, said softly, 'My father was in the resistance. He died, too. My mother was left with me, just a baby.' He paused, then decided to risk it. 'The Doctor's on our side, believe me.'

Cleomides's eyes flashed, and Daniel knew he'd got it wrong. '"Our side"! He's an alien! Did you see his blood? It's not blood – I don't know what the hell is in it. Could be any sort of Dalek slime. In the name of God, what were you thinking of?'

In her anger she seemed to have forgotten that the Doctor

looked human, and that Daniel hadn't had any reason to think he wasn't.

But she stormed on, before Daniel could even think of a reply. 'It's obvious to me that he can bend people's minds – he got past Sergeant Kelly, and that Besiddian fool, and you. He's a danger to everyone here. I'm not even sure he's safe locked away.' She looked up. 'They can do that, you know. Bend people's minds.'

Sure they can, thought Daniel. And some people's minds need bending. Need the knots straightened out of them. But he didn't dare say it.

Cleomides folded her arms, her manner suddenly brisk and official again. 'Very well, O'Ryan. If Tiydon hadn't spoken to me about you, I would have you locked up too. As it is, you're free to go. But a full report will be made to company HQ regarding your conduct.'

Daniel nodded, stood up. He thought about saluting – memories of his draft days – but decided against it. He wasn't in the marines any more.

Outside, the sergeant was guarding the door. To his surprise, she gave him a rueful grin, touched the side of her head. She must have heard the shouting.

Yes, thought Daniel, Cleomides is a bit over the edge. But you're too young to remember why. Lucky you.

He smiled back at the woman anyway.

He was waiting for the lift when he heard Cleomides's door open. He glanced over his shoulder, saw the woman setting off in the opposite direction, the anti-Dalek gun balanced in her hand.

She's going to the cell, thought Daniel. She's going to kill him. She doesn't trust anyone else to do it, so she's going to do it herself.

Then: She can't do that. This isn't the Earth. Whatever she thinks, we're not being invaded by monsters here. And the Doctor's certainly not in charge of them.

He hesitated, then set off after Cleomides at a run.

For a moment Anton thought it was a dream, then he was sure it was a nightmare.

The grey monster glided silently across the surface, legs moving with a machine's precision. Between the plates of its metallic armour gaped things that looked almost like gun ports. At the front, bulbous eyes sprouted like twin planets.

It was over ten metres long, and it was Anton's friend.

Anton opened his eyes, saw only the milky plastic of the cocoon. But the afterimage of the grey monster was still there.

It was coming. It was coming to get the men who had rescued him from Innell's mine.

He reached up with his free hand, banged on the cocoon. Vague shadows moved outside, but there was no response.

'Hey!'

A flash of light.

A crackling sound. A man's voice. 'What the hell –'

'Ixcallex!' shouted someone else.

Then there was a brief scream, suddenly cut off.

Anton could see it. He could see the dwarfish, stumpy figures of the men, could feel the monster's jaws *his jaws* cutting through plastic and flesh and bone and *another scream* and Anton was screaming too, screaming himself hoarse because the men who had saved his life were dying and he could see it happening and it was *all his fault* –

The surface was a mess. The stark, smooth landscape that Sam had crossed only four days earlier was gone, as if Dreamstone Moon had become a different planet. Everywhere the rock was newly faulted, making small, glittering cliffs. There were cracks in the ground, long stripes of darkness with a deadly similarity to the long, thin shadows cast by the setting sun. Step on the wrong shadow and you could find yourself falling.

To the south, what had been the gentle slopes of a range of low hills had been transformed into sharp, fractured jumbles of gigantic boulders. Every so often a rock would shift a little, sending a scatter of smaller rocks tumbling down from the heap to bounce across what was left of the plain. One of these had already come dangerously close to the little party of spacesuited refugees.

Aloisse and Jess were taking turns to watch the sky, while the other one checked the ground ahead. Sam had been detailed to help Sono with her injured friend: in practice this consisted of walking immediately ahead of them, checking the ground for danger.

The DMMC base had become visible ahead, a messy collection of domes and tall, cylindrical outgrowths.

'It wasn't nuked, then,' said Jess.

'No,' said Aloisse. 'And anyway, this wasn't done by any bombing.'

'You seen rockbusters?'

'If they'd used rockbusters, the Moon would be in several pieces and all of us would be dead,' said Aloisse wearily. 'This is a natural phenomenon. A moonquake.'

As she spoke, the ground trembled a little. They all froze, as if stillness would protect them, as if the quake were a predator. On the horizon, Sam saw a flickering movement, trails of light like meteors flying upward.

'That a natural phenomenon too?' said Jess.

'Outgassing,' said Aloisse. 'The stores of air used by the ecosystem are leaking. The pressure's sending pieces of rubble up.'

That's another way she's like the Doctor, Sam thought. She doesn't know that's true – she just thinks it might be. And all of us will panic less if we don't think we're being bombed, so she presents it as the truth.

Clever. Shame it doesn't make me feel any better.

Aloisse had ruled out any attempt to rescue others from the base. 'I *know* Cirbnekk's dead,' she'd said, without elaborating. 'And no one else had a chance. The common room was crushed flat.'

They'd seen it, from the outside, with half a mountain of rock on top of it.

A buggy rolled past in front of them, red autopilot lights winking, bringing Sam back to the present. She saw the pale, cocoon-like shape of a medical support tent on the back of it and shuddered. How many people had been killed by this thing? How many injured? Getting away from the Doctor didn't seem to have got her away from death and destruction.

She wondered if they could have saved Madge. Jess had said she was dead, but he couldn't have been sure. She'd been losing blood – her suit hadn't been sealed –

Sam shook her head. She knew she was kidding herself. Aloisse would have carried Madge out if there'd been any chance of saving her.

She hadn't yet told the big alien that the 'rescue' had been her idea, her way of paying back Aloisse for saving her life. She hadn't yet told her, in short, that her friend had died because she, Sam, had decided to go in for unnecessary heroics.

She told herself that Madge had come of her own free will, but then remembered the relief she'd felt when the woman had stepped after her, and the fact that she'd made no attempt to tell her to go back.

The Doctor would have said it wasn't her fault, but then he always did.

She wasn't sure what Aloisse would say.

'I'm afraid,' said Kyono, the injured Besiddian. 'There's something watching us.'

'Nothing to be afraid of,' said Aloisse. 'Just keep going carefully, now. We're nearly there.'

'No,' said Jess. 'She's right. There's something moving in the rocks.'

Sam could see it now, a grey steel carapace sliding across a jumble of boulders about a hundred metres away. Big spherical eyes, with tiny black pupils. Some sort of robot?

'Ixcallex,' said Aloisse. 'It's probably very confused, poor thing.'

Sam could see something like antennae, now, the whole form of the thing like a huge millipede, or perhaps a caterpillar, a series of connected segments each on its own set of legs. She could see fluid bubbling from one of the joints, and guessed that the thing was injured.

Suddenly, it saw them.

The pinpoint eyes rolled in their direction.

The antennae pointed.

'I think –' began Aloisse.

The animal pounced.

Sam saw the flare of the rocket exhaust from its tail, saw the speed building up, and dived flat for the ground, pushing Kyono underneath her. She saw the other Besiddian roll in panic, Aloisse picking up a rock.

Jess had a gun.

Sam saw it – some kind of energy weapon, with a flared muzzle – and heard Aloisse yell, 'No!'

Light blazed.

The front of the creature imploded. Then something punched Sam in the body and she was rolling, flying, the landscape below her and her arm hurting *have I broken it?* and –

'Watch how you land!'

Aloisse's voice. Sam could see the ground approaching, faster than she would have liked. But in the low gravity there was just time to roll – no –

Not quite enough time. She sprawled on the sharp rocks, slithered across them.

Stopped.

'Sam? Sam, are you OK?'

'Y-yes, I think so,' said Sam shakily. She realised it wasn't such a bad fall. She'd just expected it to be worse. 'What happened?'

'Ixcallex use peroxide propellants. When Jess killed it, they exploded. Luckily, no one's hurt. Except the poor Ixcallex, of course.'

Sam grinned. Trust Aloisse to worry about animal welfare in a situation like this. Sam wondered if she would have killed the thing, if she'd had a weapon.

Maybe not. She remembered the Tractite. Burned, dead. *Her* work. Had she had a choice then? Would she have had a choice this time, if she'd had the gun instead of Jess?

She realised that she didn't know the answer.

She struggled to her feet. Her arm was hurting, but it clearly wasn't broken. The suit seemed OK, too: a cluster of red impact lights on the visor display were slowly switching themselves off as the machine satisfied itself that no damage had been done.

She walked back to the others.

Then she realised that one of the red lights on the suit panel hadn't gone out.

And that she could hardly breathe.

Oh, no. I don't believe this.

'Aloisse,' she said. 'My air supply's damaged. I think it's some kind of –' She broke off, struggling to understand the diagnostics on the visor display.

But the alien was already stumping across the ground towards her, dodging a sharp, metallic fragment of the dead Ixcallex. A tentacle whipped out, and Sam felt a sharp jolt through the frame of her suit.

The light went out, and fresh, cool air flowed over Sam's face.

'Design fault on that model,' said Aloisse. 'External hoses can disconnect even in vacuum conditions. You're OK now. Come on.'

Sam followed the alien sheepishly. Suddenly she said, 'I'm sorry I didn't trust you.'

'What?'

'After the memorial service – I said –'

'Oh, that. Don't worry, I didn't take it personally. I told you, *I* don't know what's going on. You can hardly be expected to. And this –' She gestured at the shattered landscape. 'This only makes things worse. A quake like this has never happened here before. Geologically speaking, it's nonsense. It just shouldn't happen. It's something to do with the mining, I'm sure it is. I just wish I knew what the connection is. And I wish we'd managed to stop the mining in time. Before this happened. Before people died.'

They'd caught up with the others now.

Jess said, 'While we're apologising, sorry about the Ixcallex. I panicked.'

Sam blushed, as she realised that her privacy with Aloisse had been illusory. She'd been thinking of normal conversation, had forgotten that they were all linked by radio.

She decided not to talk about Madge for the time being. Perhaps one of the others would tell Aloisse what had really happened.

Or perhaps it would be better if Aloisse didn't know.

Following Cleomides was easier than Daniel would have expected. It helped that the corridor followed the gently curving surface of a pressure shell – which meant that Daniel could stay out of sight just by staying fifty metres behind, and walking quietly.

At first he'd thought he should challenge Cleomides – then he'd realised that if he didn't win the argument, there wouldn't then be anything else he could do to stop her. He'd thought about that stony face, the frame of iron hair, and reckoned his chances of winning an argument as pretty low. So he'd shadowed her, keeping just out of sight around the curve of the corridor. He'd expected her to stop and turn round at any moment – but she didn't.

Now she'd reached the Doctor's cell. Daniel could hear her talking to the guard, the words echoing along the bare metal of the walls, but he couldn't make out what they were saying.

Footsteps approached. Daniel quickly started walking forward. He saw the guard approaching.

'I need to see the captain,' said Daniel, quickly, before the man could speak.

But the guard merely nodded and pushed past.

Probably glad to be off duty, thought Daniel. An hour in the bar, rather than an hour guarding a dangerous alien. Much to be preferred.

He could see Cleomides now: she was standing with her back to him, looking at the door, gun in hand.

Cautiously, Daniel backed along the curving corridor until he was just out of sight.

The silence lengthened.

After a long while, Daniel realised that Cleomides wasn't going to go straight in. She was thinking about it.

Or maybe she just hadn't trusted the guard.

Or maybe the Doctor had mind-bending powers after all.

Daniel sat down against the wall, waited for the sound of the cell door opening. But he wasn't sure what he would do when that happened.

The buggy was an eight-wheeler, hauling itself up the slope, red warning lights winking on its four corners and on the top of a long pole attached to the steering column.

There was no one steering: it was coming in on auto, called by the base Emergency Systems beacon. On the trailer was a medical oxygen tent, milky plastic like a man-sized cocoon. Inside, a single figure.

When the buggy reached the G-airlock door of the DMMC base, the machines talked, and the lock cycled to let the buggy in. Further inside, a single DMMC security man saw the buggy pass, checked that the figure in the zipped-up bag was alive, and redirected the machine to a ship waiting in the launch bay area. He had his instructions.

In the launch bay area, the buggy stopped, awaiting clearance to cross the area and board the ship.

People passed by. A few glanced at the dark figure in the life-support cocoon.

Finally, the figure stirred.

There was a sharp thud as the emergency restraint release rolled back. A hiss of escaping air as the plastic was peeled back. A few people glanced at the man sitting up, at his blood- and vomit-stained face. No one took much notice, among all the other injuries, the pain, the fear. Nor did anyone get close enough to hear the words he was muttering to himself.

'I killed them. I killed them I killed them I killed them. I'm dangerous. You've got to stop me.'

But when he stood up and began to walk across the concourse towards the inner airlock, no one stopped him. People made way for him, assuming he was drunk or mad.

He was still muttering, but the words had changed: '– *Mummy help me, Mummy the monsters are here, Mummy ple-ee-ase –*'

CHAPTER 12

The outside entrance to the DMMC base was surrounded by a panicky scrum. Buggies, manned and unmanned, humans in spacesuits, aliens in spacesuits, medical trolleys - everything mixed up, jumbled like the boulders on the plain. Sam saw an Arachnon climbing over the heads of the crowd, delicate legs picking their way from helmet to helmet to metal strut to, finally, the scratched and dusty steel wall of the base. There the alien clung on, waiting for the airlock light to go green.

The radios fizzed and staticked, strange voices blowing in on overcrowded frequencies, making conversation impossible: '- don't understand what -' '- got to get her in before she -' '-nothing like it, never seen anything like it, my grandchildren will never believe -'

Sam was exhausted. Adrenalin had kept her going since the quake, but it had worn off now. She realised her throat and chest hurt, and she was short of breath even though her suit insisted that she had plenty of air. She wanted to lie down and go to sleep, but there was no room even to sit.

Kyono was moaning softly every few seconds, on every breath it seemed, and Sono kept saying, 'She's in pain, oh, can't we get *in*?' Jess cursed from time to time. Aloisse just stood there, like a big, tentacled rock. Every time there was a gap in the crowd, she used her size and muscle to make sure they were the first to fill it.

At last they reached the door, and Aloisse pushed her way in. There was just room for Kyono in the airlock with her, but Sam and the others had to wait outside.

Sam forced herself to stay alert, not to let anyone else get between them and the battered metal of the airlock door. Jess helped. He didn't draw his gun, but the sight of it in a showy holster at his waist kept most people back. At last the doors opened again, and they spilled in at the front. There were two guards in the lock, wearing military-style black-and-gold uniforms. They were checking everyone: Sam assumed that they were trying to sort out priorities. Sono was separated from Sam and Jess, and the guards took Jess's gun.

When the inner doors opened, Sam realised that the chaos merely continued inside. People were moving about everywhere, mostly still fully suited up, although the air was comfortably breathable, even for Sam. They were in a part of the base that she didn't recognise: a hangar-like space with a curved roof supported by steel girders, from which hung various pieces of heavy machinery. Huge white letters on one wall told her it was PRESSURE SHED NINE. A set of doors big enough to allow the passage of a fair-sized spaceship towered on the far side of the room, partly obscured by a half-disassembled hull, steel plates and ribs in a white plasteel matrix. It looked like a colossal piece of discarded fruit peel, or perhaps an abstract sculpture. A metal gallery ran around the walls of the room, about ten metres up. Sam noticed four or five soldiers there, in the same style of black-and-gold uniforms as the airlock guards, carefully watching the crowd. They had long guns in their hands.

Sharpshooters.

And there were more troops at ground level, far more than could possibly be needed for crowd control. What were they doing here? Did they think there was a murderer on the loose?

She looked around, caught sight of the bulky form of Aloisse, towering over the rest of the crowd. She couldn't get through to her on the radio, so pushed her way towards the Krakenite.

One of the troopers moved to stop her.

'That's the alien area, ma'am,' he said.

Sam stared at him. He had blue eyes, and a short fuzzy gold

beard. His skin was black.

'Alien area?'

'Aliens are under military supervision, ma'am,' he said. 'If you would care to make your way to Exit Five over there, we'll get you a ship off the planet.'

Sam blinked. 'You what?'

'We're getting all non-DMMC personnel out. For the time being. I'm authorised to tell you that any claims you've made will be respected, and full compensation will be given for any loss of business.'

Sam realised that he was assuming she was an external contractor, or an independent miner, something of that sort. She decided to use that advantage.

'That Krakenite was working with me. I need her –'

'Sorry, ma'am. As I've said, they're all under military supervision. Just a precaution, I'm sure your colleague is quite blameless, but –'

Sam huffed impatiently. 'I need to talk to her!'

The man's expression hardened. His gaze fixed on Sam's face, as if he was locking a missile on to a target. 'Not right now, ma'am. I'm sorry.'

Sam would have called out, but Aloisse was still suited up. And she was nearly a hundred metres away by now. Sam realised that the whole of the alien contingent were being shepherded towards the spaceship-sized door, which was sliding open, with an almost glacial slowness.

Sam shivered. She didn't like this. She could understand people being shoved around in an emergency, but human soldiers separating humans from aliens felt like the beginning of something bad.

She turned to the soldier, in the hope of getting more explanations, but he was frowning, muttering into a lapel mike. Sam heard the words, 'OK, I'm on my way.'

Then he raced off through the crowd. Sam looked around,

hoping to see Jess, but he was nowhere in sight.

Dumbly, reluctantly, Sam let herself be shepherded towards the exit with the others.

The click of the lock woke Daniel from a half-doze.

Damn that whiskey, he thought. He hadn't felt drunk earlier, but the stuff had still been there in his body, and now –

Now he was standing, swaying, his vision muzzy, but starting to run anyway, run because she was going to *shoot the Doctor* –

He stopped, confused. Cleomides had her gun trained on the cell door, but it wasn't open.

No, it *was* open – just a crack.

Daniel's head cleared as he realised what was happening. The Doctor was breaking out from the inside, and Cleomides –

The cell door opened, and the Doctor stood there. 'Hello, Captain.'

Daniel was already running. 'Don't kill him!'

He saw the charge light on Cleomides's gun turn from green to red. She was twenty metres away, he was never going to make it in time.

The Doctor was dropping towards the floor. Cleomides half turned her head, saw Daniel.

The gun went off, a blaze of light exploding above the Doctor's head. Smoke filled the corridor, and an alarm went off.

The Doctor was scrambling to his feet, running towards Daniel. 'Well done!' he shouted. 'Now if you can just –'

Daniel collided with Cleomides. The gun went off again. Daniel felt the wave of heated air wash over him, the stinging on his skin as tiny fragments of hot metal hit it.

He pinned Cleomides to the ground. She was big, and tough, but Daniel was younger, and heavier.

He put an arm across her throat. 'What the hell are you doing? You could blow a hole in the walls with that thing!'

She let go of the gun. The alarm was still going off. Daniel heard footsteps running down the corridor. The Doctor? No. These were moving closer.

'OK!' The young sergeant's voice. She was standing behind them. 'Get up now!' Daniel could hear a slight quiver, wondered if the young woman had seen any serious action before.

'There isn't a problem here, Sergeant,' said Cleomides. 'Go after the Doctor.'

A pause. 'Sir?'

'Just go!'

The footsteps clattered away.

Daniel stared down at Cleomides in amazement. Then, slowly, he lifted his hand from her throat.

She coughed, once, and they both sat up. The smoke was clearing, but the alarm was still shrilling.

Cleomides looked at the hole in the ceiling and, abruptly, laughed. 'You're right. I shouldn't have used that gun. It was stupid. But I wanted to be sure. Killing people isn't so easy.' She stood up, helped Daniel up. 'We'll blame the Doctor for this, yes?'

Daniel met her eyes. 'We'll see about that,' he said.

Cleomides nodded, then frowned. Daniel saw a red light flaring on her wrist. She tapped the communicator there, put it to her ear.

He saw her eyes widen. She spoke briefly into the communicator, low, coded phrases: Daniel heard the words 'cat', 'pigeons' and 'nest'. When she'd finished, she set off along the passageway at a jog.

Daniel started after her. 'What's happening?'

'Where's the nearest spacesuit locker?' she responded. 'We need emergency suits.'

'First left, a hundred and fifty metres,' said Daniel automatically.

She nodded, accelerated to a run.

'What's happening?' he repeated.

She looked at him over her shoulder, briefly, as she ran. 'Something that shouldn't be happening,' she said. 'I think it's an exercise.'

Daniel didn't believe this, and he was sure that Cleomides didn't either.

'And if it isn't…?' he asked.

This time she didn't bother to glance around, just said, 'Then we are all in serious trouble.'

Yes. And you've just frightened off the only person who could help us.

But Daniel didn't say it, just followed Cleomides to the locker. They were halfway there when the base evacuation alarm sounded.

'The monsters are coming!'

Sam jumped in shock at the hoarse, urgent voice. She realised she'd almost been asleep on her feet. The crowd was still around her, the exit somewhere ahead. Echoing orders sounded over a loudspeaker: she couldn't make out the words.

'Monsters!' repeated the voice.

Sam looked around, her heart still jumping, and found herself face to face with an unshaven, ugly little man in a battered, dusty spacesuit. His eyes met hers, and he grabbed her arms, breathing into her face. She shuddered at the smell of stale vomit.

'The monsters are coming!' he repeated. 'They're going to destroy us!'

This is just what I need, thought Sam blearily.

'Help me!' The man shook her gently, wouldn't let her go. His eyes seemed unfocused, as if he were half asleep or – more likely – drugged.

'There aren't any monsters in here,' Sam said quietly. 'Everything will be fine. Now I'll just find you a doctor –'

'I have to kill them all!'

Sam shivered again, but made herself keep calm, keep her eyes on the man. He seemed to be pleading, rather than threatening, but she knew that psychotics and drug users could change their behaviour very quickly. 'You don't have to kill anyone,' she said. 'I'll find you some help.'

He let her go. 'They won't believe me, they won't believe me, the monsters –' He took an unsteady breath. 'I'm not insane.'

'No, of course not. I just think you're very frightened and upset.' It occurred to Sam that he might really have seen something, perhaps one of the creatures that had killed the Arachnons. He might even know something useful. If she could get him away from this crowd, talk to him…

She looked around at the black-and-gold uniforms, noticed that the humans were now being urged on towards Exit Five, a smallish door in the far wall. The big doors were slowly closing behind the aliens. Sam could only hope that Aloisse was OK.

She began walking, holding the man's arm to guide him. 'Perhaps if you tell me just what you saw, I can help you.'

'It made me kill them! I called the monster and it killed them!'

'I'm sure it wasn't your fault…'

'Ixcallex!'

Sam jumped. Had he been following their party outside? Had he seen the attack?

'They said it was an Ixcallex. I made it attack them. They were helping me – they dug me out – and I called the monster and made it kill them.'

Sam noticed that, even though what he was saying was still nonsense, the man seemed to be waking up, or sobering up.

'You didn't,' she said. 'It was just frightened, that was all. I'm sorry we killed it.'

'No. That's not right. It killed them. I saw them dying.'

Sam began to feel cold. The man was out of his head, but it was beginning to look as if this was shock, not drugs or insanity. What had he seen? Not the attack on her party, that was for sure. It didn't seem unreasonable that there was more than one Ixcallex around, and that they should all be unnerved by the quake. But were they all attacking people, suddenly? And if so, why?

Before she could ask the man any more, there was a shout, then the booming of an amplified voice. 'I will count to three then fire a warning shot.'

She saw someone running along the gallery, his footsteps booming on the bare metal. Someone who looked like –

Who *was* –

No.

It couldn't be.

But it *was*.

The Doctor. The *Doctor*.

Sam felt a wild surge of joy, and at the same time her face flushed deep red. This was going to be very embarrassing, and there wasn't time to explain –

Perhaps that was just as well.

And how could she be thinking about such things? He was alive!

He was running madly down a flight of spiral steps, yelling at the top of his voice.

'Sam! Sam!'

There was an explosion of light, and a yell from the Doctor. Sam saw smoke rising.

She couldn't see the Doctor any more.

He was *hurt*.

She dived through the crowd, yelling, 'Don't kill him! *Don't kill him don't don't don't* –'

She caught a glimpse of the Doctor being lifted up, being carried over the shoulder of one of the soldiers, then her view was blocked by a wall of backs.

'No! He's not dead!' she bawled. 'I have to help him!' She pushed her way through the crowd, pummelling on people's backs, kicking their legs.

She caught a glimpse of the Doctor's hair, surely it was his hair…?

A flash of light.

Were the soldiers firing again? But surely they wouldn't just kill him! Was there someone else there? What was *happening*?

Suddenly Sam became aware that people were screaming, moving, pushing her off her feet, that the crowd were flowing towards the exit in a flood tide. A man in front of her was struggling with a spacesuit helmet, pushing it over his head.

Then she felt the air moving past her, heard the scream of breaking metal.

The light got brighter, hotter, as if someone had switched on a sun.

She looked up.

There was a hole in the roof.

There was a blazing light above the hole, a jewel-like shape almost too bright to look at. Girders were bending back like fingers being broken; steel plates were lifting away like leaves in a storm.

Someone grabbed Sam's head, pushed it down, pushed something over it.

Her helmet.

Sounds were fading away, becoming ghostly as the outside atmosphere died. Sam heard the hiss of oxygen above the ringing in her ears.

A clunk of plastic. Helmet clamps.

'Keep with me!'

She saw the unshaven face of the loony in front of her, his wild eyes staring into hers through two layers of plastic.

A hand grabbed her arm.

'Run!'

The man's face was gone, and she was running towards the exit, behind the crowd. The wall seemed to be getting closer too fast, as if the floor itself was moving. No – it was the wall. The wall was falling, falling on to the crowd ahead of her and the man was still pulling her arm, steering her away, *keep with me* he said *keep with me* and she was following him and the steel plates were falling in pieces all around them, red-hot sheets of metal *no convection or conduction only have to worry about radiation* or being hit on the head and the staircase that the Doctor had come down was loose, waving about like a demented insect like a dying Ixcallex and her chest hurt her leg hurt where she'd fallen and *I can't breathe enough to keep running* and the roof was gone and the sky was full of jewels, jewels glowing like fire and *the Doctor's dead he's dead that's why this is happening* the gallery was falling the walls were buckling there was a huge black mouth in the ground ahead of them pieces of white-hot metal were flying past her head and the mouth was opening and she could *see its teeth –*

CHAPTER 13

Tim Carr decided that war, so far, was pretty much like training. The cold, hard, airless rock was the same. The landing procedure was the same: blast a ring with the podship's guns; land in the middle of the ring; set up the small, milky dome of the pressure shelter; mount four quartering guns on the edge of the zone. Then watch out for aliens as the ground cools down. Or, as Sergeant Higgins had said in training, 'If anything moves, kill it.'

But Carr knew there was a difference. He'd seen that difference in the eyes of his friends as the podship had begun its roller-coaster power-dive to the surface. He could hear it now, in the longer-than-usual silences, the raw tension in the voices when anyone spoke. The flashes and explosions might all be distant, well over the horizon, but they were real explosions, killing real people.

His squad might be next. *He* might be next.

They'd been given perimeter duty, but nobody was sure how far the perimeter was from the action. All they'd seen were those flashes of light, and glimpses of sunlike things that might have been the alien ships. Carr glanced up nervously, but saw only the dropship *Royale*, a black shadow on the stars, its flying-skyscraper shape detectable only through the faint residual shimmer of the warp jump crawling over its surface like a rippling spiderweb. The dirty brown disc of the airless little rock's mother planet rippled in the field as if it were reflected in water.

'Carr!' Sergeant Higgins's voice.

Carr looked down, realising that he'd let his attention stray from the sector he was supposed to be watching. He returned his eyes to the jumbled rocks, the long stripes of shadow, waiting for the sergeant's rebuke.

But Higgins only said, 'Take Hunter and Wu to the fault line at 350-A.' A mark appeared on Carr's visor. 'Check it out – carefully. There's some kind of gas release there.'

Carr felt a cold hand clench around his guts. This was *real*. He was going to be in charge of a detail. An attack. People could die. *He* could die.

But he knew he couldn't allow himself to think about it. That was a sure way of ending up dead.

He pulled up enhanced pictures of the target, saw the effects of the gas release: dust glinting in the air, a crystalline deposit forming on the shattered rocks. Mostly water ice, the spectrographic analysis told him. Then he checked with Hunter and Wu and agreed a 3D-fan approach, with Wu floating ten metres up, balanced against the Moon's light gravity on his suit's jets. Finally, Carr armed the systems in his own battle suit. Red lights flickered on his status display as he began his advance.

His heart began thudding in his chest. He widened the window in his visor that showed the outside world, wondered if he should have made some attempt at a concealed approach.

No. Whatever was in there could see the landing point. It would already have fired on them if it could. Probably there was nothing: a damaged water conduit, a –

Something moved near the outgassing.

Carr blacked his visor, switched his body guns to auto. They refused to lock on.

He could see a face now: a bug-eyed face, long teeth, thin spidery arms.

He locked the guns on manually, fired.

The thing vanished. Had he hit it? A ghostly radar display flickered in his helmet: nothing.

Carr made a decision. He opened a channel to Hunter and Wu, told them to keep point. Then he lowered the weapons status of his battlesuit and moved in towards the rift.

Higgins's voice spoke softly in his ear. 'The area might be booby-trapped, kid. I suggest you proceed with care.'

Carr acknowledged the transmission, but didn't stop his steady advance.

Closer. He jumped over a little spine of rock that had looked like nothing from the landing point, and turned out to be higher than he was. Through its shadow, to the rift.

Look down.

Nothing.

No. A face.

Carr fired instantly, a low-intensity bolt.

The face vanished.

He opened a channel to Higgins. 'It's as if they're made of vapour,' he said. 'They don't show up on targeting; they disappear even after a low-intensity bolt.'

The sergeant didn't reply.

An alarm beeped in Carr's helmet. At the same time, light flooded his visor. Automatically, it blacked out. Radiation diagnostics flared everywhere: Carr saw that he had to take cover – no: the light was dimming again. A near miss.

'The ship!' Wu's voice.

Carr looked up, saw that the *Royale* had grown a sunlike ball of fire near the bridge end. As he watched, he saw the rear hull begin to tumble away, a huge, too-fast, mile-long spin. Then he saw the scatter of debris moving at meteor speeds, outward, downward, *towards them*.

'Take cover!' he bawled. He looked down, jumped forward, over the rift. If there was really anything down there...

Nothing happened.

A short scream from Wu. Carr glanced up, saw the man's battlesuit spinning, then with a shock saw that it was in two pieces, broken along the waist seal. Wu was in the upper half. Carr had a brief glimpse of his legs in their silver undersuit, kicking desperately before the suit crashed into the side of a rock.

More debris was falling, flickering explosions everywhere. Secondary infalls were hitting the battlesuit – Carr saw damage reports flash up.

He was going to *have* to go subsurface, whatever the risks, whatever might be down there.

But Wu –

He saw Hunter, hovering over the broken battlesuit, grappling on, lifting it up on the jets, speeding back to Higgins and the pressure shelter.

He peered down into the rift, saw nothing. He checked that the suit was recording, then flicked open a comms channel.

'Sergeant?'

Silence.

'Sergeant Higgins?'

A crackle of static. 'Wu here.' A gasp. 'Get out, Tim, get –' A moan of pain.

'What's happening?'

Silence.

Carr felt panic then. He'd lifted on his jets before he'd thought about what he was doing, then realised too late that if Higgins and the others were under attack he was making himself visible to the attackers. He turned quickly to look at the landing site, ready to dive back to cover, and saw with a shock that the pressure shelter was gone.

Simply gone.

Something was moving –

A long, curling tentacle, as high as a small tree, glittering with crystals.

No. Several tentacles. The others must be somewhere in the middle of that thing –

He called Wu's name again. No response. Carr saw a tentacle

whipping out towards him – saw the gnarled, demon-like face on the end of it –

No.

An eye.

An eye about a metre across, looking back at him steadily.

He fired, fired with both guns, full power, without thinking, without challenging, without following any of the rules. The creature collapsed into a thrashing heap of smoke and dust.

He pulled up an enhanced image, saw a charred body bubbling in vacuum.

Got you this time.

Another tentacle. Another eye. Another bolt of plasma. Carr even allowed himself a feeling of satisfaction as the thing collapsed.

Vapour dispersed, quickly leaving nothing but vacuum, rocks coated with black ash, a few glowing fragments.

I've killed –

Killed what?

Carr waited a full minute, then opened a comms channel.

Nothing.

He waited another two minutes, calling at thirty-second intervals. Just like it said in the manual.

No movement. No comms activity.

At last he flew over to where the pressure shelter had been, weapons on full alert.

Jumbled rocks. A broken spacesuit, a lump of charred flesh. A shred of the silky plastic material of the pressure shelter.

Another spacesuit, cracked open at the front.

Charred flesh.

Human flesh.

I've killed –

'Higgins?' called Carr. 'Hunter? Wu? *Anyone?*'

Silence. Carr saw another spacesuit, a fragment of a visor.

- I've killed them oh my God I've killed them -

Carr's body began to shake. He fumbled for the comms control, couldn't make his fingers work properly. His visor misted with sweat.

But however hard he looked, there was no trace of the tentacled things. No giant eyes, not even remnants of flesh.

Only his comrades.

His *friends*.

Carr closed his eyes for a moment in prayer, then felt a little calmer.

He knew what he had to do.

When Daniel and Cleomides reached the emergency control room the battle was already well under way. Several soldiers were manning the stations in full armour, helmets sealed, faces invisible behind black visors. Daniel, like Cleomides, had had to make do with snatching an e-suit – all there had been in the emergency locker. Daniel's was thin, buff-coloured, and the air in it smelled of rubber and stale sweat.

Aril Tiydon was staring at the huge three-dimensional status screen that filled one wall of the room, dressed only in his office clothes, dwarfed by the armoured bodies of the soldiers. He looked around when Daniel and Cleomides came in, and Daniel saw the panic on his face, the beads of sweat standing out on his forehead.

'They've got four of the pressure sheds,' he said, 'and the main dome's got a couple of breaches.' His voice was trembling. 'I've put out an evacuation order –'

'Calm down!' barked Cleomides. 'There's half a fleet up there, and a division of marines is on its way in to relieve us.'

'People are already dead!' snapped Tiydon. He turned to Daniel. 'I just can't make them understand. This is about people's lives.'

Yes, thought Daniel. A bit late for you to be thinking about that now. But the situation was beyond any worries about blame. That was for later.

He looked at the status display. It was covered in red lights and damage-control icons. Pressure was out on most of Level Zero, the dormitory level. The doors were sealed: hopefully most of the people there would have had time to get e-suits. Below that, the pressure was OK, but there were hot spots – probably fires – and some flooding. Finally, there were structural-integrity alerts up on the main dome, though none of them were critical yet.

Daniel turned to Cleomides. 'We need to get patch teams to Level Four and Level Two. Where's maintenance?'

'Out of touch,' said a woman's voice – the blonde sergeant? It was impossible to tell who was in the huge black suits. 'Internal comms are down – there's some kind of interference. We're only hoping they haven't been –'

The room shook. The sound of metal breaking shuddered through the walls.

Daniel glanced at Tiydon. 'Ri, you should suit up.'

Tiydon ignored him. 'People have died,' he muttered. 'We should have evacuated sooner. I should have realised.'

Daniel grabbed his arm. 'What do they teach you in management training now? That you can breathe vacuum? You have to suit up. This place could lose pressure any minute. You can see the situation.'

'This has become a full war zone,' observed Cleomides, leaning over the comms board. 'Nonmilitary personnel should leave. I've contacted the *Serendipity* – I can order an evacuation.'

'I can't leave –' began Tiydon.

'Order it,' snapped Daniel.

Tiydon glanced at him, then at Cleomides, then nodded. Cleomides began talking quietly into the board.

Another shudder. A shattering of glass. Daniel sensed the air move even through his sealed suit. He pushed Tiydon towards the door.

'Everybody out! This is a pressure emergency!'

'No!' said Tiydon. 'I can't leave the control room until the base is secure and everybody is safe. I must –'

The floor bucked, like a small boat hit by a huge wave. Part of the display board crumpled inward, a shower of glowing shards, tiny out-of-phase images of base schematics and damage reports dancing in the air for a few seconds before dying. Behind the broken panel the metal guts of the station were laid bare. A pipe was broken: water flooded out, dark and blobby with faeces and waste food.

The lights went down as circuit breakers tripped. For a second there was nothing but darkness filled with the whirling sparks of the dying holoboard: then, one by one, the armoured suits lit up, blue-white halo beacons that cast overlapping half-shadows on the walls and the debris-strewn water flooding across the floor.

Cleomides was already by the door, pulling it open, her hand jamming the manual override switch to stop the base systems from shutting it in response to the pressure drop. Tiydon had lost his footing: Daniel grabbed him, pushed him in the direction of Cleomides, who threw him into the passage outside. Daniel staggered after them, clumsy in his e-suit, aware of water pulling at his legs, of impacts against his back which he hoped were only soft materials – anything sharp might damage the relatively flimsy suit.

The soldiers bundled Cleomides through the door. As soon as they were all out, Daniel let the door close and seal behind them. Black water had sloshed through into the passage, ankle-deep, and flowed along it, slicking the walls like oil in the low gravity.

Cleomides was shouting something to the soldiers, the e-suit broadcasting her words on audio. Daniel heard the words 'battle group' and 'point 378-G'.

'Where?' he bawled at her.

She pointed at the ground. 'Here. We stay here.'

'There's two levels above us,' said Tiydon. 'They'll never get a podship down here.' He was leaning against the wall, studying his folding computer. Its comms light winked, red-green-red.

Cleomides was pulling an e-suit out of one of the wall lockers. 'Get this on, we're losing pressure.' Tiydon stared at her. 'Get it on or you're dead!'

Tiydon began struggling with the suit.

The floor shuddered. Another quake? An attack from above? The arrival of the rescue fleet? It was impossible to tell.

The shuddering became more violent.

Daniel saw Tiydon closing the e-suit seals around his neck, saw the suit puff out with air. Then saw him walk down the passageway and stop at the steel doors of an emergency stairway.

'Where's he going?' asked Cleomides.

But Daniel had already started after Tiydon. The man was struggling with the bolts on the doors.

'Ri. They're going to pick us up. There's no way we can help anyone by –'

'I'm going down to be with my people.' Ri's voice sounded almost comic through the e-suit's speaker, as if he were an electronic toy.

'Mr Tiydon,' said Cleomides. 'I don't think you should risk –'

But Tiydon was already hitting the last bolt back, and the doors folded inward quickly –

– too quickly because there's no pressure behind them –

'Ri!' Daniel rushed forward. Air buffeted his body. By the time he got to the doors, Tiydon was gone. Daniel half fell through the doorway, saw a wall of broken metal, the edges glowing red. Jagged shadows stretched down into a pit with burning walls. Pieces of metal and other debris were still falling down the pit, with a terrifying slowness.

Daniel realised that the shadows on the walls were moving. This wasn't sunlight. He looked up, saw a giant crystal floating in empty space above the domes, as big as a spaceship and as bright as a sun. As he watched, horrified, it brightened further, then began to split in half. Rings of fire rushed out, like ripples in a lake of superheated plasma.

He struggled to push himself back into the corridor, but the air was still flooding out. He lost his balance, slammed into the frame of the doors, struggling to grip the metal, but the pressure forced him slowly out into the vacuum. The light got brighter still: he could feel the skin of his face burning through the thin e-suit visor. Shielding his eyes with a hand, he looked up again, saw the blunt square shape of an Earth ship moving towards the breaking remains of the alien ship. No – wait –

Where the alien crystal had been, Daniel could see the outlines of a dropship. He saw the metal sheeting peeling back. Plasma fire poured into its sides, but he couldn't see the aggressor.

What had happened to the crystal? But there wasn't time to worry about it. White-hot fragments were flying out – down – towards him –

He felt something grab his legs, pulling him back. A weight descended on him, compressing his suit against his body and pushing the air out of his lungs. Then he was being rolled around, pushed against a wall.

Inside. Safe.

But Tiydon…

Daniel could see the doorway, sidelong, above him, still open. A few pieces of debris were fluttering out with the last of the air. Then his view was eclipsed by a face in front of his visor, half hidden by a visor of its own.

Cleomides. She had her knees against his chest, physically holding him against the wall. Brown eyes met his, and the lines of a smile formed around them.

'We must stop getting physical like this, Mr O'Ryan. My husband will get jealous.'

Daniel had to grin back.

But Tiydon…

Cleomides rolled away, stood up. Almost all the air had escaped by now. Silver-and-red-striped emergency pressure doors had closed, sealing them off in a forty-metre section of the passageway.

Daniel got up. 'Ri?' he asked.

'Mr Tiydon?' She shook her head. 'Sergeant Douvlos is speaking to the *Serendipity* for me now. There is a podship launched for us – we can hope that they will pick him up when they get here.'

Daniel thought of the pit outside, the slowly falling debris. 'We can hope,' he said.

Another friend gone, he thought. The Doctor was right. Aloisse was right. Sam was right.

We shouldn't be here.

When Sam woke up she was walking in darkness.

She struggled for a moment, confused, felt the plastic inlay of the suit tighten against her. A red light flickered in her eyes. A hand touched hers, and she stopped walking. A face appeared, dimly lit, haggard, unshaven, red rims around the eyes.

The loony!

– the diamond sun-bright spaceships the pressure shed disintegrating around her the Doctor was dead and the mouth in the ground she could see its teeth –

A clunk of plastic as the two helmet visors touched, and then the man's voice, hollow and muffled. 'I put the suit on automatic follow. Innell showed me.' The man's face screwed up quickly, a nervous tic. 'Innell's dead now, I expect.' A pause. 'But you're not going to die. I won't let it happen!'

– the Doctor's dead he can't be dead –

'Where are we?' she asked, trying to keep the panic out of her voice.

'Underground.'

The mouth in the ground. Yes. It must have been a cave of some sort. But it had looked *alive*.

'Who are you?'

A pause. 'I'm not supposed to tell anyone.' A pause. 'Oh, I don't suppose it can matter any more now. I'm Anton La Serre. I used to do dreams.' A giggle, which Sam realised was almost purely hysterical. 'Now –' a gulp of laughter. 'Now I do nightmares.'

'OK, Anton. I'm Sam. I'm –' she hesitated. 'I'm one of the people protesting against the mining operation. Is –' She started shaking, involuntarily. She took a breath, forced herself to speak clearly and simply. 'Look, I had a friend. A man with light-brown hair. He dressed a bit strangely. Old-fashioned. He was shot and injured by the guards just before the attack on the pressure shed. Did you see him?'

Anton frowned. 'Lots of people died.' A pause. 'But I'm sure your friend didn't!'

This was obviously wishful thinking. But for some reason, Sam felt equally sure about it. The Doctor wasn't dead. He was too old to die now. He always found a way out.

Talking of which…

'How do we get out of here, Anton? Where are we going?'

'We're not going out, we're going in.'

'In what?'

'Inside the Moon. I know how it sounds, but I know what I'm doing. Follow me.'

Before Sam could react he had let her go and was walking on, a faint, disembodied halo in the darkness.

Sam checked her suit's air supply, found that she had less than an hour left. And one of the electrical circuits was showing an amber light.

'Anton?'

Silence.

She found her suit lights, switched them on.

And stopped dead in her tracks.

A giant eye was watching her.

An eye framed by a crown of tentacles which reached out, over her head, behind her...

She turned, saw another eye, a little further away. The two creatures sealed off the passageway behind them and ahead of them.

Her heart jerked in panic. 'Anton!'

No response. He was still walking, and now she noticed that the mass of white flesh ahead was slowly retreating in front of him.

She remembered what he'd said in the pressure shed – *'I called the monster and made it kill them.'*

Could he call the monsters?

'Anton! Talk to me!'

She caught up with him, grabbed his arm.

At last, his voice spoke over the comms link. 'It's all right, they won't hurt you. I think.'

'But where are we going?'

'I've told you. Inside the Moon.'

'I think I'd rather go back to the surface.' This time, Sam couldn't keep the shake out of her voice.

'You can't.'

Sam looked over her shoulder, saw that the wall of flesh behind them was advancing, the eye still fixed on her. She realised that Anton probably didn't have any more choices than she did. Whatever he thought was happening, these things were in control.

They were going inside the Moon, and there was nothing that either of them could do about it.

It was at least half an hour before the podship arrived. Nobody spoke much in the interval. Cleomides sat apart from everyone else, propped up against the emergency pressure doors, occasionally talking into her wrist comm. The broken doors were guarded by two of the black-suited troopers. Weapons pods flickered and twitched on their arms and backs, as if the machines were eager for the kill.

Eventually, Cleomides spoke over the open channel, telling them that the podship had arrived. She didn't say anything about the state of the battle, or about Tiydon.

The troopers stood back and the doors were cautiously opened from the outside. Dim, red light seeped through, as if the passageway had become an anteroom to some medieval vision of hell. A black shape drifted in through the doors. Daniel peered at the dark visor, hoping for a clue to the situation outside, but he couldn't even see the soldier's face.

Lights moved outside the doorway. Daniel looked out, saw the familiar shape of a podship, a steel sphere with dull-green insignia, not very different from the ships he'd trained on a decade before. The dark, insect-like figures of perhaps a dozen armoured soldiers were hovering around it. There was no sign of Tiydon, but Daniel hadn't really expected that.

The soldiers hovering around the ship unfolded a pressure corridor and sealed it against the broken doors. A squad of marines in light battle armour crossed, saluted Cleomides, then urged Daniel outside. Although he couldn't see through the tube, Daniel crossed quickly. He didn't want to think about what might be below. How many bodies might be down there. How many of his friends.

He passed more marines on the way over. He saw Cleomides talking to them for a moment before she followed him across.

Inside the podship it was dark, and crammed with more of the young marines, most of these in full battle armour. They were strapped to the walls, the ceiling, the floor, cocooned like pupating insects in acceleration webbing.

Cleomides touched his shoulder, put her helmet against his. 'Daniel. There are some spare HD suits in the engineering section. Put one on. We'll need your help in the base.'

Daniel hesitated, then decided that Cleomides was right. And if there was any hope that Tiydon was still alive, it would give him a chance to help with the rescue. He squeezed past more of the marines until he found the dropshaft that led to the engineering section.

He was just about to haul himself over the steel rim of the shaft when a hand tapped him on the shoulder.

'Mr O'Ryan?'

Daniel swung around, saw a young marine blinking at him.

'There's a prisoner insists on speaking to you, sir.'

Daniel frowned.

'Daniel! How nice to see you again! Sorry I can't shake hands.'

Daniel recognised the voice. He turned, saw a cluster of marines in their black armour, helmets tight, visors dark and faceless.

In the middle of them, with a bandage around his leg and plasteel cuffs on his wrists, stood the Doctor.

Sam stumbled, and had to put a hand on the wall for support. She looked down, realised there had been a change in the texture of the floor. The smooth, marble-like surface had become striated, long grooves forming in the stone as if it were a liquid swirling towards a plughole. The slope was getting steeper, too. Soon the floor was so grooved and fractured that Sam found it difficult to keep her balance. The alien ahead of them no longer filled the entire width of the passage: Sam could see empty space above and to either side of it, the walls streaked with long shadows from the suit lights.

'Turn your lights off,' said Anton suddenly.

Sam hesitated, then complied. After a moment, as she'd half expected, she saw that there was another light ahead. For a moment she had the bizarre impression that she was standing in a cave looking out at the sky – a dim twilight sky flickering with sparks from a fire, or perhaps fireflies. As her eyes adapted to the dimness she realised that what she was seeing was dreamstone – but quite unlike any dreamstone she'd seen so far. A huge slab of the crystalline material, shaped in a rough disc, formed most of the wall on the far side of the cave. It had to be a hundred metres across. On the slope below the dreamstone, crawling across the crystalline surface, and hanging from the ceiling above it, were more of the tentacled aliens. They looked like insects creeping across a pane of glass.

The light from the dreamstone brightened, then faded again. For a moment Sam could see only the slope in front of them, and the retreating alien, a pale ghost.

She glanced behind her, saw that the other alien, the one that had been behind them in the passageway, was gone. They were free, it seemed.

Sam switched her suit lights on again, and saw that Anton was still walking. He was crossing the base of the chamber now, up to his knees in a pool of oily-looking water, which sloshed up over the rocks around him.

Sam hurried after him as he started up the opposite slope.

'Anton?'

He'd raised his hands to his neck. With a shock, Sam realised that he was removing his helmet.

'Anton!' She glanced at her suit's air monitor, saw that the atmosphere outside was barely breathable. Had he run out of air? Perhaps she could share her supply, or something. She ran up to him, saw his wild face, his hair glued to his forehead with sweat.

She heard his shout even through her sealed helmet. 'It's calling me.'

Sam felt a jolt of fear. 'The dreamstone?'

'We have to join with it.'

'*What?*'

'I know it's frightening but we have to – we have to tell it –'

He was breathing hard, as if he were running.

Sam realised that she could feel it too.

Fear.

Raw, terrible, fear. Pain. Fever.

'Anton. We have to go back.'

But he was still climbing the slope.

'*Anton!*'

Shapes were crowding Sam's vision, dim, flickering shapes of terror and delirium, some of them human, some alien.

Anton screamed, a hoarse, terrible sound.

– the monsters are here –

'Doctor!' she yelled.

– he's dead he's dead –

'– you've got to help you've got to stop them they're killing me *they're killing me* –'

CHAPTER 14

When Daniel and the Doctor climbed back up the dropshaft, Cleomides was waiting at the top, still wearing her e-suit, though she'd taken the helmet off. Daniel followed her into the jump bay, squeezed along the space between the young marines. Beside him, the Doctor limped along, looking around him with growing bafflement.

'I don't suppose they found Tiydon?' asked Daniel suddenly.

Cleomides shook her head, and Daniel cursed under his breath.

'Is he dead?' asked the Doctor softly, looking at Daniel.

Daniel nodded, gestured at the external viewscreen above the lock doors. 'Be more than one friend dead,' he said.

The Doctor stared at the screen, at the wreckage that had been Sector Six of the DMMC base. It was receding slowly: Daniel could feel the podship's engines running, acceleration as gentle as that of an elevator. More of the base came into view: Daniel was relieved to see that some of the other sectors were relatively undamaged.

The floor shifted under their feet. The ship was manoeuvring, looking for a place to make a landing.

Suddenly, unexpectedly, the Doctor spoke.

'How many people have died in this?' He was staring at Cleomides, his voice trembling with anger. 'And you knew there was a fleet ready to evacuate the place. You *knew*. Why didn't you do anything?'

The young men in their battlesuits looked up at him in amazement.

Cleomides stopped and turned, but instead of facing the Doctor she looked at Daniel. 'It wasn't my decision!' she shouted. 'I didn't know that an incident on this scale was likely! I ordered an evacuation as soon as –'

'What scale of incident were you expecting, then?' interrupted the Doctor.

Cleomides looked away. 'That's classified.'

Daniel stared at her. He could see the blush of anger over her brown skin. Slowly he realised that she wasn't angry because of what the Doctor had said, but because she knew he was right, and that she had been asking the same questions of herself.

She was only a captain, after all. The ultimate responsibility for all this lay higher. Judging by the number of ships around, a *lot* higher.

'We seem to have had this conversation before,' the Doctor was saying. 'Last time you didn't tell me what you knew, and now hundreds of people have died. Well this time, I can at least tell you what I've found out. This dreamstone your people are mining isn't just a crystal: it's part of a living system, quite possibly an intelligent –'

But Cleomides started to walk away. 'I have to get into a proper suit,' she said to Daniel. 'There's a job to do. We're docking with the *Serendipity* in –' she glanced over her shoulder at a wall screen – 'ninety seconds. Daniel, get to the comms room there and see if you can help them organise the evacuation. You know the base better than our people.' A pause. 'And get him –' a glance at the Doctor – 'locked away safely.'

'Locking me away won't solve any of your problems,' said the Doctor. 'You need my help. This situation is *dangerous*. You can't just use military tactics against it.'

Cleomides ignored him.

'We should listen to him, you know,' said Daniel.

But Cleomides was already climbing the stairs to the next level, her boots clicking on the metal stairs. Daniel realised that it was his turn to acknowledge that she was right, at least about some things. There *was* a job to do. Recriminations would have to wait.

He turned to the Doctor. 'Look, just go quietly. I'll see what I can do for you.'

The Doctor met his eyes. Daniel was suddenly sharply aware of the almost mesmerising power there, of the alienness of this so often warm and human-seeming person.

'I hope you can do something, Daniel,' said the Doctor, with quiet intensity. 'I really hope you can. All our lives could depend on it.'

The cave was dark when Sam woke up. She felt as if she'd slept for an hour or more, though her suit timer told her it was only ten minutes.

Gradually she realised that the faint sobbing sound she could hear was Anton. She switched the suit lights on, saw him curled up against the now dark slab of dreamstone, his helmet off, rocking slowly back and forth like a child.

It must have been much worse for him, she realised. He was already sensitive to this stuff, and he'd been much closer to the huge crystal. But what had happened? It had been like every childhood nightmare made real. She'd been convinced she was dying, and she felt now as if she'd been feverish – her throat was dry, and her limbs were weak as she stood.

She looked around the dim cavern, wondering if any of the aliens were still here.

Natives, she reminded herself. Not aliens. They lived here. She didn't. Aloisse would have made that distinction. So would the Doctor, probably.

Aloisse. The Doctor. Where were they? Was either of them still alive? What was happening on the surface?

No way of finding that out, without going back there.

She walked across to Anton, leaned over him. His eyes were open, but he made no response to Sam, just carried on rocking to and fro, whimpering softly. There was a mark on his cheek: a dark graze, bleeding.

'Anton.'

Still no response.

'We've got to get out of here. Our suits are going to run out of air.' Actually, Anton still had his helmet off and was evidently breathing the air in the cave, but Sam wasn't willing to risk doing that herself unless she had to.

'Anton. Please.'

Something was glittering in the graze on his cheek. A fragment of rock? Of *dreamstone*?

She reached down, touched the wound as gently as she could with the clumsy gauntlet of her suit. The crystal was pea-sized, and lodged more deeply than she'd thought. It wouldn't come out. She pulled at it, not caring if she hurt Anton, half hoping that the pain would shake him out of his stupor.

'No.'

The response surprised her, because his eyes still hadn't moved. It was almost as if he hadn't spoken.

She waved a hand in front of his face. 'Why not? If it gets infected –'

'It's part of me.'

Oh no. But Sam was surprised at how calm she felt. The nightmares induced by the dreamstone seemed to have washed all the fear – all the feeling – out of her. It was as if the last few days had been sandpapered away, leaving her clear-headed and rational. It was probably just a physical aftereffect of the nightmares, a piece of brain chemistry trying to compensate for the effects of the dreamstone, but she welcomed it.

Then it occurred to her that Anton might not be the only one with dreamstone lodged inside him.

No. It couldn't get through the spacesuit.

Could it?

She looked at the suit, searching for holes, until she realised that she was being ridiculous: the machine itself would certainly have informed her of any puncture.

When she looked up, Anton was rocking back and forth again, silently.

The briefing room was light, the wood polished, the fabrics white and gleaming. A ceremonial sword, too beautiful to be real, hung over a false marble fireplace, and a low incense candle burned in front of an elaborately wrought Buddha. The entire holographic projection was perfect: Cleomides felt as if she was standing in front of the big, shining desk. She could almost smell the incense.

She looked at the tiny man sitting behind the desk with a mixture of fear and awe. He looked ordinary enough, a plain, round, Oriental face, a shaven scalp, simple black clothes: he could almost be a monk. Only the golden starbursts on his shoulder told the world that this was a general: *the* general, Supreme Commander of the Space Marines, killer of more Daleks and other assorted aliens than any man alive, and probably the most powerful man in Earth space.

A fuzz of static moved across the image. Then the general spoke: slowly, softly.

'Captain Cleomides, we have a security problem in your sector. A problem related to aliens.'

A pause. Cleomides realised that this was an interview, not a recording. Shaiko was, somehow, linked up to her in real time. She'd heard about technology like that, but never seen it.

She realised that she was expected to reply.

'There was an attack on the base. As far as I'm aware, everything is in hand.' But Shaiko would already know that. Cleomides desperately tried to think of something else to say, couldn't.

The General nodded. 'And you have had dealings with a being called the Doctor?'

'I arrested him.' She swallowed. 'He escaped, but has been recaptured.'

After a moment, Shaiko said, 'Don't worry. From what I have heard, that's not unusual. You definitely have him now?'

'Last time I looked.' Did Shaiko know something she didn't? 'He's being held by some of the toughest marines we could find,' she added quickly, in an effort to make her reply sound less flippant.

To her relief, Shaiko merely nodded. 'There may be a use for him. We have evidence that the enemy are capable of inducing... delusions.'

A pause. Then the view in front of Cleomides changed to what seemed to be a small perimeter camp. A pressure dome. A battle seemed to be going on – soldiers fighting – soldiers firing on –

Firing on each other.

Falling. Dying.

A flash of plasma fire: Cleomides realised she was watching the scene from the point of view of one of the soldiers. As she watched, he fired prolonged bursts with plasma cannon at the others.

The suits split open. Cleomides saw an arm waving desperately, perhaps trying to stop the man from firing.

Perhaps in death agony.

A jump cut, then the camera advanced, examined the bodies.

Suddenly gauntleted hands clawed at the visor, huge as monsters. Cleomides jumped back.

'That's when he realised what he'd done.' Shaiko's voice. The briefing room reappeared. 'Fortunately, he didn't kill himself. He didn't try to cover the incident up. He was intelligent enough to know he'd been the victim of an enemy deception, and made all the records available to us.' A pause. 'The captain of the dropship *Royale* was less forthcoming, until we interrogated him. Then he admitted he'd destroyed his own ship. He was convinced it had been taken over by –' a slight pause, a faint smile – '"monsters".'

'The *Royale*? But that's –' *A dropship. A thousand people.* 'Did they evacuate?'

'The officers escaped. Not the men.'

Cleomides swallowed.

'There is worse.' The general's voice was ice-cold.

The view changed suddenly, dizzyingly, to an orbital panorama of Dreamstone Moon. Cleomides could see the base, the domes and towers, a cruising Earth ship hovering protectively.

Without warning, the ship opened fire on the base. A dome burst open, debris spread in a slow bloom of fire.

Another shot. A podship methodically firing at nothing, each shot closer and closer to the main radar tower of the base. The last shot destroyed the tower.

'The alien ships...?' asked Cleomides.

'Did not exist,' said Shaiko. 'Except in the minds of the people affected by the enemy – that is, almost everyone. All the damage, all the killing, was done by the fleet itself.'

Cleomides felt a sense of numb shock. 'But... surely the monitors – the weapons systems –'

'Were overridden. Naturally, people assumed the machines had been deceived. But in fact their own minds were affected. A full investigation is under way. That's where our friend the Doctor comes in. We need his help.'

'*The Doctor's* help?' Cleomides looked at Shaiko in amazement. 'I have to say, sir, that he's not reliable. He's not even human. He's already –'

The general held up his hand. 'Your objections were expected, Captain Cleomides. I hope you continue to object, and to be suspicious of the Doctor, because I need you to be vigilant during the operation.' A pause. Black eyes looked up and met hers. 'A ship is being provided. You will take that ship to the mother planet, Mu Camelopides VI. There is no evidence of substantial settlement on the Moon – we would have known about that years ago. The only possible site for the enemy base is the planet.

'Once you are there, the Doctor will investigate the causes of the incident. When he has found the answer, we will act to prevent a similar disaster from ever recurring. You will understand that, to protect the morale of our troops and of the local civilians, you must imagine that the present conversation did not happen. It will not be referred to at any time to anybody.'

Cleomides nodded, though she wasn't happy with the situation. What if the Doctor couldn't find a solution? What if he wasn't even on their side, but a spy, another part of the deception?

'One more thing, Captain.' Shaiko's even voice cut into her thoughts before she could formulate any coherent objections. 'If the Doctor deviates from the planned objective at any time, you are authorised to kill him.'

Cleomides nodded again, this time with a little more enthusiasm. It was the one part of her orders she could clearly understand.

CHAPTER 15

It had taken the best part of thirty minutes, and half Sam's air, but Anton had at last stopped rocking to and fro. Several times she'd contemplated forcibly pulling the dreamstone out of his cheek, but each time she'd chickened out. He might go mad. He might fight her.

He might die.

She wished the Doctor was here. He would know what to do. *If he's still alive.*

'It's better to be part of it,' whispered Anton suddenly, touching the dreamstone set into his cheek. His eyes moved, his gaze meeting hers. 'Isn't it?'

'I don't intend to find out,' said Sam quickly.

Anton began rocking to and fro again.

Sam felt her temper snap. She hit him across the face, not too hard, but hard enough to hurt. He stopped rocking again, stared at her, his eyes unfocused.

'We're going to die if we stay here, Anton,' she said.

'I've always wanted to be part of something,' muttered Anton. 'Something that mattered.'

But the last thing that Sam needed now was an existentialist dialogue. 'I don't want to die, Anton. I'm only seventeen.'

He looked up, gave her a sudden, unexpected smile. 'No, I suppose you don't.' He stood, swaying slightly. Sam caught his arm.

'We can't go back up,' he said. 'We'll have to go further down.' He began walking back across the cave, back through the oily water.

'Hold on! How do you know where we're going? Are the alie – er… natives going to lead us again?' She couldn't see any.

Anton just carried on walking.

Sam ran to catch him up, her boots clunking on the stone. 'Don't just ignore me again! Tell me where you're going!'

Anton turned and looked at her. 'I don't know,' he said. 'But we don't need guides any more. I know what it wants.' In the dim light his face seemed grey. Sam realised he was probably much more exhausted than she was, and maybe just as frightened.

'What does it want, then?'

Anton turned round, carried on walking, leading her down into a dark tunnel. He switched on his lights, revealing marbled walls, sloping downward.

Sam hesitated, then followed. After all, she didn't have any better ideas.

After a while, he spoke, his voice echoing from the walls. 'I always wanted to communicate with people. Perfectly. I tried writing – tried painting – but I just couldn't get the hang of it. It was so *complicated*. It just seemed that people could never understand me – what I was saying, what I was trying to do. I was fourteen when the first BELs came into use. It was – I can't describe it.' A pause. 'Words again. Useless things. The BELs were easy. I just put the thing on my head, pressed record, and it recorded what I thought. Played it back, too.' He laughed. 'Then I discovered that it wasn't so easy to play it back to someone else, or even to myself when I was in a different mood. Brains are just too complicated for that. And it was always subtly… changed. Mechanised. I fiddled with it for years, recording my dreams, learning how to make gyps, but –'

'What are gyps?' asked Sam, deciding that it was about time she reminded Anton that he wasn't talking to himself.

'General Intelligence Portable Thought Files – GIPTF – gyps. I was one of the first people on Occam's World to be able to make dreams into gyps, so that other people could experience my dreams. Or at least –' he snorted – 'they thought they were experiencing my dreams. What they were really getting was a filtered version, a nice safe dreamlike drama with a flavour of me about it. But it was almost good enough. I could almost fool myself into thinking I was communicating, that I was making people feel the way I felt.

'Then the dreamstones came along, and I realised that people didn't care where the dreams came from – they just wanted the experience. New dreams. New dreams in the easiest way possible. And dreamstones could give it to them. Anybody's dreams, without effort, without a price.'

A pause. Sam could hear Anton's ragged breathing. It occurred to her to switch on her own lights: at once she could see the walls more clearly, could see the lines of glittering crystals breaking into the marbled stone. She wondered where they were going, whether Anton knew. For all his talk about communication, he seemed to be remarkably short on facts.

'That's all I thought the dreamstones were, at first. Just an easy way of giving people dreams. I was furious, because they were undercutting me. Making all my skills irrelevant. I didn't realise – until I tried to use them – that I could – Sam, I can't explain, but I *understand*. I understand what the dreamstone wants, and it understands me. I want to be part of something. It's… offering – no, that isn't right – it's making me a part of it. I think the Krakenite-like things were something else, once. And probably all the other things that live here. The dreamstone's made them all a part of itself – perfect communication –' He trailed off, then added in a quite different tone, 'But it made me kill people. I don't know how to stop it doing that.'

'I don't think you should spend any more time down here,' said Sam, trying to keep the fear out of her voice. 'And nor should I. We should go back to the surface.' As if to confirm her words, a light flickered red on her suit display: external temperature. Fifty degrees Celsius. She stopped.

Anton's voice came over the suit comm, fizzing with static – he must have put his helmet on. 'The suit insulation should be able to stand it. Innell said it goes up to eighty degrees.'

'That's not going to be much use if we walk into an inferno,' Sam pointed out.

She checked her air supply: fifteen minutes. She felt a jolt of panic, struggled to control it. She would use up the oxygen a lot more quickly if she panicked.

She realised that she'd lost sight of Anton. She hurried after him, sliding on the steep, ridged rock, then saw his suit silhouetted against a bright light – too bright, surely, to be dreamstone. It looked almost artificial.

'Anton?' Sam picked her way down what was now almost an open slope. Ahead she saw dazzling arches of light, and a river of something that looked alarmingly like magma. The visor dimmed, and an alarm bipped on her suit: gamma rays, ultraviolet, particle radiation and temperature levels were all near the limit of the protection it could offer.

She reached the narrow ledge where Anton was standing – and almost fell back in shock. What she was looking at wasn't a cave: it was another world.

The 'river' was vast – a kilometre or so wide, flowing fast, its surface a mass of golden-white light. It stretched ahead of them for a distance that must be tens of kilometres at least. Looking down, Sam saw coloured shapes moving in the glowing fluid, tadpole-like creatures emitting almost painfully brilliant light in a variety of colours: green, magenta, and a coal-red glow. They flickered and writhed, like living flames. Glittering streams of lights moved in the flow in a suspiciously organised way – schools of smaller creatures, or perhaps marks on the side of something bigger. It was hard to tell. But it was clear enough that they were alive, which had to mean that Anton was right: it wasn't magma.

Sam checked the surface temperature with her suit's sensors and got an estimate of no more than a hundred degrees Celsius. She wasn't going swimming in it, but it wouldn't hurt her from this distance.

The ledge they were standing on narrowed on each side, and sloped down a steep rock face towards the glowing arches of rock she'd seen when she had first arrived. They, too, were huge: they had to be a couple of thousand metres high. They grew from the bed of the river, curving first outward and then in, arching overhead like vast ribs. Looking up, she could see delicate-coloured structures emerging from the tops, which looked almost like leaves, as if the rock arches were mountain-sized ferns. Light flickered between the leaves, moving along ribbon-like connections. Vines? Optical cables? What *was* this thing?

Sam remembered what Aloisse had said about the air-breathing ecosystem on the surface, and there being some sort of mystery about how the air was generated. Well, there was no shortage of air down here. It was even breathable, according to the suit: Sam could have removed her helmet, if it hadn't been dangerously hot. She remembered her low air supply and wondered if there was some way of filtering the outside air – or finding a cooler place.

She checked the banks of the river, saw that it was cooler under the rock arches. Hotter than comfortable – the temperature measurement bounced around between fifty and sixty degrees – but it should at any rate be possible to breathe. They'd just have to chance the effects of the radiation.

She examined the slope on either side of them, saw that the ledge was steep and narrow, and in places seemed to be nonexistent. Climbing down wasn't going to be easy. But they were going to have to do it.

'I don't suppose you've got any climbing equipment attached to that suit?' she asked Anton.

He said nothing, and she wondered for a moment if he'd gone

into trance mode again. She waved a hand in front of his visor.

'Anton? We're going to have to climb down.'

'Why?'

She explained about the air, asked him how much air was left in his own suit.

Anton didn't reply for a moment. Then he said, 'An hour, I think. I haven't got much air. I think they replaced the main tank when they picked me up, but it's nearly empty again. There might be a reserve tank. There was one, but it got damaged. I don't know whether it might work but it says it won't...'

Sam realised that Anton was panicking, which was a bit strange since she ought to be the one doing that. Her own suit had around ten minutes' worth of air left now.

Perhaps I'm just used to cheating death, she thought. Comes of travelling with the Doctor. He's always there to get you out of things.

Well, not this time.

'I'm afraid of heights,' said Anton in a small voice. 'I don't think I can make it. You go on without me.'

'Anton,' said Sam, speaking slowly and clearly. 'If we don't get to a place where we can breathe the air we're going to die. There's no time to go back.' And she didn't fancy her chances in that cave, anyway, without the protection of the spacesuit. Not after what had happened to Anton. The wound in his cheek was visible even through his helmet visor, a dark mass, like a cancer.

He looked at her, frowned. 'Oh. Yes. I said I'd look after you, didn't I?'

Sam nodded. She looked into his sweat-stained, fear-creased face, and came to a decision. Whatever was going on in his head, it couldn't be relied on to get them out. Or to get them anywhere.

'It's not you looking after me any more,' she said. 'It's me looking after you. You saved my life up there. I'm not leaving you behind.'

* * *

Kran was dead.

Daniel couldn't quite believe it: the old spider had seemed indestructible. He'd survived at least a couple of blowouts at Jelan 356, and an infall during the building of the base on Dreamstone Moon. Now he was just a crushed skeleton, the half-dried blood still oozing from the cracks. His neck was fully extended, the ikak-akak glyphs visible. Daniel remembered that they translated as something to do with fate, its inevitability, and the wisdom of acceptance.

Right now Daniel didn't feel like accepting anything at all.

He wondered what Kran had felt. If he'd felt anything. If he'd had *time* to feel anything.

'Daniel.'

Cleomides's voice. He realised that she'd been standing there, quietly, for some time. Daniel stood up, shaking his head, looking around at the improvised mortuary that had once been the tourist arrivals hall. Bodies, some bagged, others still bare, were laid out on the floor in neat military rows, watched over by a couple of pale-looking marines.

'You know, I've got a terrible feeling,' he said. 'I feel I should be counting the rows and the columns, multiplying them up, and getting a total. A total might mean something.'

'Death doesn't mean anything,' said Cleomides. 'Staying alive, that means something.'

Daniel nodded, but he wasn't sure he really agreed. Not right now. Not in the middle of this slaughterhouse that had been the place where he lived and worked. Later, when he got home, when he saw the kids again. Maybe then.

If he got home.

'Is it true you went to Mu Camelopides VI?'

Daniel frowned, tried to focus on what Cleomides was saying.

'The Moon's mother planet?' he asked at last. 'Yes. I've been there. Took part in a survey, early on. They were hoping there'd be some dreamstone there, but we couldn't find any. Tried about six locations.' He frowned again, looked round at the soldier. 'Why?'

'General Shaiko wants me to lead a reconnaissance. A small ship, landing capability.' She shrugged. 'It would help to have someone with us who's seen the place before. I won't make you go, but it could save lives.'

Daniel opened his mouth to say that he was saving lives here, but then realised that he wasn't. Not really. There were a hundred others recovered from the base who could help the rescue teams. Kran had been to Mu Cam VI with him, but he couldn't think of anyone else who'd participated in that early expedition who was still on the base now.

He supposed that Cleomides already knew that.

'All right. I'll go,' he said. 'But I'd better be getting overtime for it.'

Their eyes met, and Cleomides gave him an unexpected grin. 'I expect we can arrange that, Mr O'Ryan.'

'That's it,' said Sam. 'That's the end of the ledge. We're going to have to climb.'

They were about halfway to the shore of the river, and still probably fifty metres above its surface. Sam had managed to get Anton this far by having him turn his face to the wall, and by keeping a hand on his arm all the way. She'd navigated the best she could, trying to minimise the amount of actual climbing they were going to have to do, but now it was unavoidable. There was nothing but a sixty-degree slope between them and the shore, though Sam thought she could see some fissures near the river surface which might help, if they could get down that far without falling. She cursed her decision, made long ago in the wrecked protesters' base, not to waste time putting on a jetpack. True, she wouldn't have been sure how to use it, but it would probably have had some sort of onboard flight-control system. It would definitely have been safer than this.

Still, no use worrying about that now. She put a foot on the steep slope, and began looking around for handholds.

And then remembered something.

Ten per cent gravity. That slope wasn't anything like as dangerous as it looked.

Stupid, she told herself. What did the Doctor tell you? Always take every factor into consideration. And here you are, panicking when you're in no danger at all.

Cautiously, she put her full weight on the slope. Her foot slipped a few centimetres – then stopped. Very slowly, she swung her other foot across. She had to fight her instincts which were screaming *you'll fall you'll fall* – but she didn't fall. She didn't even have to hang on to the rock.

'It's easier than it looks,' she said. 'The low gravity helps.'

'Maybe,' said Anton. He, too, moved off the end of the ledge, keeping his face to the wall. Almost immediately he slipped and started to fall: Sam had to grab him and lost her own footing. They both started to slide down the slope, bumping gently against the rocks.

Anton screamed.

'Shut up!' snapped Sam. She was concentrating on a projecting rock about ten metres below and five to one side. It was big enough for both of them to stand on, certainly big enough to arrest their fall. If she could propel them in that direction before they gained too much speed –

She kicked the rock, giving them a trajectory she hoped would work, dragging Anton with her. For a few seconds they were flying through free space. Sam saw the rib-trees, flickers of coloured light running along them, the crystals in the projecting rock glinting in response.

Glinting. Crystals.

Even as they hit it, Sam realised that the rock was dreamstone.

They bounced, once, then Sam managed to grab hold of the rock and get one arm around it, while still holding on to Anton with the other.

He collided with the rock head first, came to a halt scrunched up against the cliff. Sam wriggled around until she could sit up, looked down at Anton.

'Are you OK?'

'Don't let me fall – please don't let me fall.'

'Come on,' she said quietly, 'we can't stay here.'

She stood up, but she couldn't make Anton do the same. He just clung to the steep rock. She put her arms under his, tried to drag him upright. She could feel his body shaking through that grip, through all the thickness of suits and gauntlets. Sam lifted him off his feet. It was easy enough in the low gravity – even with the suit he weighed only about twelve kilos – but she knew she had to be careful how she carried the weight: he was heavier than she was, and could easily unbalance her, sending them both falling towards the river.

'Just keep your eyes closed and don't move a muscle, OK?' she said.

She walked slowly across the slope, placing her feet with extreme care. At first it was easy. Then it wasn't. Her arms started to shake, then her legs. Sweat started to trickle down her body.

Then her suit beeped at her. 'You have five minutes' air supply remaining. It is recommended that you reduce your rate of oxygen consumption, by such procedures as reducing muscular activity, meditation, or yogic breathing exercises. See the training manual for further advice.'

'Shut up,' she told the machine. Sweat began to drip into her eyes. The crystalline landscape blurred into a mishmash of unstable colours, like neon lights through a rain-drenched window. She wondered what it would look like when she started suffering from oxygen deprivation.

'You have four minutes' air supply remaining –'

'Shut up shut up shut *up*!'

'Put me down,' said Anton. 'Just drop me, you'll make it on your own.'

'Don't be stupid.'

'– or yogic breathing exercises. See –'

'I'll struggle and we'll both fall.'

'No you won't. Now shut up, I need to save my breath.'

'You have three minutes' air supply remaining –'

Sam blinked to clear her eyes, and measured the distance between herself and the shore. She knew then that she wasn't going to make it. That she was going to have to breathe the outside air.

She quizzed the suit, saw that the air was humid, highly oxygenated, in fact technically breathable – but at eighty-eight degrees Celsius.

How long could she survive that?

Well, there was only one way to find out. Ignoring red lights and the stern electric warning voice in her ears, she unclamped the visor seals. Twice during the fiddly procedure she almost lost her grip on Anton, and felt them both teeter towards falling.

At last, with the suit telling her there was a minute's air supply remaining, she eased the visor open.

It was like opening an oven door, and breathing the air inside. The smell was worse: it was like a cross between a garage forecourt and a school chemistry laboratory after a particularly pungent experiment. She could feel the gasses hurting her damaged throat. She didn't like to think about what they were doing to her lungs.

But at least her muscles had stopped shaking.

Slowly, carefully, she began to ease her way down the slope.

CHAPTER 16

'This is an outrage.'

The translator didn't carry any of the overtones of the Krakenite's native speech, but the Doctor didn't need a translator to know that she was more than just annoyed. He suspected that she was almost out of her mind with pain and grief. Her skin was split open around her eye, and blood and pus were oozing out. She'd been secured by putting metal rivets through her tentacles and through the white plastic surface of the floor. More blood leaked from the wounds and a pool of it mixed with other bodily fluids around her legs.

The stench was terrible.

The Doctor wanted to comfort the Krakenite, to heal her, but his resources were limited. The small, white room didn't even have a water supply, let alone a first-aid kit. A single too-bright light glowed in the ceiling. A single vent let in a stream of cold air. A single globular lens stared at them from the ceiling, like the eye of a huge and very stupid animal.

The Doctor thought about Sam, running towards him through that huge open space, everything else she was doing forgotten. Begging the soldiers not to shoot. Whatever the reason she'd left him on Hirath, she'd obviously forgotten it, forgiven him. And now...

Now she might be dead.

Another one.

And when he'd so nearly found her.

From outside came bangs and thumps, the clattering of feet down metal stairways. The troops were getting ready to do something, and the Doctor needed to know what it was. He probably needed to put a stop to it. But first he had to get out.

'Do you speak my language?'

The Doctor looked round at the Krakenite, made a few clicking noises which he hoped she would understand as, 'What is your name?'

He was rewarded by the fluid clicks and booms of a Krakenite song of identity, followed by, 'What is your name?'

The Doctor hesitated, then said, 'I'm Doctor John Smith, Aloisse.'

'From Earth?' There was hate in the question, a vibrant hate expressed in the booming undertones of the Krakenite language.

'No, from Gallifrey,' said the Doctor quickly, then wished he hadn't. Telling people who you were in these situations could get you into trouble. It had happened to him often enough. But, somehow, he couldn't stop trusting people. And he trusted this one. Despite the way she had been treated, despite her anger. Or perhaps because of it.

She rewarded him for his trust in an unexpected way.

'Did you know anyone called Sam?'

Hardly able to believe his luck, the Doctor looked up, nodded enthusiastically.

'An Earth girl, I think. But not from this time.'

The Doctor beamed. 'Yes, that's her. Have you seen her? When I last saw her she was –'

The Krakenite interrupted him. 'I worked with her. We were protesting against the mining company. Against the base here, the destruction of the local ecosystem.'–

The Doctor nodded. 'That's the sort of thing she'd get involved with. Do you know where she is now?'

A pause. The Doctor didn't like that pause. It went on, and on, and on, and became a long silence.

'She was in Pressure Shed Nine. I saw it destroyed. She was wearing a suit, but I shouldn't think that anyone survived. I'm sorry.'

The Doctor felt a sickness in his stomach, the sickness of hope raised and then dashed. He'd hoped that Aloisse had seen her since then, that she'd somehow got out.

'All that messing about making futile inquiries,' he muttered. 'Why? Why didn't I just put a temporal tracer on her? Then I could never have lost her. I could at least have made sure she was safe.'

'Perhaps,' suggested the Krakenite, 'it was because you wanted to treat her as a being with her own rights. Someone who could act independently of you.'

'Yes! But I didn't want – I didn't –'

A light, rubbery touch on his face. One of the pinned-down tentacles was straining upward. The Doctor almost winced at the sight of the damaged flesh: he could almost feel her physical pain.

'She might not be dead,' said the Krakenite softly. 'And if she is, it wasn't your fault.'

The Doctor closed his eyes, forced himself to concentrate. She might be alive. Of course she might be alive. In which case there was even more reason to get out of here and to get out of here quickly. He looked at the lens on the ceiling speculatively. It should be fairly easy to disable it. There was probably a guard outside the door, but –

He looked at the Krakenite.

'If I can unpin your tentacles,' he said, 'will you help me get out? I'll help you.'

The Krakenite twitched a tentacle. 'I'm probably dead anyway,' she said. 'So I'm with you.'

The Doctor reached out, touched the Krakenite's skin. It was hot: hotter than it should be. The wounds must be infected. He tried to remember if he had any Krakenite-specific antibiotics in his pockets.

'You're not dead,' he said, fishing around in his jacket while keeping his free hand on Aloisse's skin. 'Not now, not at all, if I can prevent it. You have my word on that.'

'"If I can prevent it",' echoed the tentacled being softly. 'Don't worry if you can't. We're all responsible for our own fate. I'm choosing to help you.'

The Doctor looked at his shoes, embarrassed at the Krakenite's selfless generosity. But he had no choice but to accept – and leaving her here looked like certain death for her, anyway.

'Thank you,' he said quietly. 'Now, you don't happen to have a sonic screwdriver on you, I suppose? I seem to have left mine in the TARDIS.'

'Sorry, I don't.' A pause. 'I can see why Sam liked you so much, Doctor.'

The Doctor smiled at her. It didn't seem much of a reward, but a smile was all he had to offer at the moment.

He scrabbled around in his pockets, eventually found a small silver object which he recognised as some sort of electrical-pulse device. He frowned at it, wondering about its capabilities, then decided that the quickest way would be to try it. He stood on tiptoe and waved it about under the globular lens. After a moment, the lens deactivated with a loud metallic click and retracted into the ceiling.

'That works with most electrical devices,' he commented, for the Krakenite's benefit, with a confidence he didn't entirely feel. 'Now, those rivets.'

Sam noticed that the slope had ended only when she put her feet in the wrong place and almost fell over. The low gravity saved her. Even so, she was teetering, desperately holding on to Anton, feeling her muscles shake and her lungs strain, when she realised that there was flat ground only a couple of metres away.

That gave her the strength to make the last few steps.

'I have to drop you now,' she said to Anton. 'We're there.'

Despite her warning, he gave a yelp of dismay as she let him go.

Then she collapsed on the ground, wondering if the blue lights shifting below her were real or figments of her overstretched body and half-poisoned brain. She watched them form around her hand, making a sort of halo.

She saw Anton's face hovering over hers, saw him unseal his helmet.

'Careful,' she tried to say.

His blue-grey eyes met hers. 'My turn to do the looking after,' he said, smiling slightly. 'You need some water.'

He reached down, began fiddling about inside Sam's helmet, his fingers near her chin. 'It's amazing what you remember if it's repeated often enough,' he commented.

A tube attached itself to Sam's mouth, and she drank.

Clear, cold water. She almost choked.

When she'd had enough, she sat up, looked around her.

'We can't rest here,' she told him. 'This place smells like it could go up in flames any minute.' She didn't really think that was true, but she was anxious to get Anton out before he did any more 'communicating' with the dreamstone. At the moment he seemed to be sane enough, but –

She looked at the dark patch on his cheek, shivered.

There had to be another way up from a place this size: all she had to do was find it, find out what was happening on the surface, and –

Then what? What if the place had been taken over by aliens?

She felt the first jitterings of panic, and hastily suppressed them. She would find a way out, she had to. She had to find out whether the Doctor was still alive, if nothing else.

'Look how beautiful it is,' said Anton suddenly.

Sam looked, saw that he was pointing at a tall blade of grass – except that it was made of crystal, and light glinted along it. She remembered once at school she'd been given a prism for a science experiment: she'd spent several minutes just playing with it, spreading rainbows across the bench and the white tiles of the floor. This place was the same: pure colour flowed along the 'grass' and a hundred other blades around them. The tall trunks of the rib-trees pulsed with rings of subtle colour. Tiny wormlets of light ran along the ground under her feet: more crystal.

'They knew,' said Anton suddenly.

'Who knew what?'

'They knew!' he bawled, grabbing her arm and looking into her eyes. 'I'm not a miner but I know that you don't dig up half a planet without doing deep-level surveys! And we're not even that deep – two or three kilometres? I don't know. Call it five, at most. The top of this chamber has to be well in range of a drill. Or a microbot trawl. Innell talked about microbot trawls. Dammit, they knew they knew they *all* knew! And they carried on mining! They carried on – destroying – this!'

Sam looked around, at the huge space, the light, the air, and knew that Anton was right. The Dreamstone Mining Company were guilty as hell.

Still, she'd known that already. And at least this part of the underground environment was still here. There might be time to do something about it, and perhaps save lives.

If they could get out.

'OK, what are we going to do about it?' she said. Then, quickly, 'If we get out of here, we can find out what's happening on the surface. We can tell them – publicise this. They'll have to stop then. If they haven't been forced to already.'

Anton was silent.

'Anton, that's what the dreamstone wants. That's what it would want, if it understood the situation.'

'No. We've got to stay here. The dreamstone will keep us alive.'

'You've just said it's dying! Anton, start thinking! To stop the dreamstone dying we need to get out, to tell people to stop –'

'Look down,' said Anton suddenly.

Sam looked at the ground, saw the little blue wormlets of

light had concentrated at her feet. Perhaps the crystal was pressure-sensitive.

'What does it remind you of?'

She looked closely. The wormlets moved along branching courses, like small trees frozen into the crystal. They made tiny yellow sparks when they crossed the junctions between the trees.

'Dreamstone?' she hazarded eventually.

Anton shook his head. 'Before I started making my living from dreams, I worked in a cognitive-arts workshop – a Net showroom. One of our projects was a graphic display of neurones for schools.' He gestured at the ground. 'They looked like that.'

'So the crystals look like neurones. So?'

Anton grabbed her arm. 'So this is a brain! We're not just killing this place. We're taking it away, piece by piece by piece.' His blue-grey eyes locked on hers. 'We've been mining its brain and taking it away to make our dreams!'

The Doctor had barely begun his investigation of the lock on the cell when the door opened, seemingly of its own accord, to reveal a man in black-and-gold armour with a sergeant's stripes on his shoulder.

The Doctor glanced at the man's face and decided that this was an escort party and not an execution squad. He spoke quickly, before they could tell him their business. 'Ah, right, I see you've come to take me to Captain Cleomides.'

The sergeant's square face twitched very slightly – surprise. Good. He'd guessed right, then.

'Well, look sharp. She doesn't like to be kept waiting, you know. And bring this alien with me – she needs to see her as well.'

The sergeant's face clouded, and he jabbed the Doctor in the ribs with his gun.

Oh, dear. It hadn't worked. Never mind, it had been worth a try.

'You're still under arrest, *alien*,' the sergeant said nastily, addressing the Doctor. 'And the Krakenite is *ours*, right?'

The last word was emphasised with another jab of the gun.

One of his men giggled. The Doctor felt sick.

'I demand that you –' he began, only to be cut off by a slap across his face.

The Krakenite's voice rumbled behind him. 'Use tactics, Doctor. These people couldn't let me go even if they wanted to, and they don't want to. Get Captain Cleomides to help me, if you can.'

A pleading note entered her voice in the last sentence.

'They'll kill you,' muttered the Doctor, using Krakenite clicks.

'No, they won't,' said the Krakenite wearily. 'They're enjoying themselves too much for that.'

'Come on, alien,' snapped the sergeant. 'Move, or we'll be forced to carry you.'

A laugh from one of the men.

Reluctantly, with a backward glance at the stinking cell, the Doctor walked away. Despite her brave words, he doubted he would see the Krakenite alive again.

'I still don't see how anything this size can be a brain,' said Sam. She was trying to think as if she were the Doctor, trying to eliminate the spurious explanations and find the one that worked. It wasn't anything like as easy as he sometimes made it seem. Plus, she was tired, and she was hungry. But still, she was going to try.

She gestured at the ground. 'I mean, just because the lights in the crystal look like neurones doesn't mean they behave like neurones.'

But Anton just shook his head. 'Sam, I make my living out of recording and structuring dreams. My own – sometimes other people's. These dreams I've been having – the ones I had on Occam's World, the ones here – are all from the same mind. They have the same... I can't explain it – like paintings by the same person, but even more so. Dreams are uniquely individual. That's what confused me. Different stones should mean different dreams. But this is just one dream – just one nightmare.' He looked down. 'It never ends.'

'It couldn't be a recording? An impression, like the ones you make?'

'I don't think so. It's too big – too alive for that.' He hesitated. 'And it controls things – the Ixcallex –' he shivered – 'and me.'

'Is it controlling you?'

'I don't know. I feel as if I'm dreaming – dreaming when I'm awake.'

Sam tried to think about it. If the dreamstones recorded people's dreams, then perhaps the Dreamstone Moon itself was recording dreams. But why only nightmares? Because it was being destroyed? If it was more than a recording system – if it was a living intelligence – why couldn't it manage to communicate through Anton? Nothing he'd said about the dreamstone made any sense at all, really. If it was alive, and intelligent, surely it would have said something coherent to him by now.

'Anton,' she began, 'do you sense that there's anything that the dreamstone wants us to know?'

'Only that it's afraid.'

Afraid. A goldfish could be afraid. Perhaps this thing wasn't intelligent at all. Perhaps it was just making people afraid. 'In which case, all we have to do is stop attacking it.'

If she was right.

If Anton wasn't simply half deranged.

Oh, for the Doctor...

Suddenly Anton frowned, then crouched down, his palms flat on the ground.

'Something's happening,' he said.

Sam could feel it: a faint vibration, like an engine starting under the ground. Another quake? If so, they would probably be safer under cover. She glanced up nervously at the crystalline 'leaves', as far above her as clouds. If they started falling apart…

Almost as if she'd brought it on by thinking about it, she saw sparks of light falling from the high canopy.

'Anton…'

He was sitting up. 'I know.'

'We have to find somewhere to shelter.'

There was a rumbling in the air, like distant thunder. The light in the big cave seemed to be changing slowly. Sam looked up again as Anton scrambled to his feet.

There was a hole in the roof.

– there was a hole in the roof and she could see black space through it and a blazing light –

'Oh, no,' she said. 'It's happening again.'

'It isn't,' said Anton. 'That's an Earth ship.'

Sam looked, and saw that he was right. Behind the blazing light was the dark skyscraper-column of a spaceship. It didn't look much like an Earth ship from any period Sam knew, but she'd seen a picture like it somewhere.

The rumbling noise was increasing, and the floor beneath their feet was beginning to tremble. Something shattered on the rock near them: fragments clattered against her suit. She saw lumps of crystal skidding around on the smooth surface like ice on a pond.

'What do we do?' she yelled at Anton over the increasing noise. 'Wave at it?'

Anton was talking into his suit mike, but Sam couldn't hear the words.

'I've tried the general distress frequency,' he said. 'But I can't raise them.'

Before Sam could reply, light exploded around them. Sam saw a searing column of flame burning into the river, not far from the ledge where they'd entered the cavern. A wave of heat hit her, and the air roared. She saw the river boiling in clouds of silver steam, as a second column of searing light joined the first.

'What's happening?' she screamed.

But she knew Anton couldn't hear her, and she didn't need him to tell her anyway. The cavalry had arrived, but they weren't galloping to anyone's rescue. They were systematically blowing the place to pieces.

Sam struggled with her visor, managed to slam it back into place against the searing air.

'Signal!' she yelled at the suit. 'Emergency distress on all frequencies!'

Even before she'd finished speaking, she could see the barely detectable flicker of a red light telling her that the transmission was already going out.

But nobody was taking any notice. She doubted they'd be able to pick it up above the electromagnetic storm of the weapons fire.

– distress flare there's got to be a distress flare or some kind of visual signal –

But she couldn't find anything. The air was filling with steam. If she didn't hurry up they wouldn't be able to see her. She turned her suit lights on, but there was little hope that anyone would notice that.

'Radiation levels… exposure…' She could hardly hear the suit's electronic voice over the noise. She could hardly see the red lights against the glare.

But she could see the smoke coming from Anton's suit. She could smell the insulation burning on her own. She could taste the smoke in her mouth.

Doctor, where are you when I need you?

She saw something moving: a mass of tentacles, a huge eye. No – several eyes, moving towards her.

Krakenites? Or –

Tentacles grabbed hold of her.

'No!' she screamed. 'We're not the enemy! We can help! Anton –'

But she couldn't see Anton, couldn't see anything but the white skin of the aliens glistening in the blazing light from the weapons.

'We're your only hope!' screamed Sam, as the weight of the alien pushed her off her feet.

But she was pressed into the ground, her visor dark.

'Warning!' squeaked the suit. 'There is no functioning air supply in this appliance –'

The ground shuddered, and Sam felt consciousness slipping away. She tried to think clearly, as if aloud: 'We – are – here – to – help – you –'

No.

– to help –

help

no

CHAPTER 17

The Doctor, Daniel decided, was not in a good mood. His face had a look of manic determination that Daniel had seen only once before, when he'd said back in the lab that all the mining must stop.

The message was similar now.

'So what you want to do, having lost several hundred lives here, is go to the mother planet and risk more lives to find out something you already know?'

They were standing in what had been the Sector Six canteen, popularly known as Aunt Fanny's, although nobody knew who Aunt Fanny was. Tall terrestrial palms stood under an artificial sky. The dry, false, resort daylight was at stark odds with the weary, frightened, spacesuited or half-suited figures standing around, murmuring to each other. There was still food behind the counters; there were still blue-and-white autowaiters shimmering around trying to take orders – but no one was eating or drinking. The artificial sea had been drained, and was now a brown swamp streaked with green weed and plastic-looking fake coral.

Daniel realised that the Doctor was still waiting for a reply. He looked at Cleomides, who shrugged.

'We don't have any choice, Doctor. General Shaiko has ordered it.'

'So you're going to do it, even though it's stupid? Do the military *never* change?'

Daniel saw the anger flush across Cleomides's face again.

'Just for the record, Mister Doctor Alien Whoever-you-are, I don't think it's a stupid order at all. We need to find out what's on that planet. The alien ships – if that's what they were – were easily destroyed, but we were taken by surprise. People have died, in case you haven't noticed. More people will die if we are taken by surprise again. Now are you going to help or do I put you back in that cell?'

The Doctor looked at his shoes. 'It's a stupid order because, with all due respect, General Shaiko doesn't understand the situation. And neither, evidently, do you. Either that or one of you is lying.'

Cleomides's face coloured and her eyes slid away towards the swampy remnants of the artificial sea, and Daniel deduced without much difficulty that she *was* lying.

He wondered what the real situation was – what Shaiko was ordering Cleomides to lie about, what had killed O'Connell?

The Doctor had evidently noticed that Cleomides was hiding something. 'Let me guess,' he said. 'Your ships were firing into empty space most of the time? No one can find any evidence that the enemy actually existed? In short, all the damage in this war –'

'OK, that's enough!' snapped Cleomides. 'You evidently don't understand the situation either. It's not just a matter of the tactical position: there's morale to be considered.' She gestured around them, at the aimless crowd. Daniel noticed that several people were looking at them, wondered how much they'd heard.

'Dead people aren't going to have any morale at all!' snapped the Doctor. He raised his voice, consciously speaking to the crowd. 'I'm telling you to get out of here! It's not your world – it belongs to another intelligent species, who just happen to live underground! And part of their intelligence is expressed in the crystals you've been digging up, which is probably why they're trying to kill you at the moment. Why can't you understand?'

'Is that really true?' asked Daniel. He could hear murmurs from the crowd: it was fast becoming an audience.

'It's not just true, it's *obvious*! Why won't anyone listen to me?'

Cleomides replied quickly, 'Whatever the truth of it, there's no question of getting out, Doctor. This system is Earth colonial territory.' She too was speaking for the crowd now.

'Since when?'

'Since about three hours ago.' She folded her arms. 'This is a colony now. We have to fight to defend it.'

'But it's not your world.'

Cleomides was already stalking out of the room; the Doctor and Daniel followed her.

'It's been made into our world,' she said over her shoulder. 'And before you start arguing again, that decision was taken at the highest level.'

The Doctor hurried after Cleomides, ignoring his audience. It was obviously more important to him to convince Cleomides.

'Well, I want to see whoever's decision it was,' he said as they pushed through the double doors of the canteen area.

Cleomides shook her head. 'Doctor, the decision was taken on Earth. It's a political decision, not a military one. We have to abide by it.'

'No you don't!'

'Yes we *do*! Now are you going to help us or do I hand you over to General Shaiko, who likes aliens even less than I do?'

The Doctor looked at Daniel, who nodded. 'The marines just kill aliens, Doctor. It isn't funny.'

They'd reached a long, open corridor lined with broken shop windows. The tourist sector: Daniel saw gift packs of fake dreamstone, fluffy toys, all mixed up with mud and dust and slurry. Their boots squelched on the floor, which must have been flooded at one point.

'I didn't say they would kill you,' said Cleomides after a while.

'But it's true, isn't it?' asked the Doctor.

Cleomides looked away.

But the Doctor wasn't going to let it go. 'Hasn't it ever occurred to you that killing things for no reason is evil?'

'The "things" in question usually have the same policy towards us.'

'Doesn't make any difference,' said the Doctor. But Daniel noticed a change of tone, the manic determination leaching out of his face, to be replaced by a contemplative sadness. And he knew that the Doctor had made painful decisions of his own.

He could see that Cleomides knew it as well. Her face softened, and she said quietly, 'It will save lives if you help us.'

Daniel wondered if this line would work as well on the Doctor as it had on himself less than an hour before.

It did. Daniel could tell from the changed, softened expression on the Doctor's face that the decision was made, even before he spoke.

'On one condition,' he said.

Cleomides blinked at him. 'You're an alien – you don't make –' she began.

'Yes I do!' snapped the Doctor. 'Follow me!' He turned around and set off in the opposite direction along the waterlogged corridor.

Cleomides and Daniel looked at each other, then set off after him. They passed Aunt Fanny's again, crossed the Sector Six main plaza – now empty apart from a few black-suited marines – then went through an emergency airlock bolted to what had been a simple internal pressure door. Although the pressure was green on the other side, Daniel and Cleomides automatically sealed their helmets; the Doctor didn't bother. They found themselves in a mining-equipment bay, the equipment huge and shadowy.

Finally they entered a silver field shelter set up against one of the equipment-bay walls. Its bactofabricated surface was still glistening with stray organics. Inside, the freshly pumped air was cold. Marines slumped against the walls, visors up, their breath pluming the air. Red lights were gleaming on their weapons. For an instant Daniel felt a bizarre dislocation, as if these black, shining, battlesuited creatures were the aliens. As if he wasn't safe here.

He noticed that Cleomides was edgy, and became increasingly so as they entered the cold air of the temporary pressure shed. Marines looked up; one saluted, the others didn't bother. Daniel could understand their attitude: when he'd served in the marines the Specials had always been regarded as amateur soldiers, high on enthusiasm but low on training and discipline. Nothing that Daniel had seen from Cleomides had done anything to dispel that impression.

But he was beginning to prefer her company to that of the soldiers – especially these soldiers. There was a smell in this place that he didn't like, a smell of dirt and pain.

The Doctor was talking to a marine with a sergeant's stripes on his shoulder.

'We're here for the Krakenite,' he said. 'Just as I said we would be.'

'You are?' The man laughed. 'I was just about to take care of that one myself, *sir*.'

Daniel didn't like that last, derisive emphasis on the 'sir'. He didn't want any awkward questions being asked about the Doctor's identity. He glanced at Cleomides.

'We need it to assist with a field expedition,' she said quickly, with a furious glance at the Doctor. 'General Shaiko's orders.'

The sergeant leered at her. 'It's not in very good condition.'

Daniel noticed that the Doctor was already past the sergeant and fiddling with the airlock door. He tried to catch his eye and give him a cautionary glance – they weren't dealing with a half-witted Besiddian security guard here – but the door was already opening.

The sergeant whirled round. 'What do you think you're doing? I didn't give my permission –'

'Sergeant!' snapped Cleomides. 'If there is a problem with releasing the alien to us, I suggest you refer the matter to the general!'

But the sergeant had followed the Doctor into the dome. Cleomides and Daniel went after them, but had to stop in the doorway: there simply wasn't room for all of them to go in. Nonetheless, Daniel could see the shape of a Krakenite. There was blood on the floor, broken rivets, a severed fragment of a sucker from one of her tentacles.

With a shock, Daniel recognised Aloisse.

'Oh my God,' he muttered. 'You people never learn, do you?'

'Has anybody got a translator for the Krakenite?' said the Doctor. His voice was ominously calm.

'In the corner,' muttered the sergeant. 'By the toolkit.' Curiously, he seemed embarrassed. Perhaps he'd thought he could get away with this one. Perhaps he was now realising that he probably wouldn't. Daniel doubted that General Shaiko would openly condone torture, if Cleomides chose to report it.

The Doctor went to the corner of the shed, found a battered-looking grey unit and retreated into the dome with it.

After a moment the booming, clicking noise of Krakenite speech was followed by the translated voice of Aloisse: 'I am not an enemy but a legitimate visitor here for the purposes of peaceful protest, and my rights have been violated –'

Daniel pushed his way past Cleomides and a cluster of confused marines into the holding cell. For the first time he saw how badly hurt Aloisse was. Her eye was weeping blood, her skin was cracked in several places. Her tentacles twitched feebly. The Doctor was gently prising away a metal rivet that was pinning one of them to the floor.

'Who did this?' asked Daniel, his voice thick with anger.

'Does it matter?' said the Doctor. 'I shouldn't think there's going to be a court of inquiry.'

'There should be,' Aloisse said. 'My rights have been violated. I demand immediate transport to the nearest Kraken consular facilities.'

'We're in the middle of a war, Aloisse,' said Daniel. 'Right now we need your help.'

'I'm not giving any help to the forces of oppression and injustice.'

'You haven't got any choice,' said Cleomides from the doorway. 'If we leave you with this lot, you're dead.'

'I'm not giving any help to the forces of oppression and injustice,' repeated Aloisse. Her body jolted as the Doctor at last pulled the stake free.

'These people are barbarians who should never have been allowed off their own planet,' said the Doctor with feeling. 'But they're not all like that, and you know it and I know it. And the captain's right: if you stay here you're dead.'

'I'm not giving any help to the forces of oppression and injustice,' said Aloisse flatly, for the third time.

'Well, neither am I,' said the Doctor. 'I'm just trying to stop this thing before anyone else gets killed.'

Silence.

Cleomides spoke at last. 'Come on, Doctor, there isn't much time. If she won't co-operate I'll lock her up, put a Specials guard on her. Not that I can promise they'll...' She trailed off, glanced at Daniel as if for help. Daniel shrugged: what could you say? Aloisse was dead unless she came with them. She was probably dead when they came back, even then, unless she'd made herself indispensable in the meantime – indispensable enough to make Shaiko want to protect her. And he had simply no idea how the Doctor was going to contrive that.

'There's no need to feel embarrassed,' said the Doctor. After a second Daniel realised he was talking to Cleomides. 'You're not like our friends out there. I knew you weren't an evil person, even when you wanted to kill me.'

'Doctor, there really isn't much time,' said Cleomides, looking even more embarrassed.

'All right, I'll come with you,' said Aloisse. 'But I hope it isn't anything that requires me to be able to see. I can't do that any more.'

The Doctor knelt down in front of her. 'What? You're blind?'

'There are medical facilities on the *Unanimity*,' said Cleomides. 'We'll patch you up. We won't be leaving for an hour or two.'

'The retina was deliberately burned out with targeting lasers. I doubt I'll see naturally again. I'll need an implant.'

Daniel saw a twitch of anger move across Cleomides's face, and wondered about the woman who hated aliens. Perhaps she hadn't met too many of them until now.

But all she did was turn on her heel and march out of the room. He heard her shout orders, picking out marines to carry Aloisse to the *Unanimity*.

'I can walk,' said Aloisse. 'I don't want them to carry me. Doctor? Will you help me?'

'Of course.'

The Doctor gently took hold of one of the Krakenite's tentacles, and led her out of her prison.

CHAPTER 18

Light.

Blurry, painful, grey.

But light. Life. *Not dead I'm not dead those things protected me just like Aloisse and* –

'Hello.'

A face. It seemed strange, as if the head were a planet she was in orbit around, the shadowed eyes impact craters, the white surgical mask an icecap.

Sam opened her mouth, felt a tube there, felt a cool flow of air against her tongue. It was a bit like being in the dentist's chair, if only her chest didn't hurt so much.

'Doctor…?' she asked. But the word was muffled by the tube.

'Eliot. I'm Dr Eliot. Don't try to talk too much. You inhaled quite a bit of smoke, and there seems to be some lung damage already. You've had an exciting time over the last few days, by the look of it.'

'Anton?'

'Are you asking about your companion?'

Sam nodded.

'He's alive, but unconscious. There are… brain problems. But we think he'll be OK.'

Brain problems?

– we're mining this thing's brain –

Sam tried to sit up.

Eliot reached down and took the tube out of her mouth.

'OK,' she said. 'But talk slowly.'

Sam nodded. 'The Moon is alive,' she said. 'That place you were blowing up is part of its brain. It'll make you kill each other if you don't stop.'

'OK, OK.'

'You don't believe me?'

'I don't know. I'm a doctor, not a flight commander. But if it's the Moon you're worried about, don't. You're quite safe here. You're on a hospital ship in orbit.'

'I have to speak to the overall commanders of the operation. They need to know about the Moon.'

The woman put a hand on her arm. 'You don't need to worry. It's all being taken care of.'

'But they're killing it!'

The woman frowned. 'Yes. But that's what they're supposed to be doing, isn't it?'

The *Unanimity* turned out to be less a warship than a converted freighter. There were no decks: just a retrofitted bridge, slotted into what would have been the cargo module. They had a pilot, a Captain of Marines – a tall, blue-haired Lunar colonist called Piu, who looked almost as if he were an alien himself. He floated at a low workstation mounted on a transparent ring-rail, secured by a tether. Daniel noticed that he was wearing a light vacuum suit and a respirator.

Cleomides had disappeared with the Doctor and Aloisse into the upper part of the freighter – the old crew quarters and control section. Daniel wondered what the 'medical facilities' were like. Not up to much, most probably. He was half expecting the Doctor to come blustering down protesting that they weren't good enough.

They'd already launched: a globe viewscreen was wrapped around the bridge, giving the impression that the ring-rail, the attached workstations and people were floating in open space. The brown disc of Dreamstone Moon's mother planet, Mu Camelopides VI, floated ahead, its image enhanced by the viewscreen to pick out small variations in the surface colour, complex streaks and whorls like a distorted fingerprint: Daniel remembered that they were cloud formations, standing waves the size of continents trawling around the atmosphere in response to the gravity of the Moon and the parent star. Around the planet, in open space, green and yellow stars flickered unnaturally bright, another artefact of the viewscreen. They marked the position of Earth warships and command ships respectively. A hospital ship flickered white.

He heard an intake of breath from behind him and turned, to see that Cleomides had returned to the bridge. She too was looking at the rear part of the viewscreen. He followed the direction of her gaze, saw Dreamstone Moon, newly scarred with tiny pockmarks, some grey and dusty, some glowing with a visible red heat. The flicker of plasma discharges raced across the surface from time to time, casting spiky shadows. Daniel frowned: he'd assumed that the fighting was over. Especially after what the Doctor had said. Had the fleet found more of the enemy elsewhere on the Moon? Or was the Doctor right? Were they fighting illusions?

He thought about asking Cleomides, but decided against it. She would probably think that the right answer would lower his morale.

'How's Aloisse?' he asked instead.

'She's resting,' said Cleomides. But her voice was distracted. Suddenly she walked over to Piu. They exchanged a few murmured words. The conversation ended with a sharp nod from Cleomides.

Daniel looked at her as she walked back, but she only shook her head and strapped herself to an acceleration couch bolted to the ring-rail which mounted the workstations. She motioned Daniel to do the same. He did so, noticed that she was still looking at the view of the Moon. She looked different in profile: the snub nose, the slightly plump cheeks, the brown eyes. She didn't look like a warrior, not really. She wasn't even a good liar.

Her gaze flicked from the Moon to meet his. 'I tell you, my husband will get jealous, Mr O'Ryan,' she said with a slight smile.

Embarrassed, Daniel looked away. To his relief the ship's computer chimed, and spoke softly: 'Acceleration begins in fifteen seconds. Please ensure all personnel and loose objects are secure.'

Daniel hastily secured himself. He'd barely fixed the webbing over his body when the ship jolted as the main engines fired. The acceleration was fierce, building up quickly to about five gees; within a couple of minutes the Moon was visibly receding. It suddenly seemed less a world, more a dead rock. A silver ghost on which nothing happened.

After a few minutes the acceleration slackened, but didn't quite reduce to zero. Daniel looked at the status display, saw that the ship would take about three hours to reach the surface of the planet.

'OK,' said Cleomides, unstrapping herself. 'I want to speak with the Doctor. Mr O'Ryan, you will come with me, please?'

They left the bridge, floated up through a hatchway whose inner surface was smooth white plasteel – but above it, old, grimy metal replaced the new materials and grab-handles replaced the shining ring-rails.

Daniel manhandled his way along a passageway to a small white room whose walls gleamed with polish. Machines clicked quietly.

The Doctor was in a corner of the room, sitting on a chair with his chin in his hands, watching Aloisse. The Krakenite seemed to be asleep: her tentacles were folded around her, hooked together to make a maroon-and-scarlet mantilla. Elaborate traceries of yellow decorated its surface: Daniel wondered if they were blood vessels, or some kind of tattoo.

It occurred to him that he'd never seen a Krakenite asleep before. 'Is she OK?' he asked.

'As OK as you'd expect, after what's happened to her,' said the

Doctor. His tone had more sadness in it than anger. 'She won't see again without a retinal transplant.'

To Daniel's surprise, Aloisse spoke, a low, edgy rumbling.

'Never mind,' said the translated voice. 'As a sense, vision is much overrated.'

The Doctor touched Aloisse's mantilla gently, then stood up and looked at Cleomides. 'How can I help you, Captain?'

Cleomides looked at Daniel, looked at the Doctor, then looked around the bright, white space of the medical bay as if checking for spies. Finally she said, 'Doctor, I think it is safe for us to talk here.'

Anton's eyes were open, but there didn't seem to be a mind behind them. They moved to follow Sam's hand when she waved it above his face, but they didn't move to her own face when she pulled the hand back.

His mouth hung open slackly; a tube inside it hissed noisily, removing saliva.

'Try talking to him,' said Dr Eliot softly. 'It sometimes works, if a friend speaks to them.'

'Hello, Anton,' said Sam.

Nothing.

'Anton, I need your help.' Sam allowed a note of desperation to creep into her voice. She wasn't sure how genuine it was. 'You promised to help me.'

It had worked last time, and it seemed to be working again. His face twitched. Sam noticed that they'd shaved off the stubble, cleaned him up generally.

'Anton?'

He jolted upright abruptly, shouting words that were mangled by the tube in his mouth. It started to retract, and he was staring into her eyes, his hands on her throat.

'– killing me! They're killing me!'

Dr Eliot was there, pulling him back, her thin arms pushing his body back.

'It's OK, Anton,' said Sam, trying to keep her voice steady. 'You're safe here.'

But I'm about to take you back to where it isn't safe. If I can get away with it.

Sam wasn't sure how she was going to get herself and Anton back to the Moon – she knew only that she had to do it. She had to confront the people in charge of this operation with the truth about what they were doing.

Dr Eliot cautiously let Anton go. He sat up, fixed his eyes on Sam and asked, 'How long?'

Sam glanced at Eliot. 'Since you were picked up? A couple of hours, I think. It would take most of that time to get you here from the Moon.'

Anton nodded.

'Too late,' he said. 'It's too late.'

As if in response, the ship shuddered.

Anton's gaze met Sam's again.

'I don't think we're going to be safe anywhere,' he said quietly.

When Cleomides had finished telling the Doctor about her briefing from General Shaiko, there was a short silence. The Doctor looked more puzzled than surprised.

'What I can't understand is why, if they know what's happening – if they know that the enemy they're fighting isn't even real – they've sent me away to look at the mother planet. If they'd let me stay on the Moon, I could have helped them to evacuate the place safely.' He stood up. 'In fact I can still help them, if you let me speak to General Shaiko.'

Cleomides shook her head. 'You know that's not the plan. We stand and fight. Earth has decided. My orders are –'

The Doctor grabbed her arm. 'Captain, your orders are to

protect the people of Earth, to the best of your ability, so help you God, or whatever powers you should believe in. That's the oath, isn't it?'

Cleomides blinked. 'Yes, but –'

'Well, if you want to protect their lives – and ours – you'll let me talk to Shaiko. At least *talk* to him. You trust me that much, don't you? Or you wouldn't have told me what you already have.'

Cleomides glanced at Daniel, biting her lip. After a second he realised that he was being questioned. He remembered Ri Tiydon, also asking advice.

Tiydon, dead.

He nodded.

Without a word, Cleomides turned and led the way out of the room. The Doctor hesitated, then gently touched Aloisse's mantilla again and followed.

The hospital ship was rolling like a rowing boat in a storm. The alarms were still blaring, and a life-support pod that resembled a black sarcophagus had descended over Anton's bed.

Dr Eliot was pulling Sam away. 'Get back to your bed. You'll be safest in the life-support pod there.'

The floor shook, and the ceiling started to move. Amazingly, the lights stayed on, even when the whole plasteel sheet began rippling like a canvas shroud.

'Get in the pod!' yelled Dr Eliot. 'I've got to see to the other patients!' She was running along the length of the ward, a long-legged, awkward run. Absurdly, Sam found herself wondering if the woman ever went jogging.

The doors burst open and a squad of marines burst in, in full armour. They started firing plasma bolts at random.

Sam stared for a second, unable to believe what she was seeing. This was a *hospital*.

Then one of the bolts came near enough to sear her skin. She jumped back, dived for the pod containing Anton. Another plasma discharge whooped through the air above her. She heard a scream, and an electronic voice babbling about attack warnings.

Sam felt her ears pop, and realised that the uncontrolled firing must have breached the walls of the ship. What was happening? Why were the marines attacking? Were they mad? Seeing things, like Anton?

– no time to think no time to think no time to think just get out of here –

There was a small control panel on the side of the black pod, with several unlabelled switches and a standard pair of bowlboards. There was no clue as to what you needed to type to open the thing.

She tried 'open', but nothing happened.

'Release' just produced a red light, away from the control panel, near the head of the pod.

Then she saw the large red button next to the red light, marked EMERGENCY RELEASE.

She hit the button, hard. There was a thud of catches and the black cover rose up, revealing Anton, still lying on the bed. Various mechanical interfaces between the bed and the pod disconnected, slim plastic tubes and cables rippling away like small snakes. Anton smiled at her – then his face went pale as he saw the chaos, the marines advancing past them, still firing. 'The monsters are here again!'

'No they aren't,' said Sam. 'But these idiots think they are. Come on, get up. We've got to get out of here.'

'You'd be safer in the pod,' said Anton.

As if to confirm his words, a plasma bolt took out the medical unit above the bed, showering them with sparks and tiny pieces of smouldering plastic. Thick smoke was drifting towards them from further down the ward.

Sam realised Anton was right. She got down into the pod, pulled at the lid.

It wouldn't budge.

The floor shook crazily and a huge booming sound filled the air. The wall of smoke moving towards them suddenly started rushing away, as if someone had started running a film backwards.

Then it thinned, and Sam saw open space beyond it.

Her throat began to hurt.

Then, with agonising slowness, the lid of the pod began to descend.

Darkness.

Then air roared back around Sam's face, cool and sweet, and she was breathing again, and her lungs hurt and her throat hurt and everything else hurt and she could hear Anton's ragged breathing and her own but she'd made it again she'd got out of it she was *alive*.

A light came on.

A voice spoke. 'This is the Emergency Medical System. Please be assured that everything is under control. You are in no immediate danger, but have been isolated from the ship's systems as a precautionary measure. Please breathe deeply and keep calm. A doctor will be in touch shortly. Thank you.'

The message was repeated. Then silence.

'Are you OK?' she asked Anton.

Anton made a gurgling noise, then cleared his throat and nodded. His face was surrounded by tiny blobs of floating blood, like scattered moonlets.

Or debris after a disaster.

'This is the Emergency Medical System again. We are sorry that you are still waiting for attention. Please be assured that everything is under control. You are in no immediate danger, but have been isolated from the ship's systems as a precautionary measure. Please breathe deeply and keep calm. A doctor will be in touch shortly. Thank you.'

Sam and Anton looked at each other.

'We're dead, aren't we?' said Anton quietly. 'She said she would never see me again. She said that.'

'Who did?' said Sam.

'Jono. My girlfriend. She said she would never see me –'

'This is the Emergency Medical System again. We are very sorry that you are still waiting for attention. Please be assured –'

Anton started to hit the padded lining of the pod. 'We're going to die! We're trapped in here and we're going to die, you bloody stupid machine!' He began to scream incoherently.

Sam could smell his sweat, his panic. She felt her own heart thumping in reaction.

'– breathe deeply and keep calm. A doctor will be in touch shortly. Thank you.'

She grabbed both of Anton's arms, pulled them down across his chest.

'Stop it!' she snapped. 'You're wasting air!'

After a while, his breathing eased. 'Sorry,' he said, his voice hoarse and ragged.

'There's got to be an automatic beacon of some kind on this thing,' said Sam. 'We'll be rescued. But it might take a while, so we'll have to conserve air. The machine's right about that. OK?'

Anton nodded. 'Sorry,' he said again.

'It's OK,' said Sam. Her arms were still pinning his down. Suddenly he rolled around to face her.

'I just feel so helpless,' he said. 'Nothing we can do. We can die at any minute.'

'We probably won't,' said Sam, with a soothing confidence she certainly didn't feel.

She looked at Anton, but he was now preoccupied with mopping up the blood that was still leaking from his nose. It was still drifting around him in free fall, blobbing the spongy white plastic of the capsule lining.

Sam suddenly realised that she was feeling very sleepy. Too sleepy. Yes, she was hurt; yes, she was tired; yes, she couldn't quite remember when she'd last slept – but this sudden tiredness was bad.

And there was a red light glowing on the panel set into the padded lining of the pod. 'This is the Emergency Medical System. Please be assured that everything is under control. You are in no immediate danger. However, as a precautionary measure to reduce oxygen consumption, a mild sedative has been provided. Please breathe deeply and keep calm. A doctor will be in touch shortly. Thank you.'

Sam could feel her eyes closing.

'We're running out of air, aren't we?' asked Anton.

Sam struggled to concentrate on his voice, to stay awake. She *had* to, because if they were running out of air so soon it meant that the pod was damaged in some way, which meant – which meant –

Something.

The padded lining danced, the blobs of blood became islands in a sea of white, red islands, like Mars – if she'd ever been to Mars, and the Doctor had promised to show her Mars one day in the twenty-fifth century, or was it the thirty-fifth, and she would never go now, would she?

CHAPTER 19

When the Doctor, Cleomides and Daniel reached the bridge, the blue-haired Captain Piu was talking on holo with an armour-suited marine whose body kept shifting and fuzzing as the signal degraded.

'Escatechic distortion,' commented the Doctor. He was standing behind Daniel, his body shadowy against the receding silver bulk of the Moon behind them. He had sealed the e-suit, but left the helmet loose.

Piu glanced up at him. His eyes were as blue as his hair: a piercing, unnatural colour. 'Who are you? I wasn't told that there would be so many civilians.'

'He's my scientific adviser,' said Cleomides quickly. 'General Shaiko ordered us to bring him along.'

The Doctor was staring at the image of the planet ahead of them. He held up a finger in front of his eyes, moved it from side to side, as if testing his vision, or perhaps testing the wind.

The holo image of the marine faded away into a blur of static, which then vanished.

'Something's happening on the Moon,' said Piu. 'There must be a readout error – it seems to be moving –'

Suddenly his fingers were scrabbling at the controls. Daniel took in the panicky expression on his face, gazed around at the viewscreen display.

The planet was glowing, as if the sun were rising over it. But the sun was behind them. As Daniel watched, the glow brightened, diffused, became a thousand glinting fragments of –

Of dreamstone.

It had to be dreamstone. But at that range, those 'fragments' must each be several kilometres across.

Daniel heard Cleomides swear, felt the ship move sharply underneath him. The rumble of emergency rockets filled the bridge.

The Doctor spoke quickly. 'Captain Piu, plot a course fourteen by twelve by thirty-two.'

Piu stared at him, then glanced at Cleomides, who nodded. 'That's into the middle of them,' he objected, an edge of panic in his voice.

'They don't exist.'

Piu looked desperately at Cleomides. 'Sir –'

'The Doctor's right.' Daniel could hear the reluctance in Cleomides's voice. 'The enemy are capable of generating illusions.'

'I'm sorry but I can't risk –'

The Doctor spoke up again. 'Your orders are to go to the planet's surface, aren't they? Well, if you follow my instructions –'

'This is my ship and I'm not piloting it into the middle of the enemy!' snapped Piu.

Cleomides glanced at the Doctor, then jumped the narrow space to the captain's workstation. '*I'll* pilot the ship,' she said. 'Doctor, what are your instructions?'

The Doctor started giving Cleomides a series of bearings, speaking so rapidly that Daniel could hardly make out the individual numbers. He was a little surprised when Cleomides, leaning over Piu's shoulder, started to input them rapidly and without question.

The ship swayed, and started to move towards the swarm of glowing crystals.

The Doctor looked over his shoulder and met Daniel's eyes for a second. 'You can see them, can't you?'

Daniel nodded.

'I thought so.' He turned back to Cleomides and ran off another set of bearings, leaving Daniel to ponder the significance of the question. Was the Doctor *sure* that these things were illusions?

He looked at the crystals, now steadily growing, taking form and looking very real.

Suddenly a faint bleeping from the piloting unit attracted Daniel's attention. He focused on it, quizzed the software, and discovered that the signal was coming from a distress beacon. It was only just within the detector field, and would soon be out of range again, falling towards the planet. Shortly after that, it would burn up in the atmosphere.

He turned to Piu, who had moved away from the pilot's console and was watching the planet ahead with a surly expression on his face. 'What's a distress beacon HA-521?'

'Hospital ship life-support pod,' said Piu instantly. 'Where is it?'

Daniel read off the co-ordinates.

'That's too far away. We'll have to leave them. Unless you want to take the shuttle, but I don't recommend it.'

The Doctor glanced up. 'It should be safe enough. I'll go –'

'No,' said Cleomides. 'We need you here.'

'*I'll* go,' said Daniel. 'I've had enough piloting hours to handle the shuttle. I used to do drop runs when I was in the marines.'

'No –' began Cleomides, only to be interrupted by the Doctor suggesting a course correction.

'O'Connell died because I left it to your lot,' said Daniel simply. 'I'm thinking I need to do something to make up for that.'

Then he left the bridge, before he could change his mind.

Anton opened his eyes, aware that something had changed. The room was dark: he could hear Jono's soft breathing next to him. Still asleep.

But there was something wrong. Had he been dreaming?

– the diamond bright ships the strange stunted men the people running fever dying –

Yes. A dream. A really good dream, one of the great ones – had he been recording?

He moved his hand towards his head to check for the BEL connections, but it ran into something.

Something soft.

– the lining of the pod oh God the pod Sam the hospital it wasn't a dream it was real and he was stranded in space and he was dying and –

The pod shook, swayed from side to side, and there was a loud metallic clang.

'Sam!' he said.

No response.

He nudged her body with his elbow.

A faint moan.

The pod shifted again, jolted, settled.

A voice spoke.

'This is the Emergency Medical System. An attempt is being made to force open this pod. Please communicate with the person or persons outside and state whether authorisation can be given.'

A hissing sound.

'Hello?' asked Anton, feeling oddly foolish.

'Hello in there!' The voice was staticky, weak, as if the speaker was thousands of kilometres away rather than a couple of metres. The effect wasn't terribly reassuring.

'Hello!' repeated Anton, almost shouting.

'So you are alive, then? I couldn't get this thing to tell me anything. How do I open it?'

'I don't know.' He took a breath. 'Umm – Emergency Medical System, authorisation given.'

No response.

'He can open it, damn you!' snapped Anton.

An intake of breath next to him. 'Tell him to try the button marked "emergency release".' Sam's voice was weak, but coherent. After a moment she added, 'Hello, Doctor.'

There was a click, and the lid of the pod rose slowly, and a human silhouette loomed above them, outlined by glaring light.

Another intake of breath from Sam.

'Daniel?' She was sitting up, grabbing the man's arms. 'Have you seen the Doctor?'

'I've just left him on the *Unanimity*. He's fine. Telling everybody what to do, which seems to be what he's best at.' A slight pause. 'Came a long way looking for you, by all accounts. Come on, we've got to meet up with them quickly.' He glanced at Anton. 'Who's this?'

'A dream artist. We've been under the Moon. They're killing it – murdering it deliberately. I've got to find the Doctor and tell him what's happening. We've got to stop it –'

'OK, OK, let's just get going first. There isn't much room in here, so you two are going to be safer where you are.'

Anton saw that they were in a tiny two-person shuttle, so tiny that Daniel had only to haul himself a short distance along a wall to be at the control panel. A viewscreen showed drifting stars and, suddenly, the worryingly near horizon of a brown planet.

'What happened?' he asked.

Daniel shrugged. 'I'm not sure I know what happened. But the Doctor –' He broke off. 'Oh my God.'

Anton looked around, saw only the metal walls of the shuttle. Outside, only stars. But he knew what was happening inside Daniel's mind. And he could see it on Sam's face too.

The fear. The nightmares.

'Close your eyes!' he said. Though he doubted that it would do any good.

'It's not real, Daniel,' said Sam. 'You have to ignore –' She broke off, gasped.

'OK, I'm setting –' Daniel jumped back from the controls. The shuttle lurched.

Anton could still see nothing, nothing except the planet and the stars. But he couldn't pilot a shuttle, couldn't help them, couldn't do *anything,* damn it –

'Anton! You've got to stop it doing this!'

'I can't –' began Anton.

Then realised he could.

He could feel it: the fear.

It was *his* fear. He could control it, if only he believed that.

The shuttle lurched again. Daniel was piloting, swerving the machine from side to side, to avoid –

– rocks with demon faces human faces screaming screaming and a dying Zmm-Zmm –

'My dreams,' gasped Anton. *'Mine.'*

And he realised the truth at last.

He wondered if it would be too late to do him any good.

Less than thirty minutes after Cleomides took over the piloting, the *Unanimity* made the outer reaches of the atmosphere. She could tell it wasn't going to be an easy landing, and wondered if she should hand the comm back to Piu. The ship was rolling from side to side, the hull booming as the first tenuous waves of atmosphere buffeted it. The planet was now a roiling sea of cloud, so close that it had made the transition from object to a landscape – 'below' rather than 'ahead'. Brownish tendrils of vapour reached up towards the ship, far above the normal atmospheric levels. They looked structured, almost alive, like hooded snakes ready to strike. The sinister whispering, scratching sound of thin air rushing past the hull at high speed gave the impression that they were crawling over the metal, searching for a way in.

Cleomides shivered. She'd always been afraid of snakes.

She could have coped better if the dreamstone 'ships' had been real. That would have been something definite, something she could fight. But they'd vanished, quite suddenly, like the illusions they were. The Doctor and General Shaiko were both right about that, anyway. She shivered again, at the thought of what had happened on the Moon. The fleet turned against the civilian base, against itself. She wondered if it was still happening, how many more people were going to die.

An alarm beeped on the panel in front of Cleomides. She looked back at the screen, at the instrument display. The ship's angle of approach looked far too steep – almost vertical. They were going to burn up if she didn't make some course corrections soon.

She looked to the Doctor for advice, but he seemed to be doing nothing, his hands frozen on the console that was tracking the shuttle. He was muttering something to himself.

Suddenly she felt insecure again. Did the Doctor really know what he was doing? Was he even on their side? The side of humanity? Of life? True, he was disgusted by what had happened to Aloisse, but did that mean he could be trusted with human affairs? She wondered whether she should have been so precipitate in her decision to support him. Perhaps he could, as she'd first suspected, bend people's minds. Perhaps he'd bent hers...

She understood now why Shaiko had chosen her for this mission.

'Captain Piu,' she said.

The blue-haired man turned to look at her.

'Take over the piloting again, please.'

Piu nodded, and took Cleomides's place at the instrument banks, clearly pleased to be back in control.

Cleomides looked at the Doctor again, but he was still watching the shuttle. She wondered how Daniel was doing, whether he'd managed to rescue anyone. Whether he would ever get back to the ship. It was beginning to seem unlikely.

The ship began to tremble violently as the atmosphere thickened around it. Below, the sky brightened.

Brightened far too rapidly.

A mountain of crystal rose beneath them, too close for there to be any hope of avoiding it.

Just as Cleomides was telling herself that the thing couldn't possibly be real, the ship's alarm shrieked, and a recorded voice told her there were ten seconds to impact.

'Doctor!'

Piu was already inputting commands. The ship lurched underneath them.

The Doctor seemed to shake himself, then looked with alarm at the glittering shape rising out of the brown clouds below.

'Oh, dear,' he said. 'I was rather afraid that this might happen.'

'I don't think we'll catch up with them before they land,' said Daniel. He was hunched over the controls, his eyes on the forward screen. Anton was in the hospital pod, his eyes closed. He still hadn't explained how he'd got rid of the illusions – the *monsters* – that had made it impossible for Daniel to pilot the shuttle.

Daniel was speaking again. He'd kept up an almost continuous monologue since their arrival, mostly, Sam suspected, for his own benefit. 'I'm not altogether sure I can land this thing,' he said. 'The computer says it's OK, but the atmospheric density – Oh.'

'Oh what?'

Then Sam saw the patch of yellow light, growing in the brown atmosphere of the world ahead of them. At first it seemed impossible – like a sunrise – but then she realised that it was a geographical feature, a mountain of dreamstone.

No. A mountain range. This thing must be bigger than the Himalayas.

'Can we land?' she asked.

'It's probably why we can land,' said Daniel. 'The air's thinner because the mountains are so – oh, Jesus, they're moving.'

'What?'

'The mountain. It's moving. Upwards.'

And Sam could see the gaps between individual crystals, canyons that showed lower layers of cloud. She could see the movement as they were shredded by whatever huge forces were lifting the dreamstone.

'Don't worry.' Anton's voice, from behind them. 'I'll make it go away.'

'You can't,' said Daniel. 'This is real.'

'I can still make it go away,' said Anton stubbornly.

Sam could hear his rapid breathing. She wondered what he was feeling, whether he really had any empathy with the huge organism in front of them.

The highest peaks of crystal were now above them. Daniel was steering the shuttle towards one of the gaps. 'You realise we're not going to find the *Unanimity* in all this,' he said.

Sam nodded. The shuttle was rocking from side to side, the movement increasing – it was like being on a fairground ride when it was warming up. She wondered what the main ride would be like. Whether she would survive it.

Daniel glanced up at her, a brief, worried look. She wondered if it was intended to be reassuring. 'I'll do my best to get us down in one...' he began, but before he could finish the shuttle lurched, and Sam saw a cliff of glowing crystal rising ahead of them. Intricate lattices of yellowish light glowed through wisps of vapour, the whole panorama rushing past at frightening speed.

The shuttle lurched again, and the cliff was gone, replaced by a dizzying landscape of brown clouds. The tops of some were visibly shredding in the high-speed winds. Sam saw a speck of dark matter floating above the clouds – no, dropping –

Suddenly she realised that it was teardrop-shaped, metal, artificial.

'Daniel!'

He nodded. 'That's the *Unanimity* all right. But don't expect to make a rendezvous in these conditions. The best we can hope for is to follow them down.'

But Sam was looking at the viewscreen. There was a flare of light from the *Unanimity*, and then it was whirling away, followed by a dusty scattering of debris.

Before Sam could even begin to think about what had happened, it was simply gone.

Daniel followed her gaze, swore.

Sam just stared at the screen.

'He can't be,' she said. 'It can't be.'

'There weren't any other spaceships in the area,' said Daniel grimly.

'Then the Doctor's dead,' whispered Sam.

CHAPTER 20

The shock of the collision sent Cleomides spinning away from the ring-rail. The webbing caught her, wrenched her to a stop. She heard a shout of pain, saw Piu flattened against the hatchway that led from the rest of the ship.

'Captain Piu!' she shouted. 'Are you OK?'

No response. He fell, abruptly, as the ship began to shudder and decelerate once more. His spacesuit flopped against the forward part of the bridge like a toy discarded by a child, the sound terrifyingly loud in the sudden near-silence. Cleomides saw the red Medicaid light flashing on his shoulder pad and realised that he was probably seriously injured.

The viewscreen showed the planet's surface below, a brownish smog of clouds. The sun was gone, hidden behind the flying mountains of dreamstone.

Above the ship, she could see the dull crenellated domes of three parachutes.

She saw the Doctor at the pilot's console, his hands moving over the controls as if he'd had ten thousand hours piloting this type of ship. Perhaps he had; he'd certainly stabilised it quickly enough after the collision.

It had still been too late for Piu. She began moving hand over hand along the ring-rail towards him. Gravity was almost normal, the ship swaying slowly in the thickening air. Lightning flickered in dark-yellow clouds below the fallen suit, giving Cleomides a sense of vertigo. A faint booming sound could be heard through the hull. She wondered if it was thunder, or something to do with the drive systems of the huge crystals.

She unlocked the visor. Piu's eyes were open, but he was not breathing. The suit must have hit something sharp at neck level:

the gasket had collapsed and strangled him. The flesh around his eyes was blue, a dark bruised blue like a dead sea.

Cleomides looked at the poisonous atmosphere outside thickening around them, and wondered if the surface would be soft enough to let them bury his body.

Daniel watched the clouds rushing past, heard the scrape and tear of atmosphere on the outer shell of the shuttle.

Sam was still clinging to the plastic wall-rings and looking through the screen, rather than safely strapped into the pod with Anton, where she should be.

Daniel didn't blame her, but said softly, 'Strap in. It's going to be a rough ride.'

'I'm sure he isn't dead,' said the girl, with more than a trace of stubbornness in her voice.

Daniel looked at the violent clouds below, tried to figure out what the chances of someone in a life escape pod or a spacesuit would be in that environment.

Only slightly worse than the chances of three people in a wingless mini-shuttle, he decided. The instruments in front of him simply weren't equipped for this environment and he had doubts about the hull's ability to withstand the stresses of operating in this thick, turbulent atmosphere. But it was their only option. The dreamstone was all but sealing off the sky.

'You never think about how big a planet is,' he said conversationally, adjusting the thrusters a little in what he hoped was the right direction. 'Not until you see it up close like this. It was just a little brown pebble in the sky, and now it's a world. A whole world with its own way of doing things, and it doesn't give a damn about you.'

He realised he was beginning to sound afraid, which wasn't any good. He was trying to reassure Sam, to keep her distracted, stop her from panicking.

A hand touched his shoulder. 'It's OK. You've got enough to do here. I'll see to Anton.'

And he heard her scrambling down, heard her talking quietly to Anton, and felt slightly ashamed of himself for needing comfort from a teenager.

You've been in worse situations, Danny me boy, he told himself.

But right now, he couldn't think of any.

Cleomides could hardly believe it when, after all the drama of the collision, and Piu's death, they landed with a gentle bump. She wasn't even sure they were down until she saw the red cradle of landing lights on the viewscreen.

Nothing else was visible at first. As the control system scanned the various possible viewing systems – infrared, sonar, ultraviolet – random shapes formed and unformed, patterns in the air.

At last a landscape appeared: shimmering green cliffs, a purple ground puddled with black. Finally the system adjusted the false colours to match normal visual perceptions: the cliffs became grey, the ground a dull, cracked orange. The puddles were still black.

'Hydrocarbons,' said the Doctor. 'Lakes of boiling pitch. Charming place.'

Cleomides jumped up to the ring-rail, found a systems readout. 'Atmospheric pressure's 7.6 bars. No wind. Everything seems to have settled down.'

'Yes.' The Doctor was looking around. 'I wonder why. You know, I don't think those things even noticed us.'

Cleomides noticed a red light blinking on the comms panel, checked with the system, picked up a distress call.

Daniel. Almost certainly Daniel. She'd almost forgotten about his quixotic rescue mission in the confusion of Piu's death. Now she needed the man down here, and he wasn't down here. He was probably going to die, like Piu.

'Sam's alive!' shouted the Doctor suddenly. Then he added, 'Oh, I can sort that out.'

Cleomides saw that he was talking into a microphone.

'Daniel?' she asked him.

The Doctor was still talking, quietly, intensely. Cleomides heard course settings, and realised after a moment that he was talking Daniel down.

When she heard the Doctor's voice, a strange sense of embarrassment came over Sam. She desperately wanted to talk to him but – quite apart from the fact that any distraction could cost their lives – she couldn't think of anything to say.

When it became obvious that the Doctor's instructions were going to let them land safely – when she could see a blurry shape of the *Unanimity* on the viewscreen, and realised that she would be face to face with the Doctor in a few minutes – Sam's discomfort increased.

Just be cool, she told herself. There are far more important things going on than your personal problems.

She became aware that she wanted to kiss him.

No. He's the Doctor. He doesn't kiss or cuddle up close and –

She wondered if he ever had. In all those years, all the women he talked about, the other companions.

No. *Stop* it. He's the Doctor and he's old enough to be your great-great-great-great-grandfather. You know that it could *never* work.

Be cool. Be sensible. Just be pleased to see him.

Cleomides examined the control console. There were red lights all over it. The collision seemed to have taken out most of the *Unanimity*'s primary systems. They had limited power, limited air, and only a few manoeuvring jets were still working. The main airlock was non-functional, the outer door ripped off by the collision. A distress beacon was signalling, but would there be anybody to rescue them?

Cleomides looked at it all, feeling a sick apprehension. She should never have gone on this mission. She should have told Shaiko to send someone younger, someone more able, someone without a family.

Now she would never get home.

The Doctor was apparently unconcerned. He was busy adjusting the controls of an emergency hatch below the ring-rail, using some kind of sonic device. Presumably he was hoping to stop the corrosive atmosphere coming in when they tried to get out.

Cleomides was content to let him, for the time being. Her plan was to get out in Daniel's shuttle, if that was possible. They certainly couldn't live here, not judging by the atmosphere readings – there was no oxygen, and a significant percentage of sulphur dioxide. Whatever was going on in space there was at least a chance that someone would pick them up. Down here, they would be lucky if anyone could find them. But using the shuttle meant leaving Aloisse behind – the alien was far too heavy and bulky for the smaller craft. So she wasn't telling the Doctor about her plans yet. She knew enough about him to know that he wouldn't let her abandon Aloisse, even if it meant that everyone had to die.

'Reverse the polarisation on the pressure sensor,' the Doctor was saying, apparently to himself. 'The whole system should just reverse – ah! Look!'

He was staring out of the viewscreen. Cleomides followed his gaze, saw that the tarry pools were changing. Shapes were forming: half-human images, squat and malformed. They were so grotesque that, for a moment, they seemed almost absurd.

Then they started walking towards the *Unanimity*.

'Are they real?' she whispered.

'Oh, yes. They're real enough,' said the Doctor grimly. 'Just like the thing we hit on the way down. You could call it an allergic reaction.'

Sam watched the tarry, angular shapes emerging from the pools, and tried to tell herself that it would be OK, that the Doctor would do something.

'Have we got enough fuel to launch again?' she asked Daniel, who was fiddling with the control panel. A huge chunk was missing from the side of the *Unanimity*: Sam was surprised that it had got down in one piece. It certainly didn't look likely that it would still be able to take off.

'Just about. Depends on the mass we've got to carry. There's the Doctor, Aloisse, Piu, Cleomides –' He shrugged. 'We can't even fit them all in, Sam. And we'd only just make a suborbital hop. If there's no one up there to pick us up, we just crash back and burn.'

Sam remembered what had happened to the hospital ship, and wondered whether there was still anything in the area capable of rescuing them.

A whine of machinery behind them: Sam turned, saw Anton clambering into the shuttle's tiny airlock.

'Anton! What are you doing?'

'Someone has to stop this,' he said. 'And I'm the only one who knows what to do.'

Sam opened her mouth, nearly said it, nearly said, *the Doctor will know too*, then realised she didn't know that, didn't know what the Doctor was doing or what he knew.

Inside the airlock chamber, Anton was struggling into a spacesuit, with the inner door still open. It looked lightweight: an orbital manoeuvring suit. She'd seen Jess using one to make repairs on the protesters' base. But she was fairly sure that it wasn't capable of standing up to the heat and pressure of the planet's surface.

'Anton, I don't think you should do this. I don't think –'

But the inner airlock door was already closing.

Outside, dark, half-human figures were slowly dragging themselves across the rough ground towards the shuttle.

The Doctor stood outside the jury-rigged airlock of the *Unanimity*, looking at the slowly approaching figures. He could feel the presence of the dreamstone underneath the planet's surface; he could feel an immense, aching sadness. But there were no details, no thoughts, nothing he could focus on to communicate with. He had to make them understand that not all humans were bad, that not all humans should be killed.

But now, too late, he was beginning to wonder if they were intelligent at all.

All that complexity… He remembered the cities of light he'd seen in the lab. If this was an intelligent attempt at destroying the ship, it was incredibly inefficient.

So it wasn't intelligent.

There was no intelligence.

Only fear.

With heavy hearts, the Doctor realised the truth. He'd miscalculated again. Made too many assumptions.

But there might still be time to put things right.

He set off across the ground at a run, looking for crystals before it was too late.

As soon as he got outside, Anton knew that he'd made a mistake.

He could see the ground. He could see the cracks in the ground, the vapour rising up. He could feel a deep trembling, as if something vast was dying. Perhaps if he could find Sam's friend the Doctor – if he could tell him that –

– *these are my dreams this is my power* –

231

But was it even true?

He looked around, but in the mist and the blinding light he couldn't see either of the ships. Thick yellow vapour was rising. He wiped the visor of his helmet, felt the plastic move –

– move too much and a hiss of gas and he *hadn't sealed it* he'd been rushing thinking about the dreamstone he hadn't thought and the gas was burning his eyes his nose and he struggled with the clips and the helmet rocked again and *more gas and his lungs were burning choking and Innell had told him to be careful* –

Anton fell, barely aware of falling, aware only of the pain in his chest, in his stomach, across his face, eating the skin like acid. He tried to breathe, felt only agony.

Agony fading as he lost consciousness.

Lost consciousness, and began to dream.

'Where are you going?'

Aloisse's translated voice made Cleomides jump. She'd almost forgotten that the big, injured alien was there. She couldn't remember when she'd come down to the bridge. After Piu's death? After the landing? She was awkwardly propped against the ring-rail, her eye closed. Some of the bandages on her tentacles were leaking, streaks of orange fluid.

'I'm going to join the Doctor,' Cleomides said, heaving open the inner door of the makeshift airlock.

'No you're not. You wouldn't need a gun for that.'

Cleomides wondered how Aloisse knew about the gun. She couldn't see and apparently hadn't suspected that Cleomides was going until the hiss of the airlock cycle had given it away.

'I need a gun because half the planet's trying to kill us,' she said, wondering why she was wasting breath arguing with an alien. 'I'll be back.'

'You're lying,' said Aloisse.

Cleomides got into the lock.

'I can understand why you want to leave me. I know you haven't got any choice. I can't go with you. I heard you telling the Doctor about the ship status and I know that the shuttle is the only way out. I just want you to acknowledge that I am a person, and you're leaving me to –'

The airlock door slammed shut, leaving Cleomides alone for a moment. 'I'm sorry, Aloisse,' she muttered. Then thought: *alien*. Making me feel like that.

Then the outer door opened, and a thick, vaporous smog rolled in.

'It's a one-person shuttle, Sam!' snapped Daniel. 'That means one spacesuit! We can't go out there chasing Anton or the Doctor. We've got to launch soon, or stay here and get pulled apart by that lot.'

'I'm not leaving him again!' Sam knew it was irrational, but she was sure the Doctor was still alive. Leaving him would amount to murder.

The ground was trembling constantly now, and there was an ominous pattering on the hull of the shuttle. The windows were fogged, and half covered in a black sludge. Light burned outside, shifting and slanting through the vapour, but revealing nothing. Sam didn't know what had happened to the things approaching them but a look at the rows of red lights on the panel told her that they weren't the only problem: a launch was already risky and might soon be impossible.

But she wasn't leaving him again. She'd rather go out there and die and leave Daniel to fly off on his own, if that was what he wanted to do.

There was a banging on the hull.

She jumped, expecting to see a tarry figure or glowing crystals, but a gauntleted fist appeared in front of the viewscreen.

A spacesuit. Anton? The Doctor?

Daniel was already hitting the override controls on the airlock. She couldn't hear the mechanism, but after a moment the inner door opened, admitting a smell of sulphur and a spacesuited figure.

A figure with a gun.

Not the Doctor, then.

The visor windowed, and Sam saw Cleomides's face.

The woman raised the visor, glanced at the airlock door sealing behind her, then at the control panel.

'Right,' she said. 'We launch now.'

'What about –'

'They're dead. The aliens died back at the ship, and I almost fell over someone else on the way over. He was –' She shuddered. 'He was dead all right.'

Sam's vision clouded over, and she felt herself falling. 'I don't believe –' Cold metal hit the back of her neck, her arms. She could feel the planet vibrating through the shuttle's flimsy hull.

Cleomides glanced at her. 'I'm sorry.'

Daniel was flicking switches on the panel. Sam heard the whisper of jets, felt the shuttle jolt, then lurch dangerously.

– *he can't be this isn't happening I can't be leaving him again* –

The shuttle tipped forward, and Sam caught a glimpse of the ground through the murk.

Saw a spacesuited figure, standing, staring up at her.

Cleomides had said that Anton was dead, so it had to be –

She scrambled along the metal wall, pulling at the grab-handles, shouting, 'Stop! Go back! We have to go back!'

Cleomides's face turned to her, dark inside the pale helmet of the suit. 'There isn't enough fuel. It's too late.'

'No!' screamed Sam. She dived towards the control panel, but felt strong arms pulling her back.

Daniel.

'Daniel, we have to go back, we've got to go back, I'm not leaving him again –'

But Daniel just held her, held her hard even though she kicked and screamed and tried to bite, and Cleomides kept piloting the ship up, up until the atmosphere was a brown sea below them and the sky was black and she'd left him behind, she'd left the Doctor behind.

Again.

The Doctor watched the shuttle climbing through the brown murk of the planet's atmosphere and sighed. He had hoped for better from Cleomides. He was sure, even now, that she wasn't evil.

Oh, well. He walked across the surface, through the slowly clearing smog, in the slowly diminishing light.

The tarry figures approached him, slowly, the yellow shine of dreamstone in their eyes. The Doctor noticed that all the faces were the same, a recognisable face, a human face.

'Ah,' muttered the Doctor. 'Yes. It would be.'

The figures surrounded him, reaching out their hands to touch him. As they did so, the surface of his spacesuit began to smoulder, and alarms went off inside the helmet.

But the Doctor didn't notice. He had more important things to worry about.

He was asleep.

CHAPTER 21

As the shuttle cleared the atmosphere, Daniel saw a hundred moons.

Tiny, crystalline moons, some of them trailing thin comet-tails of vapour. Beyond them the real Moon was a dull ghost, dead rock.

Cleomides was still piloting: cramped beside her in the narrow command area, Daniel could see her eyes constantly moving behind the visor, from the main screen to the positional display, from the positional display to the glittering lights of the systems readouts, and then back to the screen. Sam was somewhere behind them, in the hospital pod perhaps, sobbing quietly. The hull of the shuttle made dull metallic thuds from time to time. Daniel hoped they were nothing more dangerous than expansion noises.

'There are ships there somewhere,' Cleomides said suddenly. 'I've got some radio traffic. But I can't seem to get a reply from anyone.'

Daniel pointed at the 'moons'. 'They're probably too busy with them,' he pointed out.

'I'm not sure –' began Cleomides.

A flare of light ahead: Daniel saw tiny sparks of light flying from one of the crystals. 'Well, well,' he said. 'It looks like the marines are going to pursue their usual policy.'

'What other policy would you suggest, Mr O'Ryan?' snapped Cleomides.

Daniel glanced sidelong at her, saw the fear written in her face underneath the visor. 'A sensible one?' he suggested. 'One that might mean we get home alive, perhaps?'

Another flare of light ahead. Cleomides stared at it, but said nothing. A small mountain of debris tumbled past them; some of the smaller fragments rattled against the hull.

Then Cleomides said, 'Take over here, Daniel. You will be better at avoiding this than me. And I need to talk to Sam.'

Before Daniel could argue, she'd unstrapped herself and was clambering down the metal wall of the shuttle, her movements making the hull craft ring like a funeral bell.

Ahead, the flares of light became more frequent. The new dreamstone moons were being systematically destroyed.

In his sleep, the Doctor could hear the children screaming.

– the monsters are here and they're going to kill me Mummy help me plee-ease –

And he could see the monsters, too: the black, squat ships crawling with tiny, deadly animals, fast, ferocious, black with weapons. They were killing the children, the children that looked like crystals, like mountains, like seeds.

Killing the children. Yes. That was what the human fleet was doing.

They had always been the monsters, this time. Why hadn't he seen it?

He could sense Anton, somewhere in the matrix of impression and feeling that was the dreamstone. Anton wanted to kill the monsters.

The Doctor didn't want to kill them. It was pointless, now. And most of them weren't actually evil.

The dreamstone entity – the planet, such as it was – didn't even know what was going on. It never had. It had only been afraid. It was responding instinctively, defending itself against the horrors that it could not understand.

The Doctor realised the truth then.

The dreamstone hadn't taken over Anton's mind. Anton's mind had taken over the dreamstone.

And Anton was about to tell it what to do.

* * *

Aloisse wondered what it was going to be like to die.

She hadn't thought about it much before. There had always been too much to do, too many worlds and people that she needed to find out about, to talk to, to argue with, to save from their own stupidity.

There wasn't much doubt that her death was going to happen; she'd heard the flare of the shuttle's rockets as it had launched. Perhaps Cleomides had told the Doctor she was dead – he'd hardly have left her behind otherwise. Or perhaps the Doctor was dead himself.

She hoped not. Sam needed him, she was sure of that.

She took a breath, coughed painfully. There was hardly any air left on the *Unanimity*, and what there was had an acid taste which suggested that there were breaches in the hull. And Cleomides had behaved as if they were under attack, though Aloisse had heard no trace of it.

If only she could see. At least then she would know what was going to happen to her.

She shifted painfully, feeling the alien metal of the ship dig into the damaged skin of her tentacles. This wasn't where she would have chosen to die; there again, not many people get much choice about that, and Aloisse had a feeling it didn't really matter anyway.

She took a deep breath, felt her mouth burn again from the acid in the air.

A bleeping noise distracted her. She jumped, hoping suddenly for rescue, but then decided it was probably an alarm; most likely it would be telling her something she already knew. Nonetheless, she struggled towards the source of the sound, trying to feel her way with her damaged tentacles.

A click. 'Aloisse?'

The Doctor's voice, with a high-frequency overlay: a radio signal.

'Aloisse, I –'

'I'm here.'

' – don't know if you can hear me but there's something I need you to do. It means operating the radio, but I can't come back to the ship at the moment...' A pause. 'Can you hear me?'

'Yes. What's the code?'

'Well, I hope you can hear me.'

Aloisse realised then that the Doctor couldn't hear her. Nonetheless, he went on.

'First, you need to get the transmitter switched on. Feel your way to the pilot's station, you'll find a switch three to the left of the azimuth setting – that's a keypad –'

'Doctor, I can't do this. I don't even know which way –'

'Quickly! There isn't much time! When you've got the transmitter on, enter the following code into the keypad – remember, it's a human bowlboard, I don't know if – Anyway, the code's 454879. Then you'll need to speak to General Shaiko. Tell him we're down here. Tell him I'm talking to the Dreamstone Moon. Tell him –'

A squawk of static.

'Doctor?'

Silence.

'Doctor!'

But the silence went on.

After a while, slowly, painfully, Aloisse began to feel her way around the metal rail to the place where she hoped she would find the pilot's console.

The girl wasn't asleep; she was sitting up in the hospital pod, crying silently. She looked at Cleomides once, then just turned her face away and sobbed.

Cleomides sat down on the bed.

'I don't have any daughters,' she said. 'I have sons. Three fine sons, and a husband who loves me. I'm here because I wanted to protect them. And I wanted to get home. Can you understand that?'

'*He* was my home.'

Awkwardly, Cleomides put a hand on the girl's shoulder. 'I'm sorry. But we would have died if we'd stayed. They're going to destroy the planet altogether, you know. That's what they're doing up there. If they don't pick up our beacon we'll probably die as well.' She hesitated. 'I'm sorry.'

The girl moved away from Cleomides's touch. 'Sorry? You think it's enough to say "sorry" when you've deliberately killed two innocent people? You shouldn't have been here! Why didn't you listen to anyone? Why didn't you listen to the Doctor?'

The hull of the shuttle clanged as a fragment hit it. A rumble of jets, a momentary nudge of acceleration.

Cleomides heard Daniel muttering into the transmitter.

Sam spoke again, her voice no more than a whisper. 'He wasn't dead, was he? When you left? It was him that I saw.' The last was very much a statement, not a question.

Cleomides hesitated. 'No, he wasn't dead. The Krakenite wasn't either. I – just panicked.'

She didn't say 'I'm sorry' again. There didn't seem to be any point.

'Just go away,' said Sam. 'Pilot the shuttle or call the fleet or whatever it is you do best. Just don't come near me again. Right?'

Cleomides stood up, trying to think of something to say, some last word that would make her seem a better person than she was.

Before she could speak, the shuttle's proximity alarms blared. She looked up at the screen and saw a mountain flying through space towards them, blotting out the stars.

On the third painful attempt, Aloisse managed to enter the correct code into the human bowlboard. There was a long silence

– so long that Aloisse thought she'd failed again after all, even though there'd been no beep, no tinny human voice telling her she'd made an error.

Then a voice spoke.

'*Unanimity*? It that you, Cleomides?'

'No,' said Aloisse. 'Cleomides isn't here any more. I need to speak to General Shaiko.'

Another long pause. A fuzz of static.

'Very well.'

Aloisse took a breath of the air, felt her throat burn. Then she realised that she had no idea what to say.

The holo feed made it look as if General Shaiko's office was floating in the middle of space. Part of the tumbling mountain of dreamstone was visible behind it. At the moment, Daniel had managed to match its course and velocity; they were hoping it would shield them from any smaller fragments.

In the general's office, the incense candle was still burning, the ceremonial sword hung in its place. But when he spoke, his voice was less even, his diction more rapid than usual. 'Captain Cleomides, we need to know about the Doctor and the Krakenite called Aloisse. When you left them on the planet, were they dead?'

Cleomides hesitated. Could she –

She remembered Aloisse's cold goodbye. She knew that Sam was listening, silent, in the pod.

'No, sir. They were still alive when we left, as far as I know.'

She became aware of Daniel, looking at her sidelong from his position at the controls.

'Good,' said Shaiko. 'Now can you tell me the truth about something else?'

Cleomides nodded.

The general's image was replaced by an image of Aloisse, on the bridge of the *Unanimity*. She was speaking, the mechanical voice of the translator blurred by deep rumblings which might be her native voice or static or both.

'You have to give the Doctor some time,' she said. 'He is on the planet's surface, speaking to the dreamstone entities.'

Cleomides heard Sam's intake of breath behind her.

'They wish to avoid further conflict. If there is a conflict, everyone in the system will die. That's what he told me to tell you.' A pause. 'Please listen to him this time.'

The image vanished, was replaced by the general.

'Your observations?'

'You mean – can we trust that alien? Is the Doctor on our side?'

He nodded.

Cleomides heard Sam moving behind her. She wondered what the girl would say if she stayed silent. But she couldn't speak.

– he's an alien you can't trust aliens no one can trust –

She thought about Sam. Her anger, her disgust.

She became aware that Shaiko was watching her face closely.

'He can be trusted,' she said at last. Then quickly, 'I shouldn't have left him behind.'

Shaiko nodded.

'Very well.'

The image died.

Sam appeared beside her.

'He's alive,' she whooped. 'He's done it again! He's alive!'

And to Cleomides's amazement, Sam gave her a hug.

Flowers.

The Doctor's first impression of Anton's dreamscape was flowers. Huge, lazy, scented blooms, mostly in reds and yellows, which he suspected were Anton's favourite colours. They weren't real, they weren't even realistic; they were just there, drifting, unfocused, feelings rather than images, like flowers in a dream.

Which was exactly what they were, of course. Dimly, the Doctor was aware of the heavy feel of his body on the surface of Mu Camelopides VI, the smell of burning insulation and, more worryingly, a continuous deep vibration in the ground, like the beginnings of an earthquake. But he couldn't worry about the real world now. He had to deal with the world inside Anton's head – or rather, Anton's world inside the much bigger head it had moved itself into.

He spoke tentatively. 'Anton?'

And he was in a wasteland.

Bare, cold rock. Stunted, isolated trees. A wet, gusty, uncomfortable wind.

If you actually looked at anything, it went away.

'Anton?'

And there were stars ahead, and the stars were full of monsters. The monsters unfolded, glow-eyed, horned devils, *aliens* –

Ah.

'Anton, you have to stop this.'

'I don't want to talk any more. I want to feel. I want to communicate by feeling.'

'By feeling what? Hatred? Resentment? If you don't stop this, thousands of people are going to die.'

'I just want to talk to them!'

The words of a dream. Anton was dreaming. The Doctor rather suspected that he had always been dreaming, that there had always been only a slight, if significant, distance between what went on in the world and what went on in his head.

The dreamstone, broken, afraid, had just helped complete that divorce.

The Doctor wondered how to wake him up now. And if he woke him up, whether he would die. And at that moment he realised there might be an easier way.

'It's OK, Anton,' he said slowly. 'There aren't any monsters. You can go to sleep now.'

The flowers came back.

'No monsters? But I wanted to kill them – they took away my life, you know.'

'No one took away your life except you.'

There was a long silence.

Eventually the Doctor went on, softly, 'So you don't have the right to take away anybody else's life. Nor the life of this world. It doesn't want to destroy itself, Anton. It's only afraid.'

A pause.

Then the Doctor felt the structures of Anton's mind suddenly crumble. The flowers returned for an instant, but they wavered, drifted, wilted, blackened, filled with sand.

'Time to sleep, Anton,' said the Doctor gently. 'Time to sleep.'

The flowers faded away.

After a while, the Doctor realised that he'd just killed a man with the force of an argument.

It wasn't a very pleasant thought.

CHAPTER 22

Sam stared at the lid of the hospital pod.

There was a detailed pattern in the white plasteel, like a square fingerprint, or the wiring diagram for a computer. She followed the pattern with her fingers, counted the corners, tried not to think.

She sensed Daniel behind her, heard his breathing.

'The *Dreamstone Miner*'s going to pick us up. Tina says she'll drop you off at Ha'olam.'

Sam nodded. 'The Doctor sorted it out, then?' she asked, still following the patterns on the plasteel.

'Well, we're not dead. I think he's talking to Shaiko at the moment. He's trying to talk them out of mining the new moons, now they've agreed not to destroy them. I don't know how far he'll get. You'd think people would learn, but –' A pause. 'Aren't you glad he's alive? You sounded happy –'

'Yes, I'm glad.' Unconditionally. 'But I don't want to see him.'

'Why not?'

'Because I keep leaving him behind. Leaving him for dead.' A left corner, a right corner, left, left, right. Her fingernails were grubby. Probably all that stuff under the Moon. She should have a bath soon. Perhaps she could have one on the *Dreamstone Miner*.

'You didn't do it. You didn't leave him. Cleomides did. Damn it, *I* did.'

'I left him the first time. And –'

– *wake up goodbye kiss* –

She felt the blush, felt her whole body blush. 'Just leave me alone, please.'

A sigh. 'OK. But I'll be here until we get to Ha'olam. If you need me.'

Sam didn't reply. After a while, Daniel moved away. She heard him talking in a low voice, perhaps to Cleomides, perhaps over the comm.

A faint rumble of thrusters, a gentle acceleration.

She was on her way. She wondered where Ha'olam was. She wondered whether the Doctor would be there.

Knowing her luck, he probably would.

The Doctor looked into Aloisse's huge eye, into each of the linked pupils in turn.

'Can you see my face?' he asked.

'It's all dots. Dots here, dots there…' The Krakenite sounded weary, exasperated. 'I'm sorry, Doctor, but I don't think that this piece of technology is going to work for me.'

'Give it *time*.'

As if to emphasise his words further, one of the TARDIS clocks chimed. The Doctor counted: one, two, three, four, four and a half –

Hmm. A little slow.

Aloisse withdrew her eye. 'I think I'd prefer to be blind.'

'No, you wouldn't.' The Doctor adjusted the controls of the gaudy strap-on sensor above Aloisse's eye stalk, increasing the resolution, decreasing the sensitivity. 'Is that better?'

A pause. 'Yes. I can see you now. The colours are a bit strange, but – look, Doctor, I can't carry this thing around with me for ever.'

'Why not? It doesn't weigh any more than a translator.'

Aloisse stood up, started to walk around. She was still slow, her walk unbalanced, and several of her tentacles dragged painfully.

'So the Moon was the planet's child, in a literal sense?' she asked, when she stopped for breath, leaning on the battered frame of the Doctor's VW Beetle.

'In the sense that it was part of the dreamstone, yes. I suspect it started life as something like one of those orbiting crystals.'

A pause. 'You know, humans are always trying to make their dreams come true. Once you've seen what happens when they succeed, you really wonder why they do it.'

Aloisse began shuffling back towards the Doctor. 'Not just humans,' she said. 'Anything with a mind will dream. I dream of a world where – oh, I don't know...' She made a noise like a loud harrumph. 'Where everyone's sensible and no one inflicts unnecessary suffering.'

'A fine dream,' sighed the Doctor wistfully. 'Stick to that and you won't go far wrong.'

'The less you hope for, the more you achieve.' The Krakenite sounded as if she was quoting someone, but the Doctor didn't recognise the words. Before he could ask, she said, 'How did you get on with Shaiko?'

'I think I've persuaded them to steer clear. They lost five thousand people.' The Doctor didn't really believe the agreement would stick, but the losses should keep all but the greediest and stupidest away, for a while at least.

At last Aloisse got back to her original station in front of him. He could hear her laboured breathing, smell her pain.

'Don't worry,' he said. 'Another week in the TARDIS and you'll be fine.'

A pause. The control room hummed to itself, the clocks ticked.

'Doctor,' she said gently, 'I'm not going to stay with you. I want to go home.'

'Yes, in a week or so,' said the Doctor cheerily. 'When you're better.'

But he knew he'd been rumbled, even before Aloisse said, 'I'm not the time-travelling sort.'

'I know.'

She turned round, opened her eye experimentally. 'I know you miss Sam,' she said.

'Oh, I miss all kinds of people. And I expect she has some

growing to do, you know, that kind of thing.'

'*Doctor*.'

'Yes.'

'You are going to take me back to –' she rumbled the name-song of her own planet, in its proper voice – 'and then you're going after Sam. She needs you.'

'No, she doesn't. I've discovered that. I came all this way after her, and she was managing perfectly well. She didn't even speak to me over the radio link –'

'There were a lot of other things going on.'

'She could have said hello.'

Aloisse took a few more steps, carefully avoiding a half-empty mug of tea.

'Doctor, she didn't deliberately leave us behind. It wasn't her decision. I told you, Cleomides –'

'I know that,' snapped the Doctor. 'I just think that I should stop. Stop taking over people's lives, I mean. Assuming that because some child wants a break from home, she'll want to see the universe with me for the next few years. Perhaps she'd rather see the universe on her own.'

'And perhaps not.' Aloisse was facing the Doctor, her eye wide. The huge, bloodshot surface again reflected a distorted image of the Doctor's face. 'Perhaps she is your responsibility.'

He gazed at the image for a while, shrugged, sighed, and said, 'We'll see.'